DIARY OF A

By Simon

A DC Ruth Hunter Murder File
Book 1

CW00506135

To the lovely
Cope family

Hope you enjoy it!

Big love

Swee

X

Your FREE book is waiting for you now

Get your FREE copy of the prequel to
the DI Ruth Hunter Series NOW
at www.simonmccleave.com[1]
and join my VIP Email Club

---

1. http://www.simonmccleave.com

*For Frank, Ruth, Arthur
and Tabitha*

CHAPTER 1
April 1997

The warm wind swirled as Mersad Avdic and Katerina Selimovic made their way out of the tube train at Earl's Court underground station in West London and onto the platform. They turned right and headed for the exit. It was getting busy so Mersad put his hand gently on Katerina's arm and guided her through the crowds of commuters in a slow slalom towards the stone steps.

By the time they came out, what had been a typical spring day with sunshine was making way for sporadic, stormy showers.

Mersad made a move to say goodbye to his dear friend Katerina. He had known her since childhood and, had life been different, he imagined she might have been his wife. She was beautiful both inside and out.

'It was so lovely to see you,' Mersad said. He would have loved her to come back to his flat. To cook her dinner, talk, and drink wine.

'Yes, Mersad. Despite the circumstances, it was nice to see you,' Katerina said with a more solemn tone.

Mersad didn't want to think about the reason for their meeting. It hung on his shoulders like some terrible dark cloak that wouldn't go away. There was part of him that wished their friend Hamzar had never been to Waterloo station three weeks ago. Then none of this would have been set in motion.

'I will speak to Hamzar tonight and let you know what we're going to do next,' Mersad reassured her.

'Please ... but you must be careful,' Katerina said with a grave expression.

'We all have to be careful,' Mersad said.

Katerina took his hand and looked at him. 'Please let me know what you find out - however small. It's important.'

Mersad nodded, kissed her cheek. 'Yes, of course. Zdravo.'

Katerina kissed him back. He could smell her perfume and it made his heart do a little dance. 'Zdravo, Mersad.' It was Serbian for 'goodbye.'

Katerina smiled and then headed away into a growing stream of commuters. He watched her go for a few seconds, still mulling over what might have been. Fifty years earlier, they had held hands and even kissed very briefly while watching a dubbed version of *It's a Wonderful Life* in an open-air cinema in Prirode Park in their local town of Subotica. It felt like many lifetimes ago. So much had happened since then.

As he turned to head home, Mersad saw that the man selling *The Evening Standard* had put a brick on the papers to stop them blowing away. There was a British general election only a matter of days away and the headline read *Blair stretches lead in polls.* London's rush hour was thankfully beginning to tail off a little, but the air was still thick with the diesel fumes of buses and black cabs. Pulling up the collar on his black overcoat, he got a whiff of the musty smell of the wool. He had brought it with him when he arrived in London two years earlier. If truth be told, it had been more of an escape than an arrival.

Mersad made his way north up the Earl's Court Road. Traffic was bumper to bumper. He noticed how he was making a lot more progress on foot than those stuck in the cars. The face of a boy looked out at him from a small van as he drew shapes in the condensation. As the lights changed, the cars and lorries moved forward about ten yards, their tyres hissing on the wet surface of the road.

Glancing to his left, Mersad saw the impressive sight of the Earl's Court Exhibition Centre, with its white Art Deco architecture, that he knew had been constructed in the mid-1930s. It looked Germanic to him. Fans were already huddled outside, waiting to see a band called The Verve play a concert there. He had never heard of them. From the huge photo outside, he thought they looked a bit like The Rolling Stones. He wondered if they were Britpop. He kept reading that word, but he didn't really know what it meant. Mersad hadn't bought a record since he'd purchased a David Bowie LP in the late 1970s. He couldn't even remember what they called it. The only time he had ever bought a lot of records was in the late 1950s when he was a teenager and loved the new rock'n'roll that was coming out of the US. It sounded like nothing he had ever heard before. Compared to the traditional Serbian schlager singers such as Lola Novakovic and Dorde Marjanovic, Elvis Presley's *Jailhouse Rock* sounded like it had come from another planet as it exploded out of the radio. It was angry, aggressive, and so exciting.

Trundling along the pavement, Mersad could feel a mist of fine drizzle wet his cheeks. Rubbing his face and chin, he made a mental note to have a shave later or the following morning. As the drizzle turned to rain, he consoled himself that when he got back to his flat he would make himself his favourite hearty be-gova čorba. It was a Bosnian stew, pronounced chorba, that he would rustle up with vegetables and the chunks of halal chicken he had just bought from a specialist butchers in Hammersmith. It was a place recommended by other Bosnian Muslims who had managed to escape the war. They had settled mainly in the Royal Oak and Earl's Court areas of London.

Mersad knew that there were parts of London that would be no-go areas for a Bosnian Muslim like him. The war in his homeland had caused thousands of refugees to head abroad, and London had small enclaves of the various ethnic groups from the former Yugoslavia. But the bitterness and prejudices of the war still ran deep. The Croats had settled mainly in Paddington, where they drank their traditional grape brandy called *Popa* at the local Croatian Club. The Serbs had made Shepherd's Bush their home. The 011 Club, a small, dingy basement bar close to Shepherd's Bush Green, was where they congregated – 011 was the dialling code for Belgrade, capital of Serbia. Some Croatians moved south of the river to congregate around the Croatian Centre in Clapham. Bosnians chose Ladbroke Grove with its Bosnian Advisory Centre. Mersad had heard of a vicious fight that had broken out in a Balkan restaurant in Hammersmith where a Croat had ordered using the Croatian word for soup.

He turned right into the street where he lived and soon arrived at his basement flat. His thinning hair was now a little matted from the rain. Fishing into his pocket for the keys, he made his way carefully down the wet stone steps to the dark red front door. They were slippery, so he took his time. He wiggled the brass key into the Chubb lock and turned it. However, it didn't click open as it usually did.

For some reason, it wasn't locked.

That's very strange. I'm sure I locked it on my way out, he thought to himself. *Old age, no doubt. My memory seems to be getting worse by the day.*

Opening the front door, he peered into the darkness, and entered. He put his shopping down, un-looped his scarf and hung up his coat. The flat smelled musty, but that was Victorian basement flats for you. It felt damp all year round, but the rent was cheap and the landlord friendly, so he put up with it.

He shuffled into the tiny kitchen and clicked on the solitary bulb that hung from the ceiling.

Something didn't feel right.

As he went to the kettle, he could see someone had moved it from its usual spot. As he went to move it back, he touched its side. It was boiling hot!

Oh my God! What is going on?

His stomach tightened with nerves.

Mersad looked back out of the kitchen into the gloomy darkness of the hallway.

Is someone in the flat? Is that why the door was unlocked? The landlord, Mr Peterson, is the only other person with a key. He would never let himself in. Would he?

Mersad's heart started to pound in his chest. He took a breath to try to steady himself.

What's going on?

Then he heard a sound. The clink of china.

What's that? Someone is sitting in my living room.

'Hello?' Mersad called uncertainly as he moved into the hallway and strained to see and hear.

He was now terrified.

The door to the living room was open by an inch. There was light from inside.

How did I miss that when I came in? he wondered as anxiety flooded his body.

Pushing the door open as slowly as he could, Mersad braced himself for what, or who, was inside.

In the shadowy light, a figure was sitting cross-legged in his armchair drinking tea from one of his teacups.

'Mersad Advic?' the man asked. He was broad shouldered, with a greying beard and piercing blue eyes.

Who the hell is that? He has a Bosnian accent.

Mersad felt sick.

Maybe I should run out of the flat and call the police?

'Yes?' Mersad replied, aware that his voice was shaky.

'Don't be afraid,' the man said as he gestured to the sofa. 'Please. Come and sit down. I just want to talk. Nothing more than that.'

The friendly, warm tone of the man's voice and his familiar accent reassured him a little as he nodded.

'Please, I mean you no harm,' the man said as he sat forward, still gesturing to the sofa.

Mersad took a few steps across the room and sat down slowly.

As his eyes focussed better on the man sitting in his living room, he suddenly recognised him. The last time he had seen him, the man's hair and beard had been jet black, and he had been wearing an army camouflage jacket.

Simo Petrovic. The Butcher of Mount Strigova.

Mersad's stomach flipped.

Oh my God!

Petrovic had been responsible for terrible, inhuman atrocities against the Muslims and Croats in his hometown. He had set up a concentration camp in the old ceramic's factory called Keraterm.

'I see you recognise me,' said Petrovic.

Mersad couldn't move. His whole body was shaking, and he couldn't get his breath.

Petrovic put the teacup and saucer down on the small side table and leant forward. His blue eyes seemed to drill straight into Mersad.

'Do you know who I am?' Petrovic asked, raising an eyebrow. His voice was deep and calm.

Mersad nodded, his eyes widening with fear.

'I understand that you have been looking for me?' Petrovic asked.

Mersad shook his head. 'No, no,' he stammered.

Is that why he is here? He's come to kill me.

'Mersad, I think we know that is not true. But I do not come here to harm you. You have made a new life here. And that is a wonderful thing.'

Petrovic's words confused Mersad. He was a monster who was responsible for the deaths of hundreds of Muslim men and teenage boys.

'I'm not looking for you. I assure you,' Mersad lied in a virtual whisper.

Petrovic turned to the table next to him and patted a small pile of papers and a notebook. 'You have been busy? But I am going to have to take these with me. You understand, don't you?'

'Yes,' Mersad whispered.

Petrovic nodded and stood up. 'Very well. You have your new life here in London. Me too. I would like it to stay that way, for both of us. Do we have an understanding?'

'Of course, ...' Mersad mumbled. He didn't know why Petrovic hadn't just killed him there on the spot.

Petrovic held out his hand. 'If our heritage and traditions are to survive, we must put the past behind us, no?'

Does he really want me to shake his hand? I can't do it ...

With an overwhelming sense of shame, Mersad stood up, reached out and took Petrovic's hand. It was cold but strong.

Petrovic moved forward with a smile and embraced Mersad.

'You see? You see? My little balija friend,' Petrovic said with a sneer.

Mersad froze. He hadn't heard the Bosnian derogatory slang for Muslim in years. And Petrovic's sudden change of tone was unnerving. He no longer sounded friendly and upbeat.

What's he doing?

He felt a piercing, red hot stinging pain in his neck.

Petrovic moved back. He was holding a syringe.

'Time for me to go, little balija,' he said, this time with hatred in his face.

Mersad felt dizzy and then his legs collapsed from under him.

He fell backwards into the armchair.

Everything went black.

CHAPTER 2

Detective Constable Ruth Hunter peered around the corner of the tower block and into the central concrete atrium. The last time she was here was a few months ago, on her twenty-seventh birthday. Her birthday treat that day was to go on a drugs raid, wearing a Kevlar bulletproof vest and backed up by armed response officers. Happy bloody birthday, Ruth!

This time, the callout had been a little different to say the least.

Ruth spotted the suspect straight away. And he definitely fitted the description. A man in a large red wig, red clown nose, yellow dungarees, and a red and white stripy top.

Bloody hell! It really is Ronald McDonald.

Detective Constable Lucy Henry crouched beside her. She rolled her eyes at Ruth.

'Are you bloody kidding me!' Lucy growled, gesturing to him.

'Do you want fries with that, sir?' quipped Ruth.

'Ronald McDonald' was waving around a crowbar and shouting something indecipherable.

'I don't know why Trumpton couldn't have sorted this out,' Ruth complained.

'Trumpton' was CID's disparaging name for uniformed police officers and referred to an old children's television programme.

'I've got a horrible feeling that we've been stitched up,' Lucy said.

At that moment, the man whacked the crowbar into the windscreen of a car with an almighty crash.

'Right, that's it,' Lucy said angrily as she moved from behind the wall.

'Let's take it nice and easy,' Ruth said to Lucy.

Ruth had been working as Lucy's partner for five months. It had been apparent from the first day that Lucy was a little gung-ho in her approach to policing. At least that was the polite way of putting it.

'Oi, Ronald. Put that bloody thing down!' Lucy yelled.

The man looked at her, waved inanely, and then hit the side window of the car with another swing of his crowbar. Glass went flying everywhere.

Great! We've got a right nutter here, Ruth thought.

'Stop that! And put the crowbar down!' Lucy shouted as she approached.

Glancing up, Ruth could see that the incident had now attracted some residents who were watching in amusement from balconies and walkways of the ten-storey housing blocks.

That's all we need. A bloody audience.

'Come on. Let's see if we can sort all this out,' Ruth said in a gentle tone that contrasted with her partner's. But that was how they worked. Even though they were the same age, they were definitely good cop, bad cop. So far, it had been a pretty effective partnership.

'Go on, Ronald! Do a runner!' shouted a voice from high up. The yell reverberated around the entire estate.

Cheers, mate. We don't need your bloody input, thanks.

Ruth and Lucy continued moving slowly towards him, but the man seemed to have been encouraged by the shout. He looked over at them and grinned with his white and red made-up face.

'I think he's off his head,' Ruth said as a note of caution.

Lucy pulled out her extendable police baton. 'He'll be off his head when I've bloody finished with him.'

Ronald shrugged, turned, and then ran.

In any other situation, Ruth would have found it highly comedic.

'Jesus Christ!' Lucy muttered as they ran after him.

'*Go on, Ronald! Go on, mate!*' came the cries from the watching crowd.

As they chased Ronald across the weed-strewn concourse, a great cheer came up from the watching residents.

Oh, fuck off, will you!

Ruth couldn't believe the man was trying to run away in oversized clown shoes.

In a matter of seconds, they had gained ground on the fleeing man as the cheers reverberated around the estate.

This is like Keystone bloody Cops!

The man slowed and then bent double, trying to get his breath.

'Oi, will you stop bloody running,' Lucy panted.

Ruth unclipped the handcuffs from her belt. She was not looking forward to writing up the report on this arrest. She actually wondered if it had been a wind-up by the male officers in CID. Now that she and Lucy were partners, it was hard to be taken seriously as a detective. Two women, or *plonks,* working

together in CID was very rare, and she'd had enough *Cagney &*
Lacey and lesbian jokes to last a lifetime.

Suddenly, the man spun on his heels and started running
again. The cheers from the onlookers began once more. He
went to hurdle the raised flower bed, tripped, and fell flat onto
his face.

Serves you bloody right, you twat!

A moment later, Lucy had cuffed him and muttered his
rights.

'You do know we're never going to live this down, don't
you?' Ruth said.

As they led Ronald away with his hands cuffed behind his
back, the onlookers started to 'boo' and whistle.

Lucy had had enough as she looked up and gave them a
two-fingered salute.

'Doing your bit for community relations?' Ruth asked sardonically.

'Wankers. They'll be the first people on the phone if someone nicks their bike or a smackhead gives them a funny look,'
Lucy said dryly.

As they got to the car, Ruth's hand sank into the red, wiry
wig as she pushed his head down, making sure that he didn't
bang it as he was put into the back. She slammed the door shut
behind him.

'You okay?' Lucy asked as they looked at each other.

'I've had more productive mornings,' Ruth said dryly.

'No, I mean you haven't said more than two words since
briefing.'

'Haven't I?'

'That normally means that moron of a husband of yours has pissed you off,' Lucy said bluntly.

She's right. Dan is a complete moron. Actually, he's worse than that.

'Get off that fence,' Ruth joked, but she knew that Lucy couldn't stand him.

'You need to 'get rid' and you know it. For yours and Ella's sake.'

'I know, I know,' Ruth said with an audible sigh. They'd had this conversation on an almost weekly basis.

'What's he done this time? Gone missing in action again?'

Ruth looked at her for a second. 'Actually, I think he's having another affair. In fact, I know he is.'

They both got into the car and headed out of the estate.

PETROVIC HAD BEEN SITTING outside Caffè Bonego, a Serbian deli in West London, for twenty minutes. He pushed his plate away, feeling satisfied and full. Probably too full, but he didn't care. He had quickly devoured the pljeskavica, which was a spiced meat patty, served on a flat bread with onions and soured cream. As usual, he had ordered a turijan salad – a type of lemon balm mixed with pickled yellow bell pepper, green and red tomatoes, cabbage, cucumber, celery root and peppercorns. It wasn't as good as his deda, Serbian for grandfather, had made. Deda's turijan was the taste of Petrovic's childhood.

Petrovic remembered how his deda used to sit him on his knee in the farmer's cottage in the remote Serbian village where his family was from. He used to sing him nursery rhymes and

Serbian folk songs. The village was about fifty miles from Valjevo, the largest city in Western Serbia. Deda used to tell him how the brave Yugoslav Partisans had liberated Valjevo and the surrounding area from Nazi control in 1941. They established the Republic of Uzice, his deda used to say proudly. On darker days, Petrovic would also be told how the Germans had retaken Valjevo months later and transported partisans to the concentration camps of Eastern Europe. Deda said several thousand of them were shot or gassed. His deda had lost many friends.

Deda used to puff at big, cheap cigars which would make Petrovic's eyes sting and water. One day, as he sat on his lap, deda held him tightly and told him to give him his left hand. Petrovic was confused. Deda asked him if he trusted his grandfather. Petrovic nodded. Of course. Deda held Petrovic's left hand and pressed the hot end of the cigar onto the back of it. It had been agony. Deda said it was a warning to trust no one – not even your own family. Petrovic still carried the circular scar as a reminder of his deda's cautionary advice.

Looking at his watch, Petrovic saw that his old friend Colonel Tankovic was due to join him. Since coming to Britain, Tankovic had changed his identity and even his appearance. They were both on a list of over one hundred and sixty people indicted by the ICTY, the International Criminal Tribunal for the former Yugoslavia. The central court for the tribunal had been established in The Hague in 1993. Petrovic and Tankovic were both wanted in connection with breaking the Geneva Convention, genocide, and crimes against humanity. Petrovic knew that if he was caught, he would spend the rest of his life in prison.

Tankovic had reinvented himself in the oil business and had become a multi-millionaire. He had acted as 'a fixer' between a global oil company, Natell, and the Yugoslav state oil company, Yugopetrol. Tankovic had brokered a deal while there were still Western oil sanctions in place. When sanctions were lifted, Natell made a fortune as the chief supplier of oil to the region - and Tankovic was now a very rich and well-connected man.

A large black Jaguar drew up to the pavement nearby. An enormous figure got out of the back of the car – his old friend and comrade-in-arms, Colonel Tankovic. It was good to see him. He had slicked-back greying hair, and his broad frame filled the leather coat he was wearing. He had shaved off the trademark bushy moustache that he had worn for decades in an attempt to avoid detection.

They shook hands and Tankovic sat down opposite Petrovic.

'How was the turijan?' Tankovic asked gesturing to the plate.

'The best I've had since I've been here,' Petrovic replied.

'But not as good as home?'

'No. It is never as good as home.'

Tankovic produced a pack of filterless cigarettes, took one, and offered them to Petrovic.

'I'm not meant to smoke these anymore,' Petrovic said as he pulled one out. A doctor in Shepherd's Bush had warned him that smoking forty filterless cigarettes a day was killing him. He did not care. He had stared death in the face enough times not to worry about bloody cigarettes.

'Jebi ga,' Tankovic chortled, which meant *fuck it* in Serbian.

'Jebi ga! ... You heard about General Bosnic?' Petrovic asked him.

Tankovic nodded. 'Yes. It was in the papers. They treated him like a dog. The man was a General for God's sake! They have no respect.'

General Bosnic had led units of the Yugoslav People's Army against the Army of the Republic of Bosnia and Herzegovina in 1993. He had been brought to The Hague to face charges of war crimes and murder during the siege of Sarajevo. However, someone had smuggled Bosnic a capsule of potassium cyanide and he committed suicide in his cell.

Petrovic took a long deep drag on his cigarette, then said 'I met with our little balija friend.'

'How was he?'

Petrovic felt confident that no one would look into Mersad Avdic's death. He was just an old man who had died in his sleep. 'When I left him, he was sitting peacefully in his armchair. No signs of violence, robbery, or a forced entry. I am confident that his exit from this world will be put down to natural causes.'

'Unfortunately, my sources tell me he was working with others,' Tankovic said darkly.

'I've heard the same,' Petrovic replied. 'You have names?' he asked as he started to feel concerned.

Tankovic nodded and pulled a piece of paper from his coat pocket. 'I have one name at the moment. And an address. Do you want me to take care of it, brate?'

Brate was Serbian slang for my good friend.

Petrovic shook his head. 'No.' If there were any balija scum out there trying to hunt them down, he wanted to deal with them himself.

Tankovic looked over at him. 'You are still my commanding officer. It is my duty to protect you.'

'You've done enough for me. It is not a problem. And it is nice to catch up with people from the old country.' He looked at the address and raised an eyebrow. 'Peckham? He lives with the Africans then.'

'Not for long,' Tankovic said darkly.

CHAPTER 3

Having picked up Ella from the *Tiny Tots* nursery off Streatham High Street, Ruth sat on the 249 bus that was heading from Streatham to Clapham Common via their stop, Balham. Ella swung her legs rhythmically as Ruth clipped back her hair. Her tiny burgundy shoes, with a buckle, had blue paint on them. Ruth didn't mind. It would wipe off. Ella loved going to *Tiny Tots* and she'd made lots of friends. Her best friend was Koyuki. Ruth assumed she must be Japanese, or maybe Korean. She leant forward and kissed Ella's forehead. The blonde curls that had once hung from her daughter's head were darkening and straightening. She was growing up. The thought of it made Ruth a little sad.

She handed Ella a mini pack of raisins as the bus jolted and lurched in the chaos of the South London rush hour. Her mind turned to her husband, Dan. They lived in a small ground-floor flat in a side road, halfway up Balham Hill. Everyone told her that Dan was a waste of space. He earned a pittance working as an occasional roadie and DJ. She had pleaded for him to get *a proper job,* so they didn't have to worry about how they were going to pay the rent, bills and childcare. But Dan lived in his own little world where he still believed that when he got his big break, he would be flown out to Ibiza to DJ and earn a fortune. Sometimes her anger even turned to pity. Two of Dan's friends did earn a decent living from DJing and making House records, which made it harder to convince him to *give up and grow up.*

Having got off the bus, Ruth popped Ella into her pushchair and covered her with a thick zebra-striped blanket. As she walked up Balham Hill, she could see that South London was changing before her eyes. Gentrification had arrived, and it looked like Balham was going the same way as Clapham had gone in the last eighteen months. And the working-class families from SW4 and SW12 were migrating to places like Crystal Palace and Peckham, where housing was much cheaper. Her grandparents wouldn't recognise some parts of south-west London now.

Getting out her keys, Ruth opened her front door and immediately got a pungent waft of weed in her nostrils.

Bloody hell! He is such a twat!

Ruth could feel the anger rising already. She didn't want drugs to be the first thing their daughter smelled coming home. She had continually told Dan that he had to smoke his weed outside. Unclipping Ella from her pushchair, she scooped her up in her arms and rubbed noses as Ella giggled. She plonked her down in front of the television, put on *CBBC,* handed her a bottle of sugar-free juice, and took a breath before confronting her increasingly irritating husband.

Entering the kitchen, Ruth could see that the doors to their small patio were open. Dan was sitting outside with his friend Felix – they were sharing a spliff.

Why don't you close the patio doors, dickhead?

'I could smell that as soon as I opened the door,' Ruth snapped.

Dan let the smoke pour out of his nostrils. 'Sorry, babe. I forgot the doors were open. You okay?'

He doesn't give a shit!

Even though Ruth falling pregnant with Ella hadn't been planned, they weren't exactly teenagers. Dan was heading for thirty.

'Hi Felix,' Ruth said, ignoring Dan on purpose. Felix was another wannabe DJ and record producer. He was harmless, funny, and a bit eccentric.

'Hiya,' Felix said in a rasped voice, taking the spliff from Dan.

They laughed at nothing in particular. Ruth could see that their eyes were red and glassy – they were totally stoned!

Great! I'll sort Ella's tea, bath and bedtime out. Then cook us some food!

'I'm making curry later,' Ruth said, trying not to sound annoyed. She was too tired to have yet another row.

'Sorry, babe. I've got a DJing gig in Hammersmith. Remember?' Dan said.

Ruth nodded and smiled as she put away the shopping. He had started calling her *babe* about a month ago, and despite her piss-taking, he hadn't got the message that she hated it. She also knew that most of Dan's *DJing gigs* were in grotty little bars where he played his records to about forty or fifty people. Once he'd paid for petrol, booze and drugs, he had spent over half the £100 he claimed to be getting. Then he would slope through the front door at dawn and spend the day in bed, while they paid for Ella to be in childcare for the day. To say that Ruth's patience was wearing thin was an understatement.

By the time Ruth had showered and changed, Dan and Felix had left. There was a scrawled note on the kitchen table – *I'll be DJing at The Greyhound pub if there's an emergency. Love you xx.*

Ruth made Ella tea and then gave her a bath, delighting in watching her splash and laugh as she filled her tiny bucket. Sitting in the water and playing with her toys gave her such joy. Ruth settled Ella in bed, read her *A Squash and A Squeeze,* and then fell asleep next to her.

It was nine o'clock by the time Ruth woke and went through to the kitchen to make herself a cup of tea. Her head felt a little thick from sleeping. As she waited for the kettle to boil, she looked again at the note. And then a horrible feeling of suspicion came over her.

In previous years, Ruth had found a couple of girls' phone numbers in Dan's clothes. He always had a ready-made excuse – usually that they worked for a record label and wanted him to send in a demo. He had admitted to snogging a girl at a club called Fabric, but claimed she had literally jumped on him. Ruth knew that wasn't the half of it, but she couldn't prove anything. However, that kind of continual mistrust was exhausting.

Ruth poured boiling water into her mug and then went over to a small bookshelf. She pulled out the large Yellow Pages phone directory and thumbed through until she found the number for The Greyhound pub in Hammersmith. As she went to write down the number, she wondered if she was being paranoid.

Bloody hell, Ruth. You're a detective in London's Metropolitan Police. It's okay for you to make a phone call to see where your husband is! she told herself.

With a slightly sinking feeling of what she was going to find, Ruth picked up the phone and dialled the number.

'Hello, Greyhound pub,' answered a gruff male voice.

'Hi there. I'm just trying to get in contact with my husband who is DJing at your pub tonight,' Ruth asked.

'Sorry, love. Nothing like that here tonight. We have live music at the weekends, but nothing during the week,' the man explained.

'I don't suppose there's another Greyhound pub in Hammersmith, is there?' Ruth asked, already knowing the answer.

'No, love. I've owned this pub for twenty years and the only other ones I've ever heard of are in Kensington and Hendon.'

'Okay. Must have got it wrong. Thanks anyway,' Ruth said as she hung up the phone.

CHAPTER 4

P etrovic looked down at the scribbled piece of paper that Tankovic had given him earlier in the day – *Hamzar Mujic, 23a Comeragh Gardens, Peckham, London SE15.* He knew from his sources that both Mersad Avdic and Hamzar Mujic were working together. However, he didn't know if anyone else was involved. Somehow, they had discovered that Petrovic was secretly living with a new identity in London and planned to expose him. These men, these *balija* scum, had the audacity to call Petrovic a war criminal. Who were they to sit in judgement on him? He had acted to protect the Serbian people during a bitter civil war. The Serbs, his people, had been abused, tortured, and killed by the Turks for centuries. They had infiltrated and corrupted the Serbian land and culture with their dark skin and barbaric ways.

Petrovic remembered his trip to Gazimestan, a memorial site that had been built to commemorate the Battle of Kosovo in 1389. In Serbian, Gazimestan meant *The Place of Heroes.* In June 1989, Petrovic had been asked to attend a special day of events to mark the 600th anniversary of the battle. He heard an incredible speech given by Slobodan Milosevic, their brave leader. Petrovic knew when he heard the great man speak that day of future 'armed battles', that the Serbs would fight to take back their country as they had done 600 years earlier. Over a million Serbs came to the battleground that day and heard

Milosevic's battle cry. Petrovic would never forget the sense of unity and pride he had felt to be a Serbian. And what he was doing tonight was protecting himself from Turkish devils such as Advic and Mujic – it was part of the ongoing war.

Glancing up at the tall, three-storey late Victorian houses, Petrovic found number 23. Scanning down the list of door-bells, he saw *H Mujic* scribbled in blue biro beside the buzzer for Flat A. He was in the right place.

He pressed the buzzer and waited for an answer.

'Hello?' came a man's voice. Petrovic recognised the accent. It was Slavic, so it was definitely Mujic.

'I've got a delivery here for a Mr Hamzar Mujic,' Petrovic said, trying his best to disguise his own accent and sound confused as how to pronounce the name.

'What delivery? I don't have deliveries,' Mujic responded grumpily.

'I'm sorry, sir. I think they are books?' Petrovic replied.

There was a moment's silence.

'Very well. Come up,' Mujic said, pressing the buzzer to let Petrovic in.

Opening the door with his gloved hands, he felt in his pocket for the reassuring outline of the syringe. It was the perfect weapon for such an assassination as it left virtually no mark on its victim. The coroner would not waste time by ordering a post-mortem on another old man who had seemingly died alone in his flat of natural causes.

Petrovic pushed the light button that was on a depressed timer. The bulb on the ground floor was weak and threw a dim, apologetic light onto the staircase.

Climbing the threadbare carpeted stairs, he could smell cooking. It was spicy. Maybe he would make himself a spicy Bosnian beef goulash later. And open some wine. That would round off the evening nicely.

He heard a door opening up on the third floor. Mujic had come out to sign for his delivery.

The timed light downstairs clicked off and plunged the ground floor into darkness. Petrovic could feel his pulse quicken. He needed to get Mujic back into his flat with as little noise as possible.

Reaching the top of the stairs, he could see the landing was in virtual darkness. The third-floor light wasn't on. It was the perfect cover for his attack.

Mujic was standing about twenty yards away. The open door to his flat cast a rectangular shard of light across the dark red hallway carpet.

Petrovic made no signal that he had seen Mujic. He kept his face low with no eye contact. He turned right, pretending that he was going to another flat.

'Excuse me?' Mujic said.

'Yes?' Petrovic mumbled.

'Did you see a delivery man down there? I just let him in,' Mujic said in a confused voice.

'No. There's no one down there,' Petrovic said. He spun sharply and darted across the landing, pushing Mujic in the face and chest.

Mujic yelled as he stumbled back inside the flat. He tried to slam the door, but he wasn't quick enough. Petrovic jammed his foot into the door to prevent him from closing it.

For a moment, they just looked at each other.

Petrovic glared into Mujic's terrified eyes.

Yes, fear me you little Turk scum.

Smashing his shoulder against the door, Petrovic crashed the door open and sent Mujic flying to the floor.

Hurrying inside, Petrovic closed the flat door. He knew that his entrance hadn't been as quiet as he hoped.

'Don't kill me! Please don't kill me!' Mujic screamed as he looked up from the floor.

Shut up, you little piece of Muslim shit!

Petrovic put his finger to his lips. 'Settle down, my friend. I have not come to kill you today.'

'What do you want?' Mujic shouted.

If he keeps shouting, the neighbours will knock on the door.

'I have spoken to your friend, Mersad,' Petrovic said in a gentle voice.

'Mersad? You've spoken to Mersad?' Mujic asked, his voice trembling.

'Yes. Don't worry. Your friend is fine. Come on and get up,' Petrovic said as he pulled Mujic from the floor. 'We're going to sit down, have a nice cup of tea, and I'm going to tell you what I agreed with Mersad.'

'I don't trust you,' Mujic stammered as he backed away.

'If I was going to kill you, you would be dead by now,' Petrovic said calmly.

Mujic looked at him. 'I have nothing to say to you.'

'Please. We are both a long way from home. Let us sit down and I will explain everything.' Petrovic gestured towards what seemed to be a living room.

'You have two minutes to say what you need to say. Then I want you out of my flat or I will call the police,' Mujic said.

'Of course. No problem,' Petrovic replied as he followed Mujic through the doorway and into the darkened room.

CHAPTER 5

Ruth and Lucy had grabbed a coffee after the briefing. As they wandered down the corridor to the CID office in Peckham nick, Ruth found herself lost in her thoughts. Dan's lie about where he had been the previous evening was preying on her mind. He had been asleep on the sofa by the time she and Ella had got ready to leave this morning. She would ask him later, but no doubt there would be a feasible excuse.

'Trouble on the ranch?' Lucy asked as they got to the door into CID.

'Dan couldn't lie straight in bed,' Ruth said, realising that Lucy had noticed her preoccupation.

'Fucking men! Can't live with them - pass me an enormous glass of wine,' Lucy said sardonically. 'I wish I was gay. It would be a lot easier.'

Ruth didn't like to admit that in recent years she'd had increasing doubts and confusion about her own sexuality. She found herself attracted to women more and more. And yet her pulse could race at the sight of a fantastic-looking man. Did that make her bi-sexual? She didn't even know if that was a thing. Her friend told her that George Michael was bi-sexual. Ruth knew that was bollocks. Hadn't she seen George in the video for *Faith*? He couldn't be more heterosexual if he tried.

As Ruth and Lucy reached their desks, they could see that they were covered in McDonald's wrappers, bags, and empty burger boxes. It was the male CID officers' idea of a joke.

Big fucking joke! Ha, ha Ruth thought scornfully.

'Very funny lads,' Lucy said looking around at the male detectives in CID who were sniggering at their little joke about Ruth and Lucy's collar from the day before.

'You lot are hilarious,' Ruth said dryly.

'Sarge, didn't one of the witness statements from yesterday say they were convinced that there were two clowns at North Peckham Estate?' DC Syed Hassan asked DS Tim Gaughran.

'Yeah, and also some bloke dressed up as Ronald McDonald,' DS Gaughran replied, trying not to laugh.

Idiots, thought Ruth. She had no time for DS Tim Gaughran. He came from a family of coppers, which made him a know-it-all. Even though he was in his 20s, his attitude to women belonged to the 70s.

There was more raucous laughter.

'Comedy gold, boys. How long have you been working on that?' Lucy asked.

'About twenty minutes,' Hassan admitted.

Ruth looked at Lucy and rolled her eyes. The Metropolitan Police still had a long way to go before female officers were respected in the same way as their male counterparts.

At that moment, DCI Harry Brooks walked in. Brooks was in his mid-40s and an old school, no nonsense copper who claimed he longed for the good old days of the 70s and 80s *before all this politically correct bollocks came in.* However, Ruth knew that Brooks played up to that image too. Underneath all the bluff and bluster, he could be a bit of a softie. It just suited him to remind the young male CID officers that he took no shit from anyone.

'What have we got, guv?' Ruth asked as Brooks approached with a file.

Brooks spotted the McDonald's wrappers on their desks. 'Fucking infants, that's what you lot are, you know that?' he said, rolling his eyes at Ruth and Lucy.

'Three of them still live with their mums, so it's not a surprise when they act like toddlers, guv,' Lucy said.

Brooks gestured to the file. 'Might have a suspicious death that needs looking at.'

'What happened?' Ruth asked.

'Seventy-two-year old male. Hamzar Mujic. Found dead in his flat in Comeragh Gardens. The landlady found him. She goes in most mornings for a coffee and chat, and found him sitting dead in his armchair,' Brooks explained.

'Doesn't sound very suspicious, guv?' Lucy asked.

'Neighbour says they heard shouting and maybe some kind of fight coming from the flat last night. I need you to go and have a quick look before they cart the body away.'

'Yes, guv,' Ruth said as she collected her things together and put on her jacket.

'Wanna drive?' Lucy asked, tossing Ruth the keys.

Do I have a choice?

As they headed for the doors, Gaughran looked over and made kissing noises.

'You two lovebirds going out then? Make sure you wash your truncheons when you get back, eh?' he joked, as Hassan sniggered at his desk.

He's such an unpleasant dickhead.

'Tim, you do know that sitting in your bedroom at home next to Mummy, on your stained Postman Pat duvet, while you toss off your little dick to *Ally McBeal* on the telly, doesn't constitute an active sex life,' Ruth said with a smile.

For once, Gaughran looked lost for words as Hassan burst out laughing.

Lucy grinned at Ruth and gave her a hi-five as they marched out of the CID office and slammed the doors behind them.

TWENTY MINUTES LATER, they had found the house in Comeragh Gardens and gone up the stairs to the third floor. A young, uniformed PC stood by the open door to the flat.

Ruth flashed her warrant card. 'DC Hunter and DC Henry. What have we got, constable?'

The PC showed them into the flat. 'The landlady came in just after nine and found the deceased in here, ma'am.'

They walked through the small hallway into the living room and saw an old man sitting in an armchair. He was virtually bald and wore thin-rimmed spectacles. As a uniformed officer, Ruth had seen her fair share of mainly elderly people who had died of natural causes in armchairs, sofas, or beds. It was a familiar scene.

'And you've got a name?' Lucy asked.

'Hamzar Mujic. I found a wallet with a driving licence, ma'am,' the constable explained.

Ruth thought the name sounded Middle Eastern, but the deceased man didn't look like he came from that part of the world. She went over to the body and looked carefully at the man's face. There was a mark or a bruise on his cheekbone.

'Looks like he's been hit by someone or something,' Ruth said. However, there was nothing else about the way he was sitting, or anything else in that room, that pointed to foul play.

Ruth pulled out her forensic gloves and snapped them on.

'You've taken a statement from the neighbour?' Lucy asked.

The constable looked down at his notepad. 'Yes, ma'am. Ade Kenyatta. He's gone to work now. But he said that he heard shouting from the landing and then inside the flat. Then he heard a bang as if someone was fighting. And then it stopped.'

'Did he see anything?' Ruth asked.

'No, ma'am. I got the feeling he was scared and didn't want to get involved.'

Ruth saw that Lucy had walked over to a small desk and bookshelf on the other side of the room. 'I think he's Bosnian.'

'Why's that?'

'A few articles from the newspapers. A couple of books. And a Koran which would probably make him a Muslim,' Lucy said as she looked through the man's things.

'That would fit with his name,' Ruth said, thinking out loud.

'Maybe he came here to get away from the war? After Sarajevo and Srebrenica, it's not surprising is it?' Lucy asked as she continued to thumb through papers on the desk.

Ruth's knowledge of the complexities of the Bosnian War was a little vague.

'You seem to know a lot about it,' Ruth remarked.

'My dad was in the army. He went out there,' Lucy said as she looked through what looked like a leather-bound journal.

'I didn't know your dad had been in the army. You travel around a lot as a kid then?' Ruth asked.

'Oh yeah. Proper army brat. West Germany, Ireland, Middle East. You name it.'

'Sounds like fun.'

'It wasn't. All I wanted was to stay in one place, go to the same school, keep the same friends. It's exhausting having to start again every few years,' Lucy said as she turned the pages of the journal.

Ruth nodded as she wandered out of the living room, and back down the hallway to the front door where the uniformed officer was standing. For a moment, she stood outside on the landing looking in. She then pulled the door towards her so that it was virtually closed.

There was something on the front of it which caught her eye. A thin crack in the wood about four feet from the ground. Going closer, she examined it. The wood had split as if something or someone had crashed against it. She pushed the door open a few inches, crouched down, and saw tiny fragments of wood and paint on the carpet in the hallway of the flat.

That's happened very recently. Maybe someone hit the door with their shoulder? she thought.

Ruth then opened the door further and stepped inside so she could examine the back of it. She registered the height of the lock, and then looked down to the bottom of the door where she saw black scuff marks on the white paint.

Wandering back into the flat, she saw that Lucy was still in the living room.

'How tall do you think our victim is?' Ruth asked.

Lucy gave her a quizzical look and shrugged. 'No idea. Why?'

'Six foot, five five, or five foot?' Ruth asked.

Lucy looked at the man sitting in the chair. 'He's small. If I had to guess, about my height. Five five or something.'

'Yeah, that's what I thought. Can I borrow you for a second?' Ruth asked, gesturing towards the front door.

'You're being very cryptic,' Lucy said, raising an eyebrow.

Ruth reached the door and said, 'Just stand here for a second will you?'

'Do you want to tell me what you're up to Miss bloody Marple?' Lucy asked with a wry smile.

Ruth pulled the door slowly towards Lucy and said, 'If someone tried to force this open, the lock here would hit you in the face, wouldn't it?'

'Yes. Go on.'

Ruth moved to the outside of the door and showed Lucy the thin crack. 'This crack in the wood is about shoulder height. As if someone has hit it with their shoulder to force it open. There are fragments of wood and paint still on the carpet right inside, so it happened very recently. Also on the inside, there are black scuff marks at the bottom of the door, as if someone has put their foot against it to stop it opening. If the door does eventually fly open, this metal lock might hit them in the face.'

'And our victim in there has a fresh bruise on his face,' Lucy said, catching the direction of Ruth's theory.

'If someone forced their way in here last night, that would also explain the shouting and noise of a fight.'

'Except our victim is sitting upright in an armchair with no outward signs of any kind of violence,' Lucy said.

Ruth looked at Lucy. 'I'm going to suggest that the coroner orders a PM though. Just to cover all bases.'

Lucy nodded in agreement.

CHAPTER 6

Ruth arrived at Tiny Tots Nursery. She had nearly finished her takeaway latte. Glancing at her watch, she saw that she was ten minutes early and had time for a ciggie before collecting Ella. As she lit her cigarette, she noticed one of the other mums had arrived. Ruth had seen her before. She looked like she might be Japanese. She had a beautiful, structured face, feline eyes, and always dressed immaculately in designer clothes. She was one of those mums who made Ruth feel a bit dowdy and sub-standard.

I wish I looked that pristine after a day's work.

As they smiled at each other, the mum stopped and looked at Ruth for a moment. She then approached.

'Hi, I know this is gonna be really cheeky, but can I bum a cigarette off you? I just smelled yours and mine are at home,' the mum said. She had an American accent.

'Of course,' Ruth said, fishing the packet from her coat.

The mum went into her bag. 'I've got some money in here somewhere.'

Ruth offered her the packet with a smile. 'Don't be daft. Just take one.'

'Thanks. I'm Shiori,' the mum smiled back.

Bloody hell! She really is very attractive, Ruth thought to herself. *I could look at her all day.*

'Ruth. Here you go,' Ruth said as she flicked her lighter and lit the cigarette.

Shiori took a deep drag as though her life depended on it and blew the smoke out. 'Fuck me, that's better.'

I like her.

Ruth laughed. 'Not many of us left these days.'

'Everyone I know has quit. And there's nothing worse than a reformed smoker. I'm turning into a social pariah,' Shiori said, shaking her head.

'My husband smokes so at least he's not judging me,' Ruth admitted.

Shiori raised an eyebrow ironically. 'Now, that would be nice.'

Is she referring to having a husband that smokes, or being judged?

'Your husband doesn't smoke then?' Ruth asked.

Shiori said nothing. Ruth could see that she had hit some kind of nerve.

Oh bollocks. Too many questions, Ruth.

'God, sorry. None of my business,' Ruth said, feeling very awkward.

'No, it's fine. Just got through a messy divorce so ...' Shiori said.

This is awkward.

'Sorry.' Ruth searched for something to say to change the direction of the conversation.

'It's fine. My husband fucked his secretary. Total cliché. He's back in the States while we try and sort out what we're going to do. Bit of a mess,' Shiori explained and pointed to the cigarette. 'Which is why I keep running out of these.'

'I don't blame you. That sounds horrible,' Ruth said with a sympathetic smile.

Shiori pointed to the pram and pink blanket that Ruth had with her. 'You have a daughter?'

'Yeah. Ella. She's been coming here for about a year.'

Shiori looked at her and smiled. 'Not *the* Ella? That's all I hear at home. Ella and I did this or that.'

'Koyuki? Oh right. You're Koyuki's mum?' Ruth said, putting two and two together.

'Miss Thomas says that our daughters are inseparable,' Shiori laughed.

'We must have a play date,' Ruth said, aware that she found Shiori very attractive.

Shiori looked at her. 'I would really like that, Ruth. Great idea.' She said it genuinely. Ruth wondered if she didn't have many friends in London.

'I'll write down my number for you,' Ruth said, feeling guilty that she was so excited at the prospect of this new friendship.

LAYING BACK ON THE untidy pillows, Lucy gazed up at the hotel room ceiling. She wiped the sweat from her top lip – it tasted a bit salty. The cornice was cracked and there were stains on the paint over by the window. What did she expect from a cheap South London hotel room that she and her *bit of stuff* were only going to use for an hour or two?

She wasn't complaining. The sex had been great. Frantic, passionate, and sometimes overwhelming, as sex should be in the first months of a clandestine affair. And he was a very attentive lover, unlike most of the blokes she had been with.

For a moment, she got a glimpse in her mind of her first boyfriend, Matty Davies. She had lost her virginity in the back of his Austin Healey parked up on the Epsom Downs. Matty was a posh and went to a local fee-paying school. Lucy came from the far less affluent town of Sutton, only a couple of miles away. Her dad was a plumber and her mum a primary school teacher. They told her that made them a bit working class and a bit middle class. The fumbling sex with Matty had lasted about thirty seconds and was so underwhelming that she doubted that it even counted as losing her virginity. The last she heard, Matty Davies was a successful hedge funder earning an annual seven-figure salary.

Bloody hell. Maybe I should have stuck with him?

'Shower's free,' came the shout of a male voice from the bathroom.

'I hope you didn't piss in it!' Lucy yelled back.

'That's for me to know and for you to find out,' the man said with a laugh.

'Oh, that's really bloody romantic, Harry!'

Harry Brooks came out of the bathroom with a white towel around his waist.

Of course, he was only *Harry* while they were in the bedroom together. Tomorrow he would be DCI Harry Brooks, her guvnor in CID.

Brooks gyrated his hips around. 'I think skirts must be much more comfortable than trousers. Everything down there is much looser and can just swing about.'

'Lovely. You don't have to stop being romantic just because you've rinsed your spuds,' Lucy said, rolling her eyes.

Brooks shrugged. 'I'm just saying.'

'If you want to stroll into Peckham CID in a little skirt tomorrow morning, I think you should go for it,' Lucy said getting off the bed laughing.

Brooks took her by the hand, twirled her around as if they were dancing, and then kissed her. 'Let's do this properly, Luce. No more of these grotty bedrooms, eh?'

Here we go again, she thought.

'I quite like the grotty bedrooms. It's all part of the excitement,' Lucy said.

Brooks pulled her closer to him. 'I mean it. I'll leave Karen and we can do this properly.'

'I don't want you to leave Karen. This is fine.' Lucy moved his arms from around her waist.

'Is it?'

Lucy laughed. 'Harry, I'm just going through the whole father figure thing.'

Harry smiled and shrugged. 'I don't care. How does that song go, *I will be your father figure, put your tiny hand in mine.*'

'Oh my God. Are you actually quoting George Michael lyrics to me?' Lucy grinned and shook her head.

'Oh, is that who it is?'

Lucy went to the bathroom door. 'Right, I'm having a shower. I suggest you get dressed and get going before you're missed.'

'I do love you, you know that?' Brooks said.

'Just sod off, Harry. I'll see you in the morning.' Lucy smiled and shut the door behind her.

She knew that she was falling for Brooks, but she was afraid she was going to get hurt.

What the bloody hell am I doing?

CHAPTER 7

It had just gone 8am when Ruth and Lucy strode down the long corridor of St George's Hospital in Tooting, South London. Constructed back in the 1700s, it was one of the largest hospitals in Europe.

Ruth could feel a slight tension in her stomach. Even though she had seen her fair share of post-mortems, she just couldn't quite get used to them. She told herself to get a grip as the sound of her and Lucy's shoes echoed around the long, cold, windowless corridor.

Lucy pushed open the door to the mortuary and held it for Ruth. As they entered the cavernous examination room the hospital's Chief Pathologist, Professor Sofia Deneuve, came over. She was tall and thin, with angular features and a no-nonsense attitude to her work. Ruth actually liked her as she was a refreshing change from some of the bumbling old male pathologists who seemed stuck in some post-war time warp.

'Morning, ladies. Are you here about Mr Mujic?' Professor Deneuve asked in an accent that had a trace of Edinburgh in it.

Lucy nodded. 'Yes. DC Hunter and I aren't convinced that the death was from natural causes.'

Professor Deneuve looked down at her notes for a moment. 'The coroner asked me to get this preliminary PM done this morning and to rush through the toxicology report.'

'Anything interesting?' Ruth asked.

'Looks like you girls were spot on.' Professor Deneuve wandered over to the body.

Ruth was glad that her theory about a forced entry hadn't been as far-fetched as she worried it might have seemed.

'What's the cause of death?' Ruth asked.

Professor Deneuve beckoned Ruth and Lucy to come closer to the naked, white cadaver that was laid out on the metal gurney. Mujic's upper body was almost completely covered in hair.

He looks like he's wearing a hair jumper. Imagine being married to him! Ruth thought before realising that the poor man in front of her had probably been murdered.

'I found this,' Professor Deneuve said, pointing to the skin just behind his ear.

At first, Ruth couldn't see anything.

'Sorry, I ...' Lucy said with a frown.

Then Ruth spotted it.

'There's a needle mark,' she said.

Professor Deneuve nodded as she touched the skin to make it more visible to the eye.

'How did you see that from there?' Lucy asked.

'I grew up on a lovely Battersea estate full of smackheads. I can spot a needle mark at ten paces,' Ruth quipped.

Lucy rolled her eyes at Ruth's dark humour. 'Lucky you.'

'Someone injected your victim in the neck. The skin hasn't healed, so it was broken in the last twenty-four hours,' the professor explained. 'But I would have missed it even on a routine post-mortem.'

'Has the toxicology report come back yet?' Lucy asked.

'Yes. He died from fentanyl toxicity.'

What the hell does that mean?

'Fentanyl?' Lucy asked.

'Very strong opiate painkiller. It's fifty times stronger than morphine. In the medical profession, it's just started to be used in the treatment of pain in cancer. At the concentration that we found in the victim's bloodstream, he would have been unconscious in seconds and dead in under a minute. But if you hadn't flagged up the suspicious circumstances, we would have probably missed the injection mark and we wouldn't have done a toxicology report. It would have gone down as natural causes, which I'm guessing your killer was counting on.'

Ruth looked at Lucy – not what they expected to hear when they first walked in. Now they were dealing with a murder case.

BY MID-AFTERNOON, HAMZAR Mujic's flat in Comeragh Gardens had been sealed off as a murder scene. Ruth had organised for uniformed officers to contact every resident in the block and take witness statements. They were still waiting to talk to the neighbour who had heard shouting and some kind of struggle. His evidence was now key in narrowing down the time of the attack.

Ruth and Lucy continued to scour the flat for evidence while scene of crime officers, SOCOs, dusted for prints and anything else that could give them forensic evidence.

Ruth spotted Lucy looking at something on the wall.

'Found something?' she asked as she went over.

On the wall was a small, framed pencil sketch of a smiling woman sitting at a table.

'You think it's his wife?' Ruth asked as she peered towards the bottom of the frame where there was a tiny inscription. 'Amina Mujic, 1987, Mount Strigova.'

'Amina. Pretty name,' Lucy said. 'Given the date, her age and name, I'm guessing she has to be his wife.'

'I wonder what happened to her?' Ruth said thinking out loud. There had been no evidence that anyone else lived in the flat with Hamzar Mujic, and no sign of a woman. For a moment, Ruth felt a sadness as she thought of their victim living in a strange city, alone and a long way from home.

Lucy gestured to the wall. 'Actually, it wasn't the picture I was looking at.'

Next to the sketch was a large corkboard attached to the wall. The board itself was empty and had about ten coloured pins dotted around its surface.

'What do you notice about this board?' Lucy asked.

At first, Ruth didn't know what she was talking about. Then, as she looked properly, she could see that there was a small fragment of paper under each of the pins on the board.

'Someone tore whatever was on this board down rather than removing it carefully,' Ruth said.

'Could be nothing. But at the moment, we have no motive. There are valuables and money in the flat that are untouched. So, who wants to kill a seventy-year-old Bosnian refugee?' Lucy asked.

'No idea. But it wasn't an argument that got out of hand. Someone forced their way into the flat and injected him in the neck. It was completely premeditated,' Ruth said. 'Anything in all these papers on the desk?'

'Lots of handwritten stuff written in Bosnian. I think they speak a dialect of Serbo-Croat, don't they?' Lucy asked.

I've no idea if I'm honest.

'That sounds about right,' Ruth said with a shrug.

Lucy picked up a well-thumbed Serbo-Croatian/English dictionary. 'I could use this, but I think we'll get a translator to look at some of it.'

Ruth noticed something else about the corkboard that didn't look quite right.

'This isn't flush to the wall,' Ruth said with a frown as she went to the board and saw a half-inch gap behind it. Taking the board with both hands, she lifted it from the two nails that it hung on.

The wall behind was bare. Turning the corkboard around, Ruth could see that someone had taped a clear A4 plastic wallet to the back. Inside was a thick, dark brown leather journal with the initials *HM* embossed in gold.

Ruth pulled the journal out, looked at it, and then passed it to Lucy. 'Hamzar Mujic, I presume?'

'Whatever is in there, Mr Mujic didn't want anyone to find it or read it,' Lucy said as she opened it up.

Ruth noticed that each page had a date written at the top in intricate handwriting. However, the words were in a language she didn't understand. 'Looks like some kind of diary or journal.'

Lucy stopped at a page and then showed it to Ruth. 'Day before yesterday. The name Simo Petrovic. Then something else. Over here these four names written in a column.'

Mersad Avdic
Katerina Selimovic
Safet Dudic
Hamzar Mujic

Ruth pointed to the top of the page where a name was written all in capital letters.

BEN FLEET

'Let's run those names through the PNC when we get back,' Ruth suggested.

'This word here by the name Simo Petrovic. It's in capitals and underlined.' Lucy pointed to the word and tried to pronounce it. 'Ubijena.'

Grabbing the dictionary, Ruth flicked through to the word and looked for its English translation. 'Ubijena ... Here it is.' Then she stopped and looked at Lucy.

'What does it say?' Lucy asked with a frown.

'To kill or to murder,' Ruth replied.

CHAPTER 8

Petrovic crossed his legs as he opened up his copy of The Times. He was desperate for news of his football club, Fudbalski Klub Partizan, or Partizan Belgrade as they said in Britain. They were top of the Championship and had a good chance of winning the league.

Petrovic was fiercely proud of his childhood team. He remembered when his father had taken him to his first game at the Partizan Stadium in the late 1970s. It had been packed with men who roared and sang, fuelled by cheap vodka and strong cigarettes. The songs told of a time when the Serbs had been ruled by the cruel, evil Ottoman Turks in the 14th and 15th centuries. He remembered fondly singing along to '*The laughing eye and the weeping eye*.' It told the story of a man who had one eye that was constantly wet from laughter and one wet from tears. When his son asked him why he had two such different eyes, the man explained that one eye laughed at the joy of being surrounded by his Serbian family and friends. The other eye wept for that time before the Turkish infidels invaded their land.

Petrovic loved everything about being a Fudbalski Klub Partizan supporter. It had been drummed into him that the club had been formed from soldiers of the Yugoslav Army who had fought the German Fascists in World War II. To support any other club was an anathema to his family. The team's nickname was Parni Valjak, which meant The Steamroller. His father told him it was because in the 1950s, Parni Valjak's strong physical presence and precise passing would destroy opposing teams. Petrovic wasn't sure that was true, but it sounded heroic.

Petrovic glanced around at Brompton Cemetery in West London where he had arranged another meeting with Colonel Tankovic, who said he needed to see him urgently. They couldn't talk on the phone as Petrovic was paranoid that if MI5 suspected his true identity, then they might be recording his calls.

Before Petrovic had time to scan for the football results, he heard the crunching of Tankovic's shoes on the gravel.

'Kako ste,' Tankovic said, which was a traditional Serbian greeting, as he shook Petrovic's hand firmly. 'And at last the summer is coming.'

Tankovic hitched his trousers an inch as he sat down, so as not to sag the knees. He took out a packet of cigarettes, gave one to Petrovic, and used his lighter to light them both.

Petrovic folded his paper, took a deep drag on the cigarette, and sat back. As the warm breeze picked up, he could smell the sweet citrus scent of the nearby lime trees and their white budding flowers that hung in clusters. He knew that Tankovic had bad news for him and he was just delaying it for a moment.

'What happened, moj najbolji prijatelj?' Petrovic asked. It meant 'my best of friends'.

'The police are looking into our Peckham friend's untimely demise,' Tankovic told him.

'Why? It should have been signed off as natural causes,' Petrovic said with a sense of unease. He had been meticulous in leaving no sign of a struggle. He had positioned Mujic's body carefully in the chair. The needle mark and traces of fentanyl should never have been found.

'I don't know. It could be nothing. It's hard to get details from my source at the moment.'

Petrovic felt his anger grow. 'How worried should I be? Do I need to buy plane tickets? These fucking little materinas!'

'You must keep your calm, Simo. I am sure that it will blow over. And from what I hear, you don't need to worry too much,' Tankovic said knowingly.

'Why not?' Petrovic asked, now curious as he calmed down a little.

Tankovic raised an eyebrow. 'My source says that there are two women investigating the case.'

Petrovic smiled and snorted derisively. 'Women? What kind of a country is this?'

RUTH AND LUCY WERE now sitting in the ground-floor flat of the landlady, Mrs Dalila Thomas. She was late sixties, Afro-Caribbean, and wore a colourful housecoat. The kitchen was small, tidy, and smelled of spices such as cumin and ginger. The fridge was adorned with crayon drawings that Ruth guessed had been given to her by her grandchildren.

Lucy opened her notepad. 'And how long had Mr Mujic been a tenant here?'

'I looked earlier. He came here eighteen months ago,' Mrs Thomas replied.

'Were there any problems with Mr Mujic as a tenant?' Ruth asked.

Mrs Thomas shook her head sadly. 'No, no, no. He was a lovely man. A real gentleman, you know. I would go in most mornings and we would have coffee, and talk.'

'No problems paying the rent?' Lucy enquired.

'No. Always on time.'

'Do you know if he had any friends? Anyone that came to visit him?' Ruth asked.

'Only Mr Advic. They knew each other from when they lived in Yugoslavia. Before the war.'

'Mr Advic? Do you remember a first name?' Ruth queried.

'No, sorry. They were about the same age. And they would talk in their own language and I couldn't understand a word,' Mrs Thomas said with a laugh.

'Any idea how we can get in touch with this Mr Advic?' Lucy asked.

'No. Sorry. Mr Mujic does have a daughter though. And she gave me her number if anything ... you know, happened to him. I spoke to her this morning to tell her. She was very upset. It was terrible, you know?'

'And she lives in London, does she?' Ruth asked.

'Yes. West London somewhere. Different world over that way isn't it? I'll give you her number if that helps you?'

Lucy nodded. 'Yes, that would be really helpful.'

'And you never heard Mr Mujic rowing with anyone?' Ruth asked.

'No. He was such a nice man.'

'He didn't say that he was scared of anyone or anything? Or that someone wanted to harm him?' Lucy asked.

Mrs Thomas paused, and Ruth could sense that the question had sparked something in her mind.

'Last two weeks maybe. He was not himself, you know. Very quiet. I would say "What's the matter with you? You are sitting here with me, but your head is a long, long way away."'

'But he never told you why he was so distracted?' Lucy said.

'No. But you could see it. Something was wrong with him. I thought it was all these papers that he was reading. Stuff he brought back from the library, and newspapers.'

Ruth looked questioningly at Lucy. *What papers?*

'Where did he keep all these papers?' Lucy asked.

'On that big old desk in his living room. When I let myself in yesterday, I saw that they had all gone. I thought maybe he'd thrown them all away or had given them to somebody?'

Or maybe the person who killed him took them, Ruth thought.

THE SUN HAD CUT THROUGH the April clouds and it was warm as Lucy and Ruth wandered along the North End Road market which stretched across the border between Fulham and Hammersmith. A couple of phone calls had confirmed that Sanja Mujic, their victim's daughter, was running an aromatherapy stall in the market that day, about halfway along the street.

Striped red and blue awnings covered the fruit and vegetable stalls that were pitched next to stands selling colourful jewellery, CDs, and cheap clothing. The air was filled with the sound of Oasis' song *Wonderwall* and smelled of fish from a large fishmonger. Ruth was glad that she was smoking to mask the smell in her nostrils.

'How is Army Boy?' Ruth asked of Lucy's latest boyfriend. They never had names. Just a word to describe them and then the word 'Boy'. In recent months there had been Goatee Boy, Estate Agent Boy, and Posh Boy.

'I dumped him,' Lucy said. Ruth found her clinical, unemotional attitude to relationships refreshing.

'Bloody hell!' Ruth exclaimed as they manoeuvred through the bustling market.

'He was so thick. He thought Ikea was the capital of Sweden. When I suggested we go to Ikea, he said, *Great, I love City breaks*,' Lucy said shaking her head.

Ruth laughed. She wondered if she was jealous of Lucy's carefree love life. 'Oh dear. You really do pick them.'

'I said "It's me, not you," which everyone knows actually means "You will never see me naked again,"' Lucy said with her usual caustic wit.

'So, who is it now? It's hard to keep up,' Ruth asked.

'I like to call him Man Boy as he's a bit older.'

'Oh right. You can't beat a bit of experience,' Ruth said, wondering if she would ever get to meet one of Lucy's men?

Ruth gestured to an aromatherapy stall. A dark-haired woman in her thirties, with a nose ring, was drinking coffee and staring into space. Next to her was a girl in her late teens. Sanja had just lost her father and Ruth was surprised that she was running the stall today.

'Sanja Mujic?' Ruth said with a kind smile as she showed her warrant card.

Sanja nodded. 'Yes. Is this about my father?'

Ruth nodded. 'I'm so sorry for your loss. We wondered if we could just ask you a couple of questions?'

Sanja looked at the teenage girl and asked her to cover her stall while she went to speak with the officers.

'We can go in here?' Sanja suggested, pointing to a cheap-looking café with bright red tables.

They sat at a formica table by the window and Lucy ordered them teas.

'I'm afraid we have some bad news about your father's death, Sanja,' Ruth said gently.

Sanja immediately looked concerned. 'I don't understand.'

'We don't believe that your father died from natural causes,' Lucy continued.

'Sorry, I ...' Sanja mumbled and then stopped with a lost look on her face.

'I'm really sorry, but we think that your father was killed,' Ruth said gently.

'Oh God, no.' Sanja immediately started to tremble. 'I don't understand.'

A waitress arrived with a silver pot of tea, and mugs.

'Is there anyone you can think of who would want to harm your father?' Lucy asked.

Sanja shook her head and wiped the tears from her eyes. 'No, no. He was just a gentle, old man. Who would want to kill him?'

'At the moment, we know that it wasn't a robbery. Whoever killed your father had planned to do it,' Lucy said.

Sanja took a deep breath as she sniffed. Ruth could see how hard it was for her to process what she had just been told. 'My father wouldn't harm a fly. It makes no sense to me.'

'We believe that your father had some papers or documents that he was working on. They might have been stolen by the

person who killed him. Do you know anything about that?'
Lucy asked.

Sanja shook her head, but Ruth could see from her expression that something had clearly occurred to her.

'We also found a diary hidden behind a corkboard. We're having it translated,' Ruth explained.

'We found some names written in it. Mersad Avdic? Does that mean anything to you?' Lucy asked.

Sanja nodded. 'Yes. He is my father's best friend.'

'And he lives here in London?' Lucy asked.

'Yes. Somewhere in Earl's Court. I can dig out an address if that helps?'

'Thank you. That would be useful,' Ruth said.

She could see that Sanja had thought of something but for some reason hadn't said it.

She just needs a gentle push.

'Anything you can think of, Sanja. However small you might think it is, it could help us catch whoever did this to your father,' Ruth said, hoping she would feel brave enough to trust them.

'Simo Petrovic,' Sanja said with a puzzled look on her face.

Ruth shot Lucy a meaningful look – it was the other name that had been written in Mujic's diary the day before he died.

'Simo Petrovic?' Lucy asked.

Sanja's whole body tensed. 'You don't know who Simo Petrovic was?'

Lucy shook her head. 'Sorry, I don't.'

'The Butcher of Mount Strigavo?' Sanja said, as if this should ring a bell.

Ruth had a vague recollection of the place name but nothing she could expand upon.

Lucy nodded. 'I know there were atrocities at Mount Strigavo a few years ago.'

'Atrocities? Such a meaningless word. Our family lived in a small town at the foot of Mount Strigavo. Because we were Bosniaks and Muslims, we were told to hand over our town leaders. When we refused, the Serbs shelled and attacked our village. Then they burnt it down. My mother was raped and murdered.' Sanja wept and her hands shook with the memory of it.

After a few seconds of silence, Ruth reached over and put her hand reassuringly on Sanja's arm. 'I'm so sorry to hear that.'

Sanja nodded. 'It was Simo Petrovic who led the attacks on the Muslim villages. He ordered his men to shoot us as we ran away. Women and children. Then we were rounded up and sent to the concentration camps. My father and I were sent to different camps but somehow we survived. I saw Simo Petrovic beating men and abusing young women. He made some of them dig their own graves and thought it was funny.'

Ruth had no idea that what had happened in Bosnia had been so brutal.

'Your father had written the name Simo Petrovic in his diary for the entry on the day before he was killed,' Lucy explained.

Sanja nodded as if this wasn't a surprise. 'My father had recently become obsessed with him.'

'What happened to Simo Petrovic at the end of the war?' Ruth asked.

'He committed suicide. He shot himself in the head rather than be captured and put on trial. I've seen the photographs of the coffin and the place where he was buried, which made what my father told me so strange,' Sanja said. 'I thought he was losing his mind.'

'What did your father tell you, Sanja?' Lucy asked.

'My father said that he had seen Simo Petrovic at Waterloo station three weeks ago. He swore that it was him. He followed him onto the Northern Line but then lost him.'

CHAPTER 9

As Ruth came through the front door with Ella, she saw several leaflets from the various British political parties scattered on the hall floor. The general election was only a matter of days away and electioneering in Britain had reached fever pitch.

Ruth had always voted for the Labour party. She came from a working-class family where voting for Labour was obligatory. The Labour party had re-branded itself as New Labour and Ruth knew this was an attempt to change the party's image as being the party solely of the working classes, unions, and left-wing politics. If Labour were going to win, she knew that the Prime Minister in waiting, Tony Blair, had to appeal to the middle classes too. According to the papers and opinion polls, Blair was starting to make gains in what was now called *Middle England* – the mainstream middle classes of the Home Counties and suburbia.

Even though she wasn't highly politicised, Ruth knew that the current Conservative government had cut funding to both the police force and the prison service. She could see that this was making her job more difficult and even dangerous. Less manpower meant more crime. It was a simple equation.

As she closed the front door, Ruth could smell cigarette smoke and hear the deep vibrations of house music coming from the kitchen and dining area at the back of the flat.

I'm going to fucking kill him this time! she thought as she felt herself tense.

Plonking Ella down in front of the television, Ruth stormed through the house and flung open the door to the dining area. Dan was smoking with his headphones on as he mixed two house records together on his decks.

'You said you were going to be working all day!' Ruth thundered.

Dan turned the volume down, 'Yeah, they cancelled me last minute. Might be something next week. Sorry, babe.'

'Will you stop calling me babe!' Ruth growled, realising that she now wished Dan physical harm.

Dan continued nodding to the music. 'Woah. Calm down. What's the problem?'

Oh my God! I hate his guts!

'We pay a fortune in childcare for Ella to go to that nursery. And you're here all day doing bugger all. We can't afford it,' Ruth yelled, aware that she sounded like a mother reprimanding a child.

'I was rehearsing. I've got another gig tonight,' Dan said, still nodding and seemingly paying no attention to her.

Ruth marched over to where he was standing and kicked the table. The stylus on the record jumped, skidded noisily to a halt, and the music stopped.

Dan looked a little shocked. 'Careful! What are you doing?'

'Are you kidding me! Rehearsing for a gig? Jesus, Dan! You're playing a few records to a handful of drugged-up morons in a bar in Stockwell! It's not like you're Oasis going on a world tour. Grow up!' Ruth bellowed.

Dan put his hands up defensively. 'Hey, I think you need to calm down a bit.'

'I'm not going to calm down! Your little hobby is bankrupting us.'

'I'm working tonight. Two hundred quid for an evening's work. It's more than you earn.'

Ruth glared at him. 'I earn money every day, you dickhead. And that's if you're going there at all.'

'What's that supposed to mean?' Dan asked with a frown.

'You know exactly what I'm talking about, you feckless prick!' Ruth shouted. She was aware that she was out of control now.

'I don't need all this, Ruth,' Dan said as he walked past her and headed for the door.

'That's it. Run away, Dan!'

'I'll be back for my records later,' he mumbled, and with that he was gone.

Ruth took a few deep breaths, but she knew it was all too much. She closed her eyes and felt the tears come.

Jesus Christ! I can't live like this!

Wiping the tears from her face, Ruth went to the fridge and pulled out a bottle of white wine. She was shaking.

That's it. It's over.

Her phone buzzed with a text message – *Hi Ruth, it's Shiori, Koyuki's mum. Wondered if you fancied getting together for a coffee sometime this week?*

Ruth looked at the text for a moment and then began to type.

Hi Shiori. Do you fancy sharing a bottle of white wine and ciggies at my house now? Koyuki and Ella can play. I'll text you my address if you're up for it.

There were a few seconds. Nothing. Ruth wondered if she had been too over-familiar. Shiori probably thought she was an idiot. *Now I feel stupid.*

Then Ruth saw the following message arrive – *Brilliant idea! You must have read my mind. I'll bring more wine as one bottle is never enough! I know Koyuki will be so excited to see Ella. Text me your address. Shiori x*

IT WAS GETTING DARK and Lucy had been sitting in her car for nearly fifteen minutes. She turned the heater off and looked up at the glowing floodlights that lit up the astro-turf pitches. The Charlatans' *North Country Boy* was playing on the radio. She preferred the heavier guitar music of some of the current bands to a lot of the dance stuff that was in the charts. Even though the car windows were closed, she could still hear the various shouts of the five-a-side games that stretched across the four pitches. Reaching into the glove compartment, she took out a small bottle of Calvin Klein *Obsession* and sprayed it behind each ear. It tingled for a second. She loved its smell – it was exotic and sexy.

She knew that Harry was playing his weekly game with other coppers from various South London nicks. No one from Peckham CID played so she knew she wouldn't be spotted by a colleague. However, she didn't know what she was actually doing there. The thought of going home to an empty flat, mi-

crowaving some food, and watching the telly was too depress-
ing. The thought of a quick tryst with Harry was giving her a
buzz. Glancing at her watch, she saw it was 8pm. Harry would
be coming out to his car any minute now.

It had been several years since she'd had any form of long-
term relationship. For a moment, she wondered what her ex-fi-
ancé Steve was doing with his life. They were together for just
over four years. They bought a flat in Catford together and
planned to get married. And then one day, about two years ago,
Steve dropped the bombshell that he was in love with someone
else. A woman he had met at work. And that was that. He was
sorry but there was nothing he could do – so he moved out. It
took her a long time to get over it. In fact, she wondered if she
had yet.

The noise of male voices broke her train of thought as she
glanced up at groups of men carrying gym bags making their
way from the pitches. She spotted Harry laughing and clap-
ping a team mate on the back. Smiling to herself, she thought
how attractive he was in that moment. His broad chest, silver-
ing hair, and twinkling eyes. But did she want to take what they
had further? She was self-aware enough to know that she feared
making herself vulnerable again. Harry was older and married.
She might have joked that Harry was some kind of father sub-
stitute, but she had suspicions that's exactly what he was. And
he was her boss. It was far from ideal.

Getting out of the car, Lucy looked over as Harry stopped
at his car which was parked opposite her.

'Did you win?' Lucy called over.

'Bloody hell. What are you doing here?' Harry said with a
smile as he wandered over.

'I'm prowling for men,' Lucy said.

'Any luck yet?' he asked.

'I'm waiting for the right punter.'

Harry gestured to a dozen or so middle-aged men. 'You've come to the right place.'

Lucy laughed and looked at him.

'You're very sweaty,' she said.

'I'm very unfit.'

'I wouldn't say that,' she responded with a knowing grin.

'So, what are you doing here, Luce?' he asked in a slightly more serious tone.

Lucy shrugged. 'I was at a loose end and found myself thinking about you.'

'Are you just using me for sex?' he asked teasingly.

'Only if you have a shower first,' she replied, pulling a face.

Harry shrugged. 'No can do. Karen wants to talk to me about something and I promised that I'd be home at a decent time.'

'That sounds ominous?'

'I doubt it. She probably wants to talk to me about getting that new kitchen again.'

Not even time for a quickie then?

Lucy frowned. 'Oh right. Do you need to go right now then?'

Harry nodded. 'I'm running late already.'

'Oh, right. No problem.'

Lucy was aware that she was feeling deflated, even though she knew there had been no guarantee that Harry would be free.

'You look disappointed?' Harry said as he pulled out his car keys.

'I am. But I'll get over it,' Lucy said casually.

He looked at her quizzically. 'You do know what mixed signals are, don't you?'

Lucy nodded. 'Yeah.'

'I'll see you in the morning then, eh?' he said as he wandered back to the car.

'See you tomorrow.' Lucy tried to pretend that she wasn't deflated by her wasted journey.

CHAPTER 10

As Ruth walked into CID, she swigged her strong coffee with two sugars. Her head was a bit fuzzy from the two bottles of wine she had shared the previous evening with Shiori. It was now official. She had a *girl crush* on her new American friend.

'Listen up everyone,' Brooks boomed as he came out of his office. His shirt sleeves were rolled up and his tie loosened.

Bloody hell. He looks like he's been here since dawn, Ruth thought to herself.

Half a dozen or so CID detectives stopped talking and turned to face the front of the room. Ruth went to her desk, sat down and finished her coffee. She spotted Lucy skulking in and perching on a table. The room was already too warm and smelled of the male detectives' cheap deodorant and bacon butties.

Brooks went over to the scene board that had now been established for Hamzar Mujic's murder. There was a slightly blurred photograph of Mujic at the board's centre. Around that, the usual collection of photos, maps, and time and date of death.

Brooks tapped the board with his folder. 'Where are we with this murder? Lucy? Where are you?'

Lucy stood up so Brooks could see her. 'Hiding at the back, guv.'

'We're ruling out robbery as a motive, is that right?' Brooks asked.

Lucy nodded. 'Victim had his wallet. No valuables were taken so it's not robbery. We think someone forced their way into his flat and then injected him with fentanyl.'

'Very elaborate,' Gaughran said raising an ironic eyebrow.

'That's what came up in the toxicology report,' Lucy said defensively.

Brooks frowned. 'I've never come across fentanyl before.'

'Apparently it's characteristic of recent political assassinations in the Soviet Union, guv,' Ruth said.

Gaughran snorted with laughter. 'What? You two have been watching too many James Bond films, haven't you?'

Lucy growled under her breath. 'Piss off, Tim.'

It does sound a bit far-fetched for Peckham now we've said it out loud, Ruth thought.

'Not really. In fact, I've heard of something stranger,' Brooks said.

'Sorry, guv. You've lost me,' Gaughran said with a frown.

'Don't you lot remember Georgi Markov? The poisoned pellet from an umbrella?' Brooks said in disbelief.

'Are you taking the piss, guv?' Lucy asked.

Ruth now remembered the case from when she was a kid. It was in the papers.

Brooks smiled. 'Bloody hell, you youngsters don't know anything do you ... ? Georgi Markov was a Bulgarian dissident living up the road from here in Clapham. He wrote articles against the Bulgarian regime. One day, he was walking across London Bridge when someone bumped into him. He felt a little scratch on his leg. What he didn't know was that a member of the Bulgarian Secret Service had fired a tiny pellet of ricin, which is a deadly poison, from the tip of an umbrella into his calf. By the time he got home he was feeling unwell. The next day he was dead. Now that really is James Bond stuff, Tim. So, although it's rare, it does happen.'

Gaughran looked a little subdued as though he had been admonished. 'Learn something new every day, guv.'

Brooks looked pensive for a second before asking, 'Was Hamzar Mujic a politician back in Bosnia?'

'No, guv,' Ruth said.

'Anything that gives us a clue as to why he was killed like this?'

'Not yet. But we spoke to his daughter yesterday. She seems to think that Mujic had seen a Bosnian war criminal called Simo Petrovic in London, which doesn't make sense,' Ruth explained.

'Why not?' Brooks asked.

'Because just over three years ago, Simo Petrovic killed himself and was buried in Bosnia,' Lucy said.

Brooks looked directly at Lucy. 'Have you checked this Petrovic out?'

'Not yet, guv,' she replied.

'Mujic had some papers and articles, both on a desk and pinned to a corkboard. They disappeared around the time of his murder,' Ruth said.

'Fentanyl is a painkiller isn't it?' Hassan asked.

'Yes,' Lucy confirmed. 'The pathologist reckons it's fifty times stronger than morphine.'

'Who was that then? Professor sexy pants?' Gaughran asked with a grin. 'I'd love her to give me a scrub down in the mortuary.'

Gaughran is such a dick!

Ruth rolled her eyes. 'Don't you ever wonder why you're single?'

'And why your right hand has friction burns on it?' Lucy quipped as the others in CID laughed.

'I'm left-handed actually,' Gaughran joked, trying to front it out.

Brooks looked at the scene board for a moment. 'Can you infants shut up for a minute? If we think that a foreign national like Petrovic is involved and in the UK, I'll have to let Scotland Yard know. It's probably something we need to run past the Home Office.'

Ruth looked up to see a uniformed officer head her way with several sheets of a printout.

'Thanks,' Ruth said quietly as she took the sheets and had a quick look. It was a PNC check on Mersad Avdic, Hamzar Mujic's best friend.

Something immediately caught her eye.

Ruth gestured to the printout. 'Guv, I think I've got something.'

'What's that?' Brooks asked.

'PNC check on Mersad Avdic, who was Hamzar Mujic's best friend. He was found dead in his flat in Earl's Court two days ago. Cause of death was natural causes.'

A UNIFORMED OFFICER opened the door to Mersad Avdic's basement flat in Earl's Court and showed Lucy and Ruth inside. It smelled musty and damp.

'No luck finding the next of kin?' Lucy asked.

'No, ma'am. We're having to go through the Foreign Office to see if they can find anyone in Bosnia. Landlord wants the flat back at the end of the month, so all his possessions will have to go into storage,' the officer explained.

Ruth stepped over the letters and leaflets that had dropped through the letterbox and made her way down the hallway. Further along was a small shoe rack with four pairs of shoes neatly arranged on the flimsy wooden shelves.

'We found him in here,' the officer said, indicating a door to the living room.

Ruth and Lucy went into the sparse and functional room. The dark orange curtains were still closed.

The officer pointed to a large red armchair. 'Mr Avdic was sitting there when we came in.'

'And no sign of a forced entry or a struggle?' Ruth asked.

'No, ma'am. Nothing. He was just sitting there.'

Ruth spotted that beside the armchair opposite was a teacup and saucer with a centimetre of tea inside.

Lucy went over to a desk that was tidy and clear of any clutter.

'I'll have a quick scoot round,' Ruth said to them as she left the living room, headed down the hallway and into the kitchen. On the counter were two small bags of shopping.

Ruth peered inside and could see a bag of frozen peas and a tub of vanilla ice cream, both of which had now defrosted.

Why didn't he put those away? she asked herself.

She then wandered into the bedroom. The walls were covered in a sky-blue and white patterned wallpaper that looked a little bit like the sky. The small double bed was made, and next to that was a deco lamp and pine bedside table. There were two books, but the titles were in a foreign language so Ruth couldn't read what they were.

Returning to the living room, Ruth looked again at the shoe rack in the hallway. It had sparked a thought. As she entered, Lucy looked over from the desk.

'Find anything?' she asked.

'He didn't put his shopping in the freezer,' Ruth said as she went to the armchair where the teacup and saucer were.

'That's because he was dead,' Lucy quipped darkly.

'Why didn't he put it away when he came in?' Ruth said as she crouched down for a second and looked at the carpet just in front of the armchair. There was a small piece of dried mud and fragments of gravel.

'At it again, Sherlock?' Lucy said with a frown.

Ruth looked up at the uniformed officer. 'Was Mr Advic wearing slippers when you found him?'

The officer thought for a second and then nodded. 'Yes, ma'am. Those old-fashioned tartan ones you get.'

'Something up?' Lucy asked.

'Mr Avdic comes home from the shops. He takes off his shoes in the hallway and puts on his slippers as he always does. He takes the shopping to the kitchen. For some reason, he leaves it there and doesn't unpack it. He comes in here. The kitchen is immaculate and so is most of the carpet in this room,' Ruth said, trying to put together the inconsistencies as she spoke.

'Where are we going with this?' Lucy asked as she searched the drawers in the desk.

'There's mud on the carpet here, and a teacup and saucer next to this armchair. So, Mr Avdic comes in, puts the shopping down, doesn't take off his shoes, makes a cup of tea and comes and sits here. Meanwhile his frozen food is defrosting. He then decides to go and put his slippers on. Comes back in here, sits on this other armchair, and dies.'

Lucy nodded. 'You think someone else was in here with him?'

'Maybe. I think we need to persuade the coroner to order a PM and to do a toxicology report on him and look for any signs of a needle.'

'Good luck with that. It will come out of Kensington's budget.'

Ruth looked thoughtfully around the living room. 'None of this adds up.'

However, Lucy had stopped listening. She was staring at something that she had found.

'What's that?' Ruth asked.

Lucy turned and showed her a photograph of a man in his 40s. He had black hair, a thick beard, and a camouflage jacket. Ruth thought he looked a little bit like Fidel Castro. Lucy then turned the photo over. There was some writing on the back.

Ruth peered closer. 'What does that say?'

'It says Simo Petrovic. And a London address. Where's W14?' Lucy asked.

'Hammersmith.'

STUBBING OUT HER CIGARETTE, Ruth took a breath and continued turning the pages of the London A-Z map book. It was the middle of the day and the offices of Peckham CID were relatively quiet. Most of the detectives were out and about.

She glanced down again at the postcode and the index. W14 3TJ. Moving her finger across the map, she found what she was looking for. The address on the back of the photo of the man that she presumed was Simo Petrovic.

Turning the photo over, Ruth gazed for a moment at the man's face. He was handsome, in the old-fashioned sense of the word. His face looked like it was about to break into a smile. The skin around his eyes had started to wrinkle with age. His eyes looked up and past the camera. There was nothing in that photo to suggest that this man was The Butcher of Mount Strigavo. However, Ruth had been a copper long enough now to know that appearances meant nothing, despite the great British public's theory that someone should *look guilty*. The first time she saw a photo of Ted Bundy, she couldn't get over how good looking he was. The fact that he had murdered over thirty young women put a bit of a dampener on that though.

'I've got the first part of Hamzar Mujic's diary translated,' Lucy said, waving a folder as she entered CID.

'Have we heard back about that CCTV from Waterloo station?' Ruth asked.

'No. Nothing. What about the coroner in Kensington?'

'Apparently they're backed up, but they will do a PM when they have time. And getting a blood sample and a toxicology report could take over a week,' Ruth explained.

The door to the CID office opened and Brooks appeared.

'Ladies, I need to borrow you both,' he said, and beckoned them to follow him by curling his finger.

'Sounds ominous,' Lucy muttered under her breath as she pulled a face at Ruth.

Brooks led them out of CID and down the corridor to a meeting room. At the far end of the oval table sat two middle-aged men wearing grey suits.

They don't look like coppers, Ruth thought.

'These gentlemen are from the Home Office. They would like to talk to us about Hamzar Mujic's murder,' Brooks explained as he sat down and indicated that Ruth and Lucy should do the same.

Ruth shot Lucy a look and widened her eyes.

That all sounds very serious.

The older man, who was bald and wearing glasses, gestured to a folder that he had in front of him. 'DCI Brooks has been good enough to update us on your investigation into Hamzar Mujic and his untimely death. We understand that Mr Mujic believed that he had seen a Serbian national called Simo Petrovic in London a few weeks ago?'

Lucy nodded. 'His daughter said he had spotted and followed Simo Petrovic at Waterloo station. We don't have the exact date.'

'Apparently, he was adamant it was him though,' Ruth said.

The younger man gave them both a rather supercilious smile. 'That's quite impossible, I'm afraid.'

'I know that he was meant to have committed suicide and was then buried in Bosnia. But isn't it possible that was just some smokescreen that allowed him to escape justice?' Lucy asked.

The younger man reached into his file and pulled out some documents. 'The UN Security Council investigated this when they set up the ICT at The Hague.'

This man is irritatingly pompous.

'Sorry? ICT?' Ruth asked.

'International Criminal Tribunal. For war crimes committed in the former Yugoslavia,' the older man said, chipping in.

The younger man turned to show them an A4 photograph of a grave. 'This is where Simo Petrovic was buried.'

'That's what you were told,' Lucy said a little pointedly.

She's being even more feisty than usual.

Brooks shifted awkwardly in his seat.

The younger man ignored Lucy and showed another photograph to them. 'And this is a photo of Simo Petrovic's death certificate.'

'Yeah, well I can go to a bloke five minutes from here and get a fake copy of my own death certificate for about fifty quid,' Lucy said derisively.

'These documents came from the Bosnian government in 1995. We are not here to justify or debate their authenticity,' the younger man said coldly.

'Then why are you here?' Ruth asked.

Brooks shot both Ruth and Lucy a look to rein it in.

The younger man put the photographs back into the folder. 'Simo Petrovic is dead. I have shown you the evidence of that. The Home Secretary is keen that your investigation into Mr

Mujic's murder doesn't instead become an investigation into whether Simo Petrovic is alive and hiding in London. Should anything leak to the press or the media, it could spark a rather unpleasant diplomatic incident.'

Lucy shrugged. 'I guess that having a Bosnian war criminal wandering around the streets of London would be embarrassing.'

'And I'm guessing if that happened a few days before a general election it might be damaging for the current government?' Ruth added.

The younger man ignored them and got up from the table, unmoved by what Lucy and Ruth had said. He looked over at Brooks.

'I'm sure that DCI Brooks will explain to you that looking for Simo Petrovic is a waste of valuable police resources. And that it is a line of enquiry that the Home Secretary would like you to close.'

Brooks got up, went to the door, and showed the men out. He closed the door once they had gone and glared at Lucy and Ruth.

'What the bloody hell was that?' he snarled.

'You want us to turn a blind eye to the fact that there might be a war criminal killing Bosnians in London in an attempt to keep his identity hidden?' Lucy asked.

'Where's your bloody evidence, Lucy!' Brooks said brusquely. 'We've got one murdered old man who thinks he might have seen someone from his past that is buried in Bosnia. It's not much to go on.'

'What about the photograph in Avdic's flat?' Ruth asked. Petrovic being involved in the murder did explain a lot of the more unusual aspects of Mujic's murder.

'I don't want to hear any more about Simo Petrovic,' Brooks said.

'Never had you down as someone who would bend over and drop their trousers so easily, guv,' Lucy snapped.

'Lucy!' Ruth exclaimed. She had seriously crossed the line now!

Brooks looked at her for a moment. 'I'm going to pretend I didn't hear that Lucy ... Petrovic is a line of enquiry that isn't open to you. And that's an order.' Brooks then looked directly at them both. 'Is that understood?'

They nodded.

Brooks went out of the room and slammed the door behind him.

Ruth looked at Lucy.

'What?' Lucy asked.

CHAPTER 11

Ruth came back into her living room with a pizza. Lucy was sitting on the sofa drinking a beer and looking through the English translation of Mujic's diary.

Lucy had wanted to continue digging around the case. Dan was out and Ella needed picking up, so they had decided to continue working into the evening at Ruth's flat.

Ruth plonked the pizza down on the low table by the sofa. 'What is pepperoni anyway?'

Lucy was lost in what she was reading. 'What?'

'Pepperoni. It's pork isn't it? Cured?' Ruth said munching away, but realised that her words were lost on Lucy.

'I cannot believe this happened only five years ago,' Lucy said quietly. Ruth could see that she had tears in her eyes as she blinked. 'That poor man had been through so much. Too much. And for him to die like that ...'

It wasn't like Lucy to get so emotionally involved in a case. In fact, it was usually the other way around, with Lucy telling Ruth that she was too close to a case for her own good. However, it was clear that something about Hamzar Mujic and his diary had struck a chord with her.

Ruth watched Lucy wipe a tear from her face with the back of her hand. 'I guess it makes for pretty grim reading?'

Lucy nodded, and looked back down at the diary. 'I'll just read you this entry ... *March 1992. I, along with all the Muslim*

81

men from my town, had been transferred to a concentration camp at Ravnik. As we spent our days in hard labour, we could see the British troops in their reconnaissance vehicles in the distance, working as part of the UN and driving towards Kuzla. This was the first time I had come across Simo Petrovic. I had heard his name before, and it seemed to strike terror into everyone who heard it. People called him The Butcher. Petrovic hated the British and would take delight in ordering the road to Kuzla to be shelled. Once, I saw one of the British vehicles swerve a shell and get stuck in the mud. Petrovic grabbed a high-powered rifle and began to shoot at the stationary vehicle. He must have fired around twenty rounds. Later, it was reported on the radio that a British soldier had been killed in that vehicle. Petrovic spent the next few days bragging about what a great marksman he was and how he had murdered a British dog.

The next week, I was moved from this camp over to Dretelj. The Bosnian Croat army had turned the old Stolac hospital buildings into an interrogation centre. Petrovic was in charge of all the camps in the area. He wanted us to tell them where the Muslim fighters were hiding out. He was particularly interested in where the foreign Mujahideen fighters, who had come to help us from Afghanistan, had their training camp.

We were kept in a pitch-black room for days with no food or water. There were about seventy men from our town. There were no toilets, so we had no choice but to go where we sat. The smell was unbearable.

Petrovic and his men tortured us one by one. I will never forget the screaming of my friends from the rooms next to us. Every time the door opened, I felt sick as I knew it would be my turn soon. When the time came, I was dragged to a large room and tied to a chair. I couldn't see because my eyes had grown accustomed to being in the darkness. They beat me with sticks and used barbed wire to rip my skin. When I passed out, they threw urine on me until I was conscious. Then I saw a neighbour of mine, Dizdar, lying dead against the wall. He had been there for three days. His eyes were wide open, but his skull had been crushed. His face was such a strange colour. They laughed and said he was an observer from the Red Cross. Petrovic kicked his head backwards and forwards like a football while I watched. At one point, Dizdar's teeth flew out of his mouth and skidded across the floor. I was sick but I'd had no food so I retched until I couldn't breathe. I can still see Dizdar's face in the nightmares that I have nearly every night.'

Lucy stopped reading. She wiped a tear from her eye and blew out her cheeks.

'Jesus, that's horrific! You okay?' Ruth asked.

'Yeah, sorry. Reading his diary has affected me badly. That's not like me is it?' she said, sitting back on the sofa and reaching for her bottle of beer.

'Not really,' Ruth said hesitantly.

'Oh thanks,' Lucy said with a little laugh as she dried her eyes and nose.

'I can't talk. I get way too involved in cases that I'm working on,' Ruth admitted. 'But I don't blame you. It's horrible.'

Lucy's phone buzzed. She took it from the table and read the text.

'Text from one of your lover boys?' Ruth asked, aware that she was a little jealous.

'Yeah,' Lucy said as she read it. 'Man Boy.'

Ruth was secretly relieved she could put her feet up and watch the telly. 'I thought we were working?'

'Yeah, but I need a bit of me time now. And he's a little older so he knows what he's doing, if you get my drift.'

Ruth was now feeling very jealous. 'Dirty bitch! Any future in that?'

'Not really,' Lucy pulled a face. 'He's ... married.'

Ruth felt herself getting angry. 'Lucy! For God's sake. Have they got kids?'

'No. The wife is a controlling bitch who makes his life hell,' Lucy explained defensively.

'That's what *he* says. You told me that you would never do that. You would never be the other woman.'

Lucy raised an eyebrow. 'Careful Ruth. I'm not sure you're one to judge anyone given the domestic situation here.'

Ow! Bit below the belt.

There was an awkward silence.

Lucy got up and went and got her coat. 'Do you want me to leave this here?' she asked gesturing to the diary.

Ruth nodded. 'You're going right now, are you?'

'Sorry. My head's all over the place, and I'm not in the mood for a lecture. I'll see you tomorrow.'

Ruth watched as Lucy walked to the door and left.

LUCY WENT INTO HER flat, turned on all the lights, and walked into the kitchen. She was in such a rage. The text from Brooks had asked if it was okay to *drop round*. After the dressing down he had given her and Ruth that afternoon, she couldn't believe he had the balls to ask. However, she was determined to have it out with him before she went to work the following day. Reaching inside the freezer, she pulled out a bottle of vodka and poured herself an inch. She swigged it back in one go.

Right, that's better.

Hanging up her coat, she looked at her watch. Brooks was late. Fucking cheek. She wandered around the flat, eventually sitting down on her sofa. She clicked on the television and saw the BBC News was on. It was something to do with the general election. She had voted Conservative all her life. So had her father. She wasn't about to change that, and there was something distinctly creepy about Tony Blair. He looked like he worked in an advertising or marketing company. He certainly didn't look like a politician.

The doorbell rang. Lucy took a breath, got up from the sofa and went the door. She could feel her whole body tense as she opened the door.

'You've got a fucking cheek, you know that?' she snapped.

'Hi Harry. How are you? Thanks for popping over,' Brooks said sarcastically.

'You can't talk to me like that at work and then expect to just pop over for a quick shag,' Lucy growled at him.

'I thought you said we couldn't talk about work while we were together?' he said.

'Don't be a fucking smart arse, Harry.'

'Any danger of me coming inside? Or do you want to do this on the doorstep for all the neighbours to hear?'

'I don't give a shit if they can hear!'

'Lucy,' he said raising his eyebrows.

'Don't bloody *Lucy* me!' she said opening the door wider with a scowl and ushering him inside.

'Thank you,' Brooks said as he came in and then stood uncertainly in the hallway.

Lucy looked directly at him. 'I read his diary.'

'Whose diary?' he asked with a shrug.

'Hamzar Mujic's. It's heartbreaking ... If Simo Petrovic is alive and well and living in London, we can't look the other way.' Lucy was beginning to feel overwhelmed again by what she had read. 'And if you had read what that man did to people, you would feel the same. It's sickening.'

Brooks took a moment and nodded. 'Okay. But I haven't read it. And if the Home Office is telling us that he's dead and for us to accept that, what am I meant to do?'

You spineless wanker!

'Grow a pair of balls, Harry. If you found out that Adolf Eichmann was hiding out in London, you wouldn't be prepared to look the other way, would you?' Lucy asked.

'I think they hanged him in the 60s, didn't they?'

'This isn't a bloody joke! I think you should leave, Harry,' Lucy said coldly.

'You don't know that Simo Petrovic is alive. You've got the defective memory of an old man who was traumatised from his time in Bosnia, and a photograph. It's not enough for a line of enquiry, is it?' he said in an angry tone.

'I know Simo Petrovic is alive. And he's here in London. And I want you to leave now,' Lucy snapped.

He held up his hands and turned towards the door. 'Hey, don't worry, I'm going. I came here for a break from work. Not to listen to your little fantasies.'

'Fuck off, Harry. Seriously, fuck off,' Lucy said as he went out of the door and slammed it behind him.

Wandering back to the kitchen, Lucy grabbed the bottle of vodka, poured herself half a tumbler and drank it.

She took a deep breath, but it was too late. She began to sob.

IT WAS CLOSE TO MIDNIGHT and Ruth had just finished a whole bottle of wine to herself. She was more than aware that she had been drinking too much in recent weeks. However, she found that when she drank, she cared far less that she had married someone who had little interest in spending time with her or their daughter. It was a tough thing to come to terms with. And it was also hard to hear from someone like Lucy, whose opinion she really respected.

Reaching over to Mujic's diary, she sat for a moment flicking through the pages. For a moment, she sat and read it.

September 1995

I don't know how I ever made it back to my hometown alive. But I did. What had happened to my poor Esme would never leave me. However, I wanted to see if there was anything left of the town where I'd lived my whole life. The street where I was born had vanished under mounds of rubble from the mortar shells. The office where I worked had been burnt to the ground. There was nothing left of my life except for Amina. It was then that I knew that me and my daughter needed to go somewhere new and start a new life a long, long way away. There were just too many ghosts on the slopes of Mount Strigova for us to stay there.

If there was anything good to take from these few years of misery and hell, it was that life is precious and short. We must make

the most of our time on this planet because we won't be return-
ing. We must seek and give love where we find it. If something or
someone makes us unhappy, then we must seek to change that. As
we grow older, regret is something that is hard to live with.

Swigging the last of her wine, Ruth thumbed through the
diary to the more recent entries.

Remembering Amina's comment that her father had seen
Simo Petrovic at Waterloo station three weeks earlier, Ruth
flicked through the pages looking for the word *Waterloo.*

A day that I want to forget. I was waiting for a train at Wa-
terloo East station and looking up at the huge list of trains and
times. I caught sight of a man walking along and heading for the
stairs to the underground. I knew that I recognised him, but for
several seconds I couldn't believe what I was seeing. It was Simo
Petrovic. There could be no mistake. I would not forget that man
for as long as I drew breath on this earth. He still had a beard and
dark hair. He was wearing a huge black overcoat. I thought I was
going to be sick to my stomach. I felt myself shake, but I knew what
I must do. I had to follow him. The rumour I had heard that he
had faked his own death was true after all. I stood behind him
as we went down the escalator but then he disappeared into the
crowds of commuters.

Wait until I tell this to Mersad. He will not believe me.

Something about what Mujic had written struck a chord
with Ruth. She sat and thought about the situation she was
in. Somehow, she had married someone who had the emotional maturity of a toddler. Dan seemed to lurch between needy
and insecure, to pompous and aloof. And if she was honest, she
knew he was cheating on her. It was so hard to admit. A part
of her had hoped she would find evidence to contradict that

thought. Something that would indicate that she was paranoid and jumping to conclusions. But it had never happened. And that left her with only one conclusion.

Rather than making her feel drowsy, the wine had given Ruth a little boost of energy. It had also disinhibited her. Picking up her phone, she scrawled through the contacts until she found Shiori's number. From their conversation, Ruth knew that Shiori was going to hear any day now about her divorce. It was a good excuse to get in touch. Ruth couldn't stop thinking about Shiori, and now she was a little drunk, she just wanted to act on it. *Fuck the consequences.* Ruth knew that she deserved better than this.

Hi Shiori. It's Ruth. Just wanted to see if there was any news from your lawyers. I know that you're worried about it and I was thinking about you. Pick up the phone if you fancy a chat. Any time. Hope we can have another play date soon. Ruth x

Ruth pressed send and sat back. She didn't care if Shiori didn't get back to her straight away. It had just felt good to send the message.

A few seconds later, Ruth's phone buzzed with a return message.

Hi Ruth. How lovely to hear from you, and it's so sweet that you've been thinking about me. I've been thinking about you too! Yes, let's get together soon. I'm very lucky to have a new friend like you xxx

CHAPTER 12

R uth and Lucy had been across London to Kensington police station. They had picked up a folder containing pho-
tocopies of Avdic's possessions and paperwork which had now
been boxed up. CID were keeping an open mind on Mersad
Avdic's death until the results of the PM came back.

As Lucy pulled away and joined the heavy traffic, Ruth began to flick through the folder that Kensington CID had given
them. There were old family photographs of what appeared to
be Avdic's wedding. Several bank statements and utility bills. A
few letters that were in Serbo-Croat.

'Are we okay?' Ruth asked after a few minutes' silence.

'Yes. What do you mean?' Lucy asked.

'You didn't seem very happy when you left last night. And
I'm sorry if I was a bit judgemental.'

'Oh God, that. I'd forgotten about it by the time I got
home. This case is just driving me a bit mad. I don't understand
why no one thinks these deaths are connected,' Lucy said in a
frustrated voice.

'They don't think they're not linked. But until they get the
PM results back, there's no evidence that Avdic was murdered,
is there?'

'Bloody hell, Ruth. Two Bosnian Muslim friends, both
probably victims of torture by a Serbian war criminal, think
they've found out he is still alive and living in London. They

decide to try and track him down. One of them is assassinated and all his papers are stolen. But, big coincidence, his friend happens to die the day before in his flat from natural causes?' Lucy said, going into a rant.

'I've done this job long enough not to believe in coincidences. But we also have to do things by the book, don't we?' Ruth said. It wasn't a question that needed an answer.

'Do we? I know it's a cliché, but it's not like the old days where you could run with a hunch or your instinct and no one would bollock you,' Lucy grumbled.

'The good old days? Ten years ago, they would never have had two female detectives working as a team. You'd have been hard pressed to find two female detectives in any CID in any London nick,' Ruth said, getting a little bit wound up.

'Yeah, all right, sister,' Lucy said teasing her.

'*Make us a cup of tea will ya darling*?' Ruth said in a voice mocking the kind of comments she got when she first joined the force.

'Bloody hell, you think that's bad. My first DCI said to me, *Oi Doris, give us a blow job and you can come out on the next call we get.* And this was in front of the whole of Croydon CID.'

'Bastards, the lot of them.' Ruth laughed and then looked up and saw that they were heading west rather than south back to Peckham. 'Where are we going?'

'Scenic route?' Lucy replied with a mock look of innocence.

'Isn't Hammersmith about a mile down this way?' Ruth asked as they stopped at some traffic lights.

Lucy shrugged innocently. 'I don't know. Is it?'

'Bloody hell, Lucy! I know where we're going.'

The address on the back of the photo of Simo Petrovic is in Hammersmith.

'I just want to have a look, that's all.'

'Yeah, and I want to keep my job,' Ruth snapped.

This is bloody irresponsible!

'You've read what that man did. He's a monster. And I think people like Mersad Avdic and Hamzar Mujic deserve justice, don't you?'

'Of course, I do. But we don't even know if Simo Petrovic is alive.'

'Don't be naïve, Ruth. Who else wanted those two men dead? They had found out Petrovic was alive and well and living in London. And he needed to shut them up.'

'Brooks will go mental if he finds out,' Ruth said.

'Fuck Brooks. You know, as well as I do, that someone in Whitehall wants this to be sat on until after the election.'

Ruth knew that Lucy was probably right, but she needed her job. At this rate, she fully expected to be a single mum in the next year so she couldn't afford to get sacked.

'Okay. But whatever we do, we need to tread carefully. Please.'

'Trust me. This is the right thing to do,' Lucy said in a stern tone.

Ruth knew there was no point arguing any more.

A few minutes later, they reached the Hammersmith one-way system and stopped in the heavy traffic outside Hammersmith Odeon.

'Wham! Club Fantastic Tour, 1983,' Ruth said, looking over at the building and trying to change the atmosphere in the car.

'Wham!? Never had you down as a teenybopper. I went to Thin Lizzy, 1983. And they were a proper band,' Lucy said. 'Chinatown was a great album.'

'Yeah, all right. How about Wet Wet Wet, 1987? Is that better?' Ruth asked with a smile.

'No, that's much, much worse,' Lucy chortled.

'Kajagoogoo?'

'I think you need to shut up now.'

They turned into a residential road and parked opposite a tall Victorian semi-detached house. 32 Summer Gardens – this was the address that had been written on the back of the photograph.

Getting out of the car, Ruth looked around nervously. She just wasn't comfortable doing this after their conversation with Brooks and the men from the Home Office. However, she also felt that what Lucy had said was right. The two murdered men deserved justice, and for their deaths to be fully investigated.

'What are we doing to do? Knock on the door and say "Hi there. Just wondering if a man named Simo Petrovic lives here?"' Ruth asked mockingly.

Lucy raised an eyebrow. 'You can stay in the car if you want.'

'I'm not leaving you on your own. God knows what trouble you'll get into,' Ruth quipped.

'Charming.'

They crossed the road and went through a small broken iron gate, and up an old gravelled path which led to the front door.

Lucy cupped her hands and tried to look inside through the green frosted glass of the door.

'Can't see anything,' she said, standing on tiptoes.

Ruth shuffled across to the large ground-floor bay window. She looked in through a gap in the shabby curtains. The room inside was completely bare – half-painted walls, floorboards, and no furniture.

'Doesn't look like anyone lives here,' she said.

Lucy came over. She had some flyers and envelopes in her hand. 'Post got stuck in the letterbox.'

'Isn't that stealing?' Ruth asked raising an eyebrow.

Lucy gave a little grin and shrugged. 'Gathering information as part of our investigation?'

Ruth saw Lucy's smile change when she noticed something down the street. Ruth turned and spotted two men in dark overcoats walking along purposefully. They were about a hundred yards away.

Ruth's stomach tensed. 'Shit!'

'Who are those clowns?' Lucy said as she shoved the envelopes into her coat pocket.

'I don't know, but maybe we should make ourselves scarce?'

Lucy gestured to the passageway down the side of the house. 'Down here then.'

Ruth followed Lucy down the weed-strewn passageway that led to the back of the house. The garden was overgrown, and two old mattresses and a stained fridge were propped up against the stone garden wall. It smelled of old rubbish and urine.

'Now where?' Ruth asked.

Lucy pointed to the fence-topped wall at the bottom of the garden. 'What about that way?'

'Seriously? We're going over that?' Ruth grumbled.

This is bloody ridiculous.

Sprinting to the wall, Ruth climbed onto its top and grabbed the mesh fence with her hands.

How the hell am I going to do this?

Glancing left, she could see that Lucy had beaten her and already had one leg over the top of the fence.

'Come on, slow coach,' she urged.

Ruth got her footing and pushed herself up with all her strength.

She could hear male voices getting closer. Someone was coming down the side of the house.

Shit!

She rolled over the top of the fence and dropped down on the other side to join Lucy. They were in a goods yard with a long concrete bay and stacks of wooden pallets. Two Luton vans were parked to one side.

As they ran quickly across the yard, Ruth glanced back. The two men were now in the back garden. A second later, one of the men spotted them and pointed.

'Shit! They've seen us,' Ruth gasped.

'Just keep running,' Lucy said as they turned left down a small mews street with a cobblestone surface.

Ruth was seriously out of breath and getting a stitch.

Bloody hell! I'm unfit.

Looking back, she could see that there was no sign of the men – yet.

They reached a main road and found themselves back on the Hammersmith one-way system.

Ruth looked at Lucy who had already caught her breath.

'I can't believe you just made me do that!' Ruth panted.

'Perk of the job.'

'Who the bloody hell were they?' Ruth asked, holding her side where the stitch had developed.

Lucy blew out her cheeks. 'No idea. But I didn't want to find out.'

'Now we've got to get to the car,' Ruth said shaking her head.

'Give it ten minutes and they'll probably have gone.'

'Probably?' Ruth said dryly. 'Great.'

Lucy indicated a nearby pedestrian crossing. They crossed the main road, then nipped into a newsagent's and bought two cans of Diet Coke. They drank them as they walked back to where they had come from.

Stopping at the end of Summer Gardens, they looked down the road. There was no one around.

'Told you. Coast is clear,' Lucy said as they set off towards their car.

Ruth wasn't quite as blasé and kept a watchful eye out.

As they reached the car, Lucy tossed Ruth the keys. 'Do you mind driving? I think I've jarred my ankle.'

Suddenly, the doors of the car behind them opened and the two men in overcoats got out and walked towards them.

'Oh bollocks,' Lucy muttered under her breath.

I'm not running again, Ruth thought.

'Good morning ladies,' the first man said. He looked the younger of the two, and had a shaved head and a public school accent.

At least they're not Serbian hitmen.

'Morning,' Lucy said in a sing-song voice. 'Can I help?'

'You two seemed very interested in No 32 over there,' the older man said.

'We run a property company. It looks ideal for renovation,' Ruth said, thinking on her feet.

'And you normally jump over fences do you?' asked the younger one.

'No offence, but you two looked pretty bloody scary coming along like that,' Lucy said with an innocent smile.

'Cut the bullshit please ladies,' the older man said as he took out identification and showed it to them. 'Intelligence Service.'

Ruth got out her warrant card. 'CID Peckham.'

'What are MI5 doing snooping around that house then?' Lucy asked.

'We have an ongoing surveillance operation in this area,' the younger man said.

'Why's that then?' Ruth asked.

'I'm afraid that's classified,' he replied.

'Oh right. So, you could tell me but then you'd have to kill me?' Lucy quipped.

Don't take the piss out of them, Lucy!

'We're just following a lead in a murder investigation,' Ruth explained.

'If you have any enquiries regarding this property then you need to run it past the Home Office first,' the older man said gravely.

'What do you know about a man named Simo Petrovic?' Lucy asked, sounding a little confrontational.

Bloody hell, Lucy!

There was a moment as Lucy's question seemed to hang in the air.

'Have a good day, ladies,' he said as they turned and walked back to their car.

Lucy looked over at Ruth with a smirk. 'Looks like we've pissed on somebody's chips!'

IT WAS LATE AFTERNOON. Lucy and Ruth had been sitting in the CID office for several hours. The CCTV tapes from Waterloo station had arrived earlier, and Lucy insisted that they trawl through for the date that Hamzar Mujic claimed to have seen Simo Petrovic. Even though it was a bit of a long shot, Ruth knew they had a chance of spotting Petrovic – and that would confirm Mujic's story.

They knew that Mujic was waiting to get on a train from Waterloo East up to London Bridge, where he would have caught a train to Queen's Road station in Peckham. It was a journey of just over thirty minutes. They had therefore narrowed down their search to the only platform that had trains travelling to Queen's Road.

However, Ruth was starting to feel frustrated. They had looked through the footage from 1pm through to 3.30pm twice. It had taken them hours. But there was no sign of Mujic or Petrovic anywhere at Waterloo station. Lucy seemed irritated but reluctant to give up.

Ruth arched her back and stretched. Maybe she should go for a walk, get them another coffee, and have a cigarette. Her mind turned momentarily to Dan and what was happening at home. There just didn't seem to be any way forward. She wanted to take Ella on a foreign holiday in the summer, but they couldn't afford it.

'Check the date again, would you?' Lucy asked, breaking Ruth's train of thought.

She's starting to get on my nerves.

Ruth blinked, took a deep breath, and looked at the paused frame on the monitor. The platform at Waterloo East in mid-afternoon wasn't busy. There were no more than four or five passengers waiting for the trains heading south.

We're not getting anywhere, Lucy!

'It's pretty empty isn't it?' Ruth said, which was a polite way of saying shall we move on to a more productive line of enquiry.

'Ruth?' Lucy said raising an eyebrow.

Ruth tried her best not to show her annoyance. 'What?'

'Please.' Lucy gestured to Mujic's diary. 'Just have a look, eh?'

Ruth shrugged. 'Hamzar Mujic was an old man. He had been through a lot of trauma. Maybe he saw someone who looked similar to Petrovic? Maybe it was just some kind of flashback? Or maybe he just wanted to see him for some reason?'

'I just don't believe that Mujic would have got it that wrong. He didn't see him for a second and then he was gone. He says that he followed him to the underground.'

'But we can't find either of them,' Ruth said, wondering why Lucy was avoiding using basic detection principles in favour of her gut instinct. 'We can't look through those tapes forever.'

Brooks came thundering through the door and glared at them both.

'Where were you two this morning?' he asked angrily.

Lucy put on her best innocent smile. 'Kensington police station, guv.'

'Don't piss me about,' he growled. 'Why have I got a fax from Scotland Yard asking if I sent two female detectives to an address in Hammersmith?'

Oh shit! We're in trouble now.

Ruth could feel herself blush. She had never seen Brooks so infuriated.

'Are you suggesting it was us?' Lucy asked with a mock frown.

Don't take the piss, Lucy.

'No, Lucy. How could it be? Two female detectives, claiming to be from this nick, identified themselves at an address that the Security Services have under surveillance. Tell me, how many female detectives do we have in this nick?'

'Is this a trick question?' she asked.

Ruth shot her a look to say *Shut up*.

Brooks was really starting to lose his temper now. 'What the *hell* were you doing there?'

'It was the address that was written on the back of the photo of Simo Petrovic, guv,' Ruth said meekly. She needed to say something.

'I thought we had established that Simo Petrovic was dead and buried in Bosnia and that we weren't going to follow his involvement in Hamzar Mujic's murder as a line of enquiry?' Brooks was getting red in the face.

'That's what you suggested, guv. But we think he was involved. How else do you explain that address being under the surveillance of the Intelligence Service?' Lucy asked.

'Firstly, dropping any investigation into Petrovic wasn't a suggestion, it was a direct order. As for why MI5 have any property in London under surveillance is beyond our jurisdiction,' Brooks said sharply.

'But I know you don't believe in coincidences, guv,' Lucy said.

'If you two don't leave this alone, I have no other option but to give you both a written warning,' Brooks said irritably.

Lucy could not help herself. 'But, guv, what if Petrovic *is* alive and in London?'

Please don't talk Lucy.

'Ruth? You're not saying very much so I assume you're less keen to lose your job than your smart-mouthed colleague here?'

'No, I don't want to lose my job. But I do think that Simo Petrovic is a viable suspect. It's hard for us to ignore that. But you've told us to drop it, so there's not a lot we can do,' she replied, hoping that might pacify him.

'Good. Someone talking a bit of sense. What's this you're looking at then?' he asked, gesturing to the monitor.

'CCTV from Waterloo, guv,' Ruth said sheepishly.

Brooks shook his head. 'Brilliant,' he said sarcastically. 'What have you found?'

He was deliberately ignoring Lucy and focussing all his attention on Ruth.

'Nothing, guv,' she said quietly.

'You're wasting your time, ladies. It's time to move on. I do not want to have this conversation again. Understood?' Brooks said sternly as he turned and then closed the door firmly behind him.

Lucy looked at Ruth and blew out her cheeks. 'Christ, he's such a dick.'

Ruth had had enough of Lucy. 'He's not a dick though, is he? If he doesn't do what the Home Office and Scotland Yard tell him to do, he'll be out of a job. And so will we. He's trying to protect all three of us.'

Lucy nodded and pushed her chair away from the desk. She gave an audible sigh. 'Sorry. I don't know why this case has got to me so much.'

'It's all right. I read Mujic's diary too. Petrovic was an evil bastard and I hope he *is* dead in a grave in Bosnia.'

'And if he's not?' Lucy asked.

'I don't know. But until we have some concrete proof, I think we have to put it to one side. I'm sorry.'

'Please. Just check that date in the diary again. If it tallies, we'll drop it and we'll move on.'

'Bloody hell, Lucy!'

Lucy gave her a disarming smile. 'I promise. Brownie's honour.'

'You were never a Brownie,' Ruth said raising an eyebrow.

'Just look at the flipping date, will you?'

Ruth went to the translation of Mujic's diary and turned back to the page she had marked. 'Here it is. 17th April is the day he was at Waterloo station.'

Lucy pointed to the date on the timecode of the CCTV tape which read *17th April 1997.*

'Bollocks ... Mujic was imagining things then,' Lucy said, sounding deflated.

'Right, can we turn that bloody thing off now?' Ruth said, indicating the monitor and VHS player. 'I've got a headache.'

Lucy nodded and moved her chair over to the table.

'Do you want a coffee?' Ruth asked.

Lucy nodded. 'Chocolate. I need chocolate. I'll come with you to the canteen. There's that young bloke who works behind the till. Lovely eyes.'

'Eyes or arse?' Ruth laughed.

'Both actually.'

'He's about eighteen, Lucy!'

'I'm not that old,' she protested.

Ruth looked again at the diary entry as she went to close it. She saw something that didn't add up.

'Wait a second ... The 17th of April was a Thursday wasn't it?'

'No idea. Sorry. Why?' Lucy asked as she pressed eject and took out the VHS tape.

'It *was* a Thursday. It would have been my Mum's birthday. And it was definitely a Thursday because I went to Streatham cemetery to lay flowers on her grave,' Ruth said thinking out loud.

'Sorry Ruth, you've lost me now.'

'The diary entry is for *Wednesday* 17th April. What if Mujic got his dates and days muddled. What if he was a day out?'

'You mean he might have been at Waterloo station on Wednesday 16th April?' Lucy's eyes widened. She went back to the video tapes. 'They sent the whole week of CCTV over.'

Lucy grabbed the relevant VHS and swapped the tapes over. Then she whizzed through the CCTV for Wednesday 16th April and got to 2pm.

'This is it,' she said, as she allowed the tape to play at normal speed so that the image was clean.

Ruth came over, leaned in close, and peered at the screen. As with the day before, there were only a handful of passengers and none of them looked remotely like Mujic or Petrovic.

Lucy sped the tape forward ten minutes and let it play again. Nothing. Another ten minutes. Again, nothing.

'Bloody hell!' Lucy said in a frustrated tone.

'Worth a try.'

Lucy pondered for a moment then said, 'I'm just going to look at the main concourse.'

'I really think we're wasting our time here,' Ruth said pointedly.

Lucy glared at her but said nothing as she sped the tape forward several more times. There was still no sign of either of the men.

Ruth looked at her watch. It was time to leave and go and pick Ella up from nursery. She then watched as Lucy delved into the box again and pulled out another VHS. 'This is the other end of the main concourse at Waterloo station on the same afternoon.'

Bloody hell! I don't have the patience for this anymore.

Ruth shook her head. 'We're really clutching at straws now.'

Lucy looked at her and snapped, 'Are you interested in finding this scumbag or not Ruth?'

'Of course. I think that Petrovic should face justice *if* he's still alive.'

'*If?* Bloody hell, Ruth. Have you had your head up your arse for the last few days?' Lucy growled.

'Oi! What's got into you?'

'I hate being told what I can and can't investigate when I know there's something suspicious going on. We can't do our job properly.'

'We're out of our depth with this - and I can't afford to lose my job!' Ruth said, now losing her temper. 'And Petrovic might be dead and buried in Bosnia.'

'Don't be so bloody naïve! This is some kind of coverup, and you know it.'

'I don't get paid enough to try and expose political conspiracies.'

'You're being selfish.'

'No, I'm not. So where is he, Lucy?' Ruth snapped.

'Bury your head and pretend it's not happening. That's how the Nazis got away with the holocaust and how men like Petrovic got away with slaughtering Muslims in Bosnia,' Lucy thundered.

Ruth headed over to her desk and chair to get her jacket. 'For God's sake, that's not fair. And I think we need to have this conversation when you've calmed down. I need to go and pick up Ella.'

'Well off you go then,' Lucy sighed, as she switched over the VHS tapes and began trawling through the footage again.

Ruth went over to the coat stand, grabbed her overcoat and put it on. 'I'll see you tomorrow then?' she said quietly.

'I've got him,' Lucy said in a virtual whisper.

'What?'

What did she say?

'Petrovic,' Lucy said, her eyes widening as she turned to look at her. 'I've got him ... on the tape here. Bold as fucking brass.'

'What?' Ruth said approaching. 'Where?'

Lucy pointed to the screen. 'Say cheese, you murdering bastard.'

Ruth looked at the image.

There was no doubt.

The bearded man coming through the ticket barrier was Simo Petrovic.

'Jesus Christ! That's him!'

CHAPTER 13

By the time Ruth got home, she was still trying to process what she had seen on the CCTV from Waterloo station. The image of Simo Petrovic was solid proof that he was alive and living in London. It also meant that the lines of enquiry they had established for both Mujic's and Avdic's murders which implicated Petrovic were probably correct. The two Muslim men had discovered that the Butcher of Mount Strigova had faked his own death, was living in London, and they were either going to expose him or take their revenge. And that's why they were killed.

Why were there people trying to cover up his existence? Why had the Home Office ordered them to close down that line of enquiry? And why did MI5 have the property in Hammersmith under surveillance if the Home Office truly believed that Petrovic was dead and buried in Bosnia. To say that it stank of some kind of political coverup was a huge understatement. However, it did scare her to think that she and Lucy were so far out of their depth.

Putting those thoughts to one side, Ruth made Ella boiled eggs and toast soldiers. Then she went about tidying the house and getting some washing done. Dan was doing some roadie work in North London but said he wouldn't be late. If she was honest, she hoped he would be. Ruth had started to realise that she preferred life without him. She didn't trust him for starters.

He seemed to only take care of Ella when it was convenient for him – which was rarely. And even though he was about to turn thirty, he acted as if he was a twenty-year-old single man.

The worst part of it was that Ruth had allowed him to get away with it for far too long. She ignored the fact that he lied about where he was at night ... that she had found two unexplained phone numbers in his pockets ... that he rarely wanted sex with her anymore ... that he drank and smoked weed like a student. She had now reached the point where everything about him either irritated her or made her want to do him physical harm. She was aware that this was no way to live. Life was too short to be this miserable at home.

What was she afraid of? Of being alone ... or of being judged for having a failed marriage and being a single mum? She could sense there was something holding her back from packing his bags for him and chucking him out. No one would blame her.

Sitting back on the sofa, Ruth switched on the television. The build-up to the general election was growing.

A BBC journalist was talking to the news anchor. 'If the polls are to be believed, then Tony Blair is going to transform the political colour of the whole country.'

She wasn't in the mood. She turned off the television and picked up the translation of Mujic's diary again. Turning to the final entry, she wondered if there was anything that might give them a lead. The name *Simo Petrovic* was written down with the word *KILL* that was underlined. Then on the other side of the page was the list of four names - *Mersad Avdic. Katerina Selimovic. Safet Dudic. Hamzar Mujic.*

Ruth then thumbed back to the pages that covered Mujic's life before he came to Britain and began to read again.

February 1992 – By the middle of February, every Muslim or Bosniak from our village had been taken to a ceramic's factory called Keraterm. Men, women and children all lived in the same camp, but we had separate sleeping quarters. There was still no word of what had happened to my beloved Amina, but I had to fear the worst. I kept my thoughts from Sanja and said that her mother was just in another camp and she would be safe and well.

My great friend Katerina looked after my Sanja while they were in the women's quarters. I couldn't thank her enough. Some of the Serbian soldiers prowled the female quarters at night and raped girls. Katerina made sure that Sanja was hidden away and safe. For that, I thank Allah.

After about a month, Katerina disappeared. I heard many rumours of where she had been taken. A nearby barracks had a building which had become a brothel. Someone told me that Katerina had been taken there with several other women. It would be another eighteen months until I saw poor Katerina and learned of the cruelty that had been inflicted upon her.

Ruth didn't want to read anymore. It was just too upsetting. However, it had steeled her resolve to find Petrovic. She had put in requests for PNC checks on Katerina Selimovic and Safet Dudic but was still waiting to get them back. How were they linked? Were they all Bosnian Muslims living in London? Were they aware of Simo Petrovic's presence in London? And then she had a darker thought. Was Simo Petrovic aware of the identities of the four on that list, two of whom were now dead? She made a mental note to check the electoral registers and utilities records first thing in the morning to see if the other two could be located quickly.

There was the sound of a key in the lock and the front door opened. It was Dan. Ruth's heart sank. She had hoped for more time on her own to sit and watch the telly.

Walking into the living room, Dan shuffled awkwardly. He had obviously had a few drinks. He looked at her for a moment with a curious expression. It was as if he was waiting for her to say something.

He is acting very strangely. Why hasn't he just sat down?

'Are you all right, Dan?' *Not that I actually care.*

'No, not really,' he replied.

'Are you going to sit down?' Ruth asked in an almost bemused tone.

'We need to talk. Or at least I need to talk to you.'

Ruth knew exactly what was coming next. He was leaving.

'Right. Do you want to sit down when we talk?' Ruth said with a sarcastic edge. She wasn't going to make this easy for him.

Why do I feel nothing? Why do I feel a massive sense of relief?

'I think I'm going to move out for a bit,' Dan said as if he had been waiting for hours to get those words out.

Ruth looked at him dispassionately. 'Okay.'

'We're not getting on. I'm scared to come home in case we have a row. I just need some time to think.'

'I think you're right.'

Dan looked at her and frowned. 'Okay. I thought ...'

'Come on, Dan. You didn't really think I was going to dissolve into a weeping mess and beg you to stay?' Ruth sneered.

'No, I just ... I don't know. It just feels sad, that's all.'

Oh my God. Has he got a tear in his eye?

'It is sad. It's very sad. There's a little girl asleep in there. And it would have been lovely for her if she could have grown up with two loving parents in the same house,' Ruth said.

'I didn't say that it's over. I just said I needed some time.'

Ruth shook her head at his self-deception. 'Come on, Dan. You know, as well as I do, that once you've moved your stuff out, you're never coming back.'

'Don't say that.'

'Is there someone else?' She knew there probably was, but she had to ask.

'No, no. It's nothing like that. I just don't think it's working between me and you,' he said, squirming a little as he stood there.

'I completely agree,' Ruth said with no hint of emotion.

Dan gestured up the hall to their bedroom. 'Right, okay. I'm going to pack up some of my things. I'm going to stay at Felix's house for a bit.'

'What about Ella?'

'Yeah. I'll ring or text and arrange a time to come and see her,' he said.

Oh my God, you have no interest in seeing her, do you?

'Tomorrow?' Ruth asked, trying to put him on the spot and make him feel guilty.

'Erm, I don't know. Let me give you a ring. We'll sort something out.'

You are a useless, selfish prick!

Dan looked at her, nodded, and then walked out of the living room.

Ruth sat back against the sofa and gazed up at the ceiling. Even though she knew this day was going to come, and she was relieved that it had, an overwhelming sense of sadness swept through her.

She took a deep breath, but she already had tears in her eyes.

Poor Ella. Poor, poor sweet Ella. I'm so sorry I've allowed this to happen to you.

IT WAS MID-EVENING and Lucy was still working in CID. After completing a mountain of paperwork, she retrieved the VHS tape that showed Petrovic at Waterloo station. She had been right all along. It gave her a feeling of satisfaction that her initial instincts had been correct.

Glancing down into the Peckham police station car park, she saw Brooks' car - he was still in his office. She readied herself to confront him about what they had found on the tape. She didn't care that he was her DCI. They had shared a bed, with all the intimacy that comes with an affair. He needed to listen to her, both as her boss and as her Man Boy. He owed her that much. Brooks was burying his head in the sand, so it was time to have it out with him.

Grabbing the VHS tape and a photograph from her desk, she marched down the corridor, heading for his office. As she arrived outside, she took a deep breath and knocked on the door. However, she didn't bother to wait for a reply and just stormed in.

'Evening, Lucy,' Brooks said with a quizzical look. 'What are you still doing at work?'

'Don't move,' Lucy snapped as she closed the door, went over to the VHS player, and slotted the tape into the machine.

'I'm not sure it's appropriate for us to watch porn at work,' he said dryly.

'Shut up, Harry! This is serious.'

'I thought we'd agreed I was guv at work,' he said, half teasing.

'Watch this,' Lucy snarled at him as she pressed play. A moment later, the CCTV footage showed Petrovic walking to the ticket barrier and showing his ticket to the inspector.

Lucy pressed freeze as Petrovic turned to face the direction of the camera. 'Recognise him?'

Brooks sat forward on his chair and squinted. Lucy could see that she now had his full attention. He had an increasingly serious expression on his face. 'I'm guessing that's your man?'

Lucy nodded and showed him the photograph they had of a slightly younger Petrovic. 'That's Simo Petrovic three weeks ago at Waterloo station ... Ruth's seen this, and she agrees ... Look at the photograph, Harry. It's definitely him, isn't it?'

Brooks put his hand to his face and rubbed his chin as he thought for a few seconds. 'Who else has seen this?'

'Only Ruth.' She was glad to see that he was finally taking what she said seriously.

'Right, I don't want you to show this to anyone else, okay? I mean it. And not a word of what you've seen,' Brooks said gravely. 'Put that tape somewhere safe.'

I really fancy Harry when he's like this, she thought. *But his apprehension is worrying me.*

'What are you going to do?' Lucy asked. She had rarely seen Brooks this uneasy.

'I hate to admit it, but I was wrong. We can't stand by and ignore this.'

'Why didn't you believe me when I first flagged this up?' she said fiercely. Secretly she was excited that Brooks was taking her seriously, but she wanted to have a pop at him anyway. He should have bloody trusted her.

'Because until now, you were working on a hunch without any decent evidence.' He pointed to the image on the screen. 'But this changes everything.'

'What do we do now?' Lucy asked.

'Leave it with me, okay? As far as everyone else in CID, or anywhere else, is concerned, we are not looking at Petrovic, his involvement in Mujic's murder, or if he is alive and living in London. At the moment, it might be sensible not to tell Ruth that you've spoken to me either.'

'Why?' Lucy didn't like keeping secrets from Ruth. She hated the fact that she had kept her affair with Harry from her in recent months.

'My job is to protect you and Ruth as much as I can. Someone, somewhere, with a lot of power, doesn't want Petrovic found. The less Ruth knows, the less she can be implicated if anything goes wrong.'

Oh my God, Harry, you are soooo sexy ...

Lucy's face softened into a smile. 'Thank you, Harry. It means a lot ...'

'I do take you seriously, Luce. You're an excellent copper. A bit hot-headed but your instincts are bloody good,' Brooks said.

Wow. Did he actually just say that?

'Thank you, DCI Harry Brooks. I want to give you a big fucking snog.'

'But we're at work, so obviously you're not going to do that,' Brooks said, arching his eyebrow.

Lucy marched over to him. 'Wrong. I don't give a shit.'

She kissed him full on the lips, and put her hand to his face for a moment before turning and heading for the door.

'See you tomorrow, guv!'

'I DON'T UNDERSTAND why no one is investigating this properly?' Shiori said as she sipped her wine and stubbed out her cigarette.

Ruth had sent Shiori a text once Dan had left. Half an hour later, she had arrived with Koyuki, a bottle of wine, and some supportive and encouraging words. Ella and Koyuki were now fast asleep in bed.

'We've been told not to,' Ruth said shaking her head.

Shiori frowned. 'But that's your job. They can't ask you not to investigate a murder properly.'

'That's exactly what they've told us to do. It's coming directly from the Home Office, via Scotland Yard. My guvnor is wetting himself. He thinks he's going to lose his job if we carry on looking for this man,' Ruth explained.

'With my journalist hat on, my first instinct is why?' Shiori asked.

Ruth tried to summarise what she suspected was going on. 'It has to be the election. If the papers get hold of a story that shows a wanted Serbian war criminal, responsible for the torture and deaths of thousands of innocent civilians, is living in London, it will be a scandal. The buck stops with the Home Office and the current government. People will want to know how that's been allowed to happen. And with days to go before a general election, that would be very damaging.'

Shiori sat forward and shook her head. 'Jesus Christ, Ruth. They can't be allowed to cover this up because it will cost them votes. It's disgusting.'

Ruth shrugged. 'What do we do? If Lucy and I carry on, we'll probably get suspended. We can't go to any senior ranking officers because they're going to have the same problem.'

'Then you need to go to someone outside the Metropolitan Police,' Shiori said.

'Like who? We don't know anyone.'

'I do. Claire Gold. She's a human rights lawyer and she's fantastic. We went to college in Chicago together. I think we should go and talk to her,' Shiori said.

'You want to help us with this?' Ruth asked. She felt very apprehensive about going outside of the force to talk to anyone.

'Of course. We have to do this. You've told me what was in that diary, Ruth. We can't allow that man to escape justice due to political expediency. What they're doing is criminal.'

'I can't lose my job. I've got Ella to look after and I'm on my own now,' Ruth said. She had an overwhelming sense that the investigation was getting out of control.

'You're not going to lose your job. I promise you. Given what you've told me, I can't see how they can touch you or Lucy.'

Ruth thought of Ella asleep in the next room, Dan's rapid departure, and now the prospect of going outside of the Met. It was all too much for her. She was terrified. Taking a breath, she felt tears coming into her eyes.

'I'm sorry. It's just been a horrible evening,' Ruth said with a sniff.

'Hey, you don't need to apologise,' Shiori said, getting up and going over to her. 'Come here.'

Ruth stood and Shiori gave her a hug. She could smell her hair and perfume. She smelled incredible. She wanted the hug to last for the rest of the night.

Ruth sniffed again as they moved apart. 'God, I feel so stupid.'

Shiori put a reassuring hand on her arm. 'Imagine what a perfect world this would be without fucking men.'

Ruth smiled and then laughed. 'Yeah. Maybe one day, eh?'

Shiori looked at her watch. 'Right, I'd better go. I will call Claire and I'll come with you and Lucy when you talk to her. My advice up until then is to pretend that you are doing exactly what you've been told to do. Don't ruffle any feathers.'

Ruth nodded and looked at her. 'You can stay if you want ... I mean I can sleep on the sofa and you can have my bed.'

Oh God, did that sound weird as if I was propositioning her?

'That's very sweet of you, but I'd better get the little princess home. Maybe another time though.'

Ruth nodded, and put her hand on Shiori's. For a moment, they held hands and looked at each other.

'Thank you. I don't know what I would have done without you tonight.'

'No problem. You're going to be fine.' Shiori smiled. She went into Ella's bedroom, carefully lifted Koyuki, and headed for the door. 'If I'm lucky, she'll stay asleep until we get home. We'll talk tomorrow. Get some rest.'

CHAPTER 14

It was morning, and Ruth went back into CID after fetching a coffee from the canteen. She felt a little hesitant when she saw that Lucy had arrived. Even though they had found the image of Simo Petrovic, there had been a slight atmosphere between them after their cross words the previous day. She also had to broach the conversation she'd had with Shiori last night.

'Any sign of Mujic on those tapes?' Ruth asked.

Lucy shook her head but didn't meet her eye. 'No. Although if we can see that Petrovic is there, we have to assume Mujic was.'

'Yeah'. Ruth sipped her coffee and waited a few seconds. 'Sorry about yesterday.'

Lucy nodded. 'Me too.'

Ruth cast a furtive glance around the CID office. There were two male DCs chatting over by the photocopier.

'I think you're right,' Ruth said quietly under her breath.

'What do you mean?' Lucy asked, frowning.

'I think that if we know that Simo Petrovic is alive, it's our duty to find him and bring him to justice.'

'Why the change of heart? I thought you were worried about your job?'

'I am. But I have a friend. She's a freelance journalist.'

Lucy rolled her eyes. 'Please tell me that you didn't tell her any of this?'

'I kept it vague until I talked to you,' Ruth answered, aware that she was lying.

'What did she say that seems to have changed your mind so radically?'

'She said that no one would, or could, sack two female police officers for pursuing a war criminal who they suspected was involved in two murders. It would be a PR disaster for the Met. And for anyone who might be implicated in covering up the man's identity.'

'And you trust her?' Lucy asked.

'Yes. There's no hidden agenda with her.'

'Can I meet her?'

'Yes. Of course. She wants us to go and meet a human rights lawyer friend of hers.'

'Okay. We can do that ... Right, better grab your coat then,' Lucy said with a determined look.

'Why? Where are we going now?'

'I've told Brooks we're going to Kensington police station.'

'Where are we really going then?' Ruth asked, feeling uneasy.

'Portobello Road.'

'Why?'

'It's where the Serbian Cultural Centre is. If you're a Serbian in London, that's where you go.'

AS THEY QUEUED IN THE traffic going north over Battersea Bridge, Ruth clicked on the radio. *Remember Me* by Blue Boy was playing.

'Oh, I love this!' she said enthusiastically.

'God, you really do love all this dance music crap,' Lucy quipped.

'All right, grandma. You can play your Fleetwood Mac CD later,' Ruth joked. Even though they were virtually the same age, Ruth thought Lucy's taste in music was really old-fashioned.

Lucy looked out over the Thames as they stopped again in the traffic at the south end of the bridge.

'This was your manor, wasn't it?' Lucy asked.

'Yeah. Lived and worked here. Before the wankers moved in and started calling it South Chelsea.'

'Batter Sur La Mer. That's what the yuppies call it isn't it?'

'My dad called them Hooray Henrys.'

Lucy glanced over at Ruth and frowned. 'You been crying?' she asked.

Bollocks! Does it show?

'No,' Ruth said avoiding eye contact.

'Liar. Are things deteriorating on the ranch?'

Ruth wasn't sure how much to tell Lucy. She had been telling her to ditch Dan for over a year now.

'Dan moved out last night,' Ruth admitted.

Lucy looked over at her. 'Oh my god. I'm sorry to hear that.'

'No, you're not.'

Lucy shrugged and pulled a face. 'Okay, I'm not sorry that he's gone. But I am sorry that you're upset ... Did you kick him out?'

'Not really.'

'How do you mean?'

'He left me. He said he needed some time to think, and that we weren't getting on. He couldn't get out of the front door fast enough. The worst part of it was that he wouldn't arrange to meet up with Ella or even say that he'd miss her.' Ruth felt a tear well up.

Lucy reached over and touched Ruth's arm to comfort her. 'He's such a prick. I know you don't want to hear it, but it will be for the best. I promise.'

'I'll be fine. We'll be fine. And I'm not worried about being on my own or being lonely. But I feel so sorry and angry for Ella.'

'Of course, you do. But you two will be so strong and amazing on your own. Like a dynamic duo!'

Ruth looked over, wiped the tear from her eye and smiled. 'Thank you, Lucy.'

'Don't be daft. That's what we do. Imagine if you were stuck with some fat, hairy-arsed male DS in the car all day,' Lucy chortled.

Ruth laughed. 'Been there, got the t-shirt.'

'Me too ... You're going to be fine. I promise.'

The traffic cleared a little as they reached the north side of the bridge, cut through Chelsea, and headed east towards Notting Hill.

As they travelled north on the Portobello Road, they turned left. Lucy pulled the car up outside a large church and community centre on a side road just behind Portobello Market. Ruth glanced up to see a sign - *All Saints, Serbian Orthodox Church.* The front of the imposing, grey stone building had arched windows that were symmetrical with the two arched doors below.

Getting out of the car, Ruth watched two teenagers sitting outside the Cultural Centre building. They wore traditional Serbian dress. The boy had a square hat, black waistcoat, and baggy crimson trousers. The girl had red and yellow flowers in her hair, and a black patterned pinafore over a long, dark checked skirt.

Ruth couldn't help thinking how different they looked to the archetypal teenagers of Ladbroke Grove in their tracksuits and sports gear.

'I rang earlier. There's a bar and function room at the back,' Lucy said as they walked over to the entrance of the Cultural Centre.

Once inside, Ruth could see that most of the posters and signs were written in Serbo-Croat.

They marched over to the reception desk where a woman with jet black hair, pulled into a tight bun, was on the phone. She hung up just as they arrived, and smiled at them.

'DC Henry and DC Hunter, CID. I wonder if you can help us. We're trying to track down this man,' Lucy said as she reached into her pocket and pulled out the photo of Petrovic that they had found in Mujic's flat. 'Have you ever seen him before? He's Serbian.'

The receptionist's face didn't register when she saw the photo. She shook her head.

She doesn't know him, Ruth thought.

'No. Sorry. I've never seen this man before.'

'I understand that you have lunchtime entertainment in the bar. Mind if we ask around?' Lucy asked, although it wasn't really a question.

'Of course not. It is down the end of this corridor and then you must turn right,' the receptionist said, gesturing.

'Thanks,' Ruth said as they turned and went.

'She's never seen Petrovic before has she?' Lucy asked under her breath.

'Definitely not,' Ruth replied as they headed down the corridor, turned right, and found large open double doors that led into a function room and bar.

Folk music was playing and a group of Serbian teenagers, dressed in the traditional clothing that Ruth had seen outside, were performing a dance in couples.

Ruth watched for a few seconds. 'Who would have thought you would find a place like this slap bang in the middle of fashionable Notting Hill?'

It reminded her of some traditional Greek dancing she had seen when on holiday in Crete. It was the first holiday she and Dan ever went on. For a moment, she remembered the events of the previous evening and her heart sank a little.

On the other side of the room were around twenty or so older people nursing drinks, smoking, chatting, or watching the dancers.

'Come on - unless you want to join in?' Lucy quipped.

Ruth laughed as they walked over to the bar. 'I would need to be hammered to do that.'

A tall barman came over and said something that Ruth didn't understand. She showed her warrant card to him. 'Do you speak English?'

'Of course. Is there some kind of problem?' he asked with a frown.

'No. We're just looking for someone. He's Serbian,' Ruth explained as she took the photograph from Lucy and showed him.

Again, the man's face showed no recognition as he shook his head. 'No sorry. And you're sure he's Serbian?'

'Yes,' Ruth nodded and looked at Lucy.

Bugger. We're not getting very far.

'Maybe talk to Novak over there? He's the president of the centre. He knows everyone,' the barman suggested. He pointed to a man in his sixties, with a bulbous nose and large wrinkled forehead. 'Novak Pupin.'

Ruth and Lucy approached the table where Pupin was drinking a beer and smoking.

'Mr Pupin?' Ruth asked.

He nodded with a curious look on his face. 'Can I help you ladies?'

'We're police officers and we're looking for someone. We know that he's Serbian and wondered if you could help us,' Lucy explained.

'Of course, of course,' Pupin said with a smile as he gestured to chairs at the table. 'Please, sit down. Would you like a drink, ladies?'

'We're fine. Thank you, Mr Pupin,' Ruth said as she sat down. She couldn't help but look at his craggy face that seemed to have been chiselled out of stone.

'Novak, please. And how can I help two such beautiful ladies?' Pupin said in a slightly brazen way.

All right, mate. Tone it down a bit.

'We're looking for someone. We know that he is Serbian so we thought he might have been here,' Ruth explained.

'It's as good a place to try as any,' he said with a chortle.

Lucy took the photograph and slid it over the table for Pupin to look at. He took out his glasses from his jacket pocket. Ruth saw an enormous sweat stain under his armpit and got a waft of body odour a moment later.

One word. Deodorant.

'Let me take a look,' he said, taking the photograph and studying it. After a moment of reflection, his forehead wrinkled even more with an accusatory frown. He put the photograph down and looked at them.

'Yes. I know who this man is,' he said in a sombre tone.

'Can I ask who you think he is?' Lucy asked, sharing a look with Ruth.

'It causes me great displeasure to say his name out loud to you. This man is Simo Petrovic. And he would not be welcome in this place. But you will not find him.'

'Why not?' Ruth asked.

'He's dead. He was buried in Serbia a few years ago.'

Ruth noticed that his hand had clenched into a fist at the thought of Petrovic.

'We're not sure that he was,' Lucy said.

'No, no. Of this fact I am sure. And that man, and men like him, brought such shame on the Serbian name in your country. You have seen the church next door?' Pupin asked, pointing in its direction.

'Yes. It's an incredible building,' Ruth said.

'It was given to us by Lady Paget who was the wife of the British Ambassador to Belgrade after the Second World War. Serbians, like my father, were heroes in London after the war. The Serbian partisans fought the Nazis with guerrilla warfare for years. My family fled here when General Tito took power, and we were welcomed with open arms. But since this war in my homeland, the atrocities ... this has all changed. Serbians are seen as monsters,' he said. 'And it makes me very sad.'

'And you're sure that you haven't seen Simo Petrovic?' Lucy asked.

Pupin snorted. 'Of course not! I would have killed him with my bare hands if I had.'

'Okay. Thank you for your help,' Lucy said as she and Ruth got up from the table.

'I'm afraid you ladies are wasting your time.'

'Thanks again,' Ruth said with a polite smile.

They walked back across the function room, watching the folk dancing as they went, then headed past reception and out towards the car.

'Back to the drawing board,' Ruth muttered.

Ruth squinted. The sun was now out, and it was turning into a warm spring day.

As Lucy unlocked the car, Ruth could see the disappointment on her face.

'Don't worry. We'll find him,' she said reassuringly.

'I was banking on getting something from here,' Lucy grumbled.

'Excuse me. Excuse me, please,' came a voice from behind them.

An old man, with a bushy grey moustache, was heading towards them. He walked with a limp. Ruth recognised him from the Serbian Centre bar. He had been sitting with a group of elderly women.

'Please. I need to speak to you for a moment,' he said, looking around furtively.

He clearly doesn't want anyone to see that he's talking to us.

'How can we help?' Ruth asked quietly.

He looked scared. 'I heard you were looking for someone. I think I might know something.'

Sounds promising.

'Anything you help us with would be held in the strictest confidence,' Lucy said as she came around the car and approached him.

'Simo Petrovic, yes?' He hunched his shoulders and his breathing accelerated. It was as if just saying the name out loud terrified him.

'Yes,' Lucy said.

'I heard some men talking in there this morning. And I thought if you were police officers, you should know,' he said with a slight tremble in his voice.

'Sorry? Know what?' Ruth asked.

'They said that Simo Petrovic left the country last night. He got a plane to Germany.'

Lucy looked over at Ruth – not good news.

'Which men?' Lucy asked.

'They come here in the mornings for coffee. They're younger than me, but I do not know their names. They're not here now.'

'Do you know which airport, or where he was going?' Lucy asked.

'Dusseldorf. I think that's what they said. Dusseldorf.'

CHAPTER 15

It was early evening and still light outside. The weather was warm enough for Ruth to have the door to the tiny garden open. Ella was tottering around, playing with her toys.

Ruth looked over at Lucy who was sitting on the sofa in the flat, drinking wine and sifting through evidence. Ruth was grateful that Lucy was more than happy to sometimes use the flat as a makeshift office when she needed to pick up Ella and get her home. None of the male detectives in CID seemed to have that problem. They had wives at home or that worked part-time.

Ruth poured more wine into her glass and gestured to Lucy.

'Not if I'm driving,' Lucy said as she squinted at the fax in her hand. They had managed to get the passenger lists of all three flights from Heathrow to Dusseldorf from the previous evening.

Ruth grabbed the list that was marked *BA137 LHR to DUS 19:25*. 'We're assuming that he's using a false passport?'

Lucy shrugged. 'I don't know. Petrovic is officially dead. His name wouldn't be flagged up at airport security.'

'It's pretty brazen to walk through Heathrow with your own passport when you're supposed to be dead,' Ruth said.

'Simo Petrovic doesn't strike me as a man to worry about that.'

'No. If MI5 suspect that he's alive, he would be on their no-fly list. False passport?' Ruth suggested.

Lucy sighed. 'We know how easy they are to get. If he's got one, we'll never find him.'

'Although I suspect that he would be travelling under a Serbian name,' Ruth said.

'Which would end with a *-vic* then,' Lucy said. Ruth spotted Lucy's expression change. 'Hang on a bloody second.'

'What is it?' Ruth asked, watching as Lucy got up and went over to her coat.

'Those letters that I borrowed from that house in Summer Gardens,' Lucy said, fishing the envelopes from her pocket.

'I thought you said they were all bills?'

'They are. But they are all addressed to an Oliver Stankovic. I didn't put the two together.'

'You think Oliver Stankovic is Simo Petrovic?' Ruth asked.

Lucy shrugged. 'Could be. Has to be worth having a look.'

Ruth went back to the list she was looking at and began to scan for both names.

She got to the bottom but neither name appeared.

'Anything?' Lucy asked as she continued to look at the fax.

'Nope. Nothing,' Ruth replied as she grabbed the passenger list for another flight. She scanned it and immediately saw what they were looking for. 'But now I have.'

'What is it?'

'Oliver Stankovic. On flight TK564 to Dusseldorf, last night at 9.30pm.'

'Shit! Then we've lost him,' Lucy said despondently.

'Interpol?' Ruth suggested.

'We don't have any hard evidence that Oliver Stankovic is Simo Petrovic. We'd be wasting our time.'

Ruth nodded. It looked like the end of the line.

'Petrovic must have got spooked and fled the country,' Lucy said.

Ruth glanced back at the passenger list. 'Any idea what FF means?'

Lucy's face lit up. 'FF? Are you sure?'

'Yes ...'

'There is an FF beside Oliver Stankovic's name?' Lucy asked with renewed energy.

'Bloody hell, Lucy! Yes. What does it mean?'

'Failure to fly. Oliver Stankovic didn't check in or board the plane even though he had a seat bought and paid for.'

'Petrovic might still be in the country,' Ruth said.

'Yeah, but where? We need to get to him before he does fly somewhere else.'

KENSINGTON GARDENS was still busy as Londoners made the most of a warm spring evening. Colonel Tankovic looked over at the magnificent architecture of Kensington Palace which had been designed and constructed by Sir Christopher Wren in the late 1680s. He caught sight of a black Range Rover, with blacked-out windows, cutting up the gravel driveway to the Palace. He wondered if Princess Diana was inside. He had seen photos of her in the papers recently when she'd visited a nearby hospital in Paddington.

Tankovic moved out of the way of a speeding mountain bike and saw the pond where he had arranged to meet Novak Pupin. Pupin said he had important information to pass on to him but was too scared to do it over the phone.

Glancing at the rows of green-striped deck chairs that faced what was known as the Round Pond, Tankovic spotted Pupin coming the other way. They nodded an acknowledgement to each other before shaking hands.

'Kako ste. Thank you for seeing me,' Pupin said.

Tankovic gestured to the deck chairs. 'Shall we sit down?'

'Yes, of course, Colonel,' Pupin said with deference.

Tankovic was pleased to see that a foot soldier such as Pupin still respected his rank within the Serbian army.

'Cigarette, Colonel?' Pupin said, offering Tankovic the kind of strong cigarette that was favoured by those who had served in the Serbian army.

'Thank you.' Tankovic took it, cupped his hand to light it and took a deep drag. 'Where do you get these?'

'A man comes into the centre once a week with them. I can get you some if you like?'

'Yes. I would like that ... You've heard about some of the young people from our community going to this club in the West End?'

Pupin nodded with a sombre expression. 'This place in So-ho? It is no good.'

'A friend told me that there are Croats and even balija dogs in there. They drink, dance, and listen to music all together,' Tankovic said. When he had heard what the twenty-something Serbs from their community were doing, it made him so angry.

'I'm afraid that I heard the same. They just don't understand what we fought for,' Pupin said sadly.

Tankovic nodded and took another drag of his cigarette. It was time to talk business. He looked around cautiously.

'You have something to tell me?' he asked, lowering his voice.

'Two police officers came to the centre this morning. They were looking for information about the Major.'

'Two women, yes?' He knew who they were.

'You know about them?'

Tankovic nodded. 'I know that they are looking for the Major. What did you tell them?'

'We did what you told us to do, Colonel. I told them that the Major was dead and buried in Serbia. And as they left, Milos told them he had heard a rumour that the Major had flown to Germany.'

'You think they believed him?' Tankovic asked.

Pupin nodded. 'Milos said that they seemed to be very interested in what he had told them.'

'Good. We'll keep leading them down dead ends until they give up looking.'

'Can I ask about the health of the Major? Is he well?' Pupin asked.

'Yes, quite well. He is hidden away somewhere safe until all this dies down. No one knows where he is, which is as it should be.' Tankovic felt proud to be a member of the Major's trusted circle.

'But what if it doesn't?' Pupin asked with a concerned expression.

'What do you mean?'

'What if it doesn't die down? What if those women police officers continue to stick their noses into our business and try to find him? Then what?'

Tankovic smiled. 'Do not worry yourself, my friend. I have the officers' names, and it won't be long before I know where they live. And if they continue to buzz around us like irritating flies, they will be persuaded to go away or they will be swatted.'

CHAPTER 16

Ruth sat back at her desk and finished her coffee. It was still early, and CID was its usual hive of chatter and movement as officers prepared to assemble for the morning briefing. Gaughran went over and pulled down a blind to cut out some of the sunlight.

Lucy approached holding some papers. 'I've got something.'

'That's nice. Well, don't give it to me,' Ruth quipped.

Lucy groaned. 'Very funny.' She then put down the envelopes that she had taken from the house they had visited in Summer Gardens. 'One of these was handwritten to Oliver Stankovic. I didn't see it until I got home last night.'

'What's inside?' Ruth asked, wondering why Lucy hadn't mentioned it before now.

Lucy pulled out a folded piece of paper. 'It's a newspaper article from a Serbian newspaper called Politika. I can't read it, but we can get it translated.'

'Do we know anything about Politika?'

'It's the oldest paper in the Balkan region and published out of Belgrade. Right-wing politics and fiercely loyal to Serbians. Just before the war started, it was under the control of Slobodan Milosevic.'

'Which would make it Simo Petrovic's paper of choice. How does that help us?' Ruth asked, wondering where Lucy was going with this.

'We think that Oliver Stankovic might be Petrovic's new identity don't we?' Lucy asked.

'Yes.'

'Whoever addressed and sent the article was in contact with Petrovic and knew he had changed his name.'

'But that doesn't help us, does it?'

Lucy turned over the envelope and showed Ruth the postage mark. 'It was posted in Cobham, Surrey. I've checked, and it's a small post office.'

'And you expect them to remember one person?'

'No, but if Petrovic has gone into hiding, he would have to go somewhere he has friends.'

'Which could be Cobham,' Ruth said, not sounding particularly enthused.

'It's all we've got. Has to be worth checking out.' Lucy turned and went back to her desk.

Ruth wasn't sure.

Clicking open her phone, she saw that she had a missed call from Dan at 4am.

Bloody hell! He's such a knob.

The time of the call told her that Dan had been off his head somewhere and, in a fit of self-pity or rage, had decided to ring her. It seemed strange that she didn't miss him. In fact, it was a relief to wake up and not worry about whether he'd managed to get home. And it was a relief not to have to usher him to bed from the sofa at 8am, or go home to a house that smelled of weed. Even the horrible, nagging feeling that he was cheating on her had dissipated.

Just as she went to close the phone, a text arrived. It was from Shiori. *I've spoken to Claire. She's very keen to meet as soon as possible. Let's talk later X*

Ruth couldn't help feeling a tingle of excitement. She tried to persuade herself that it was because Shiori was her new, slightly exotic friend and they got on like a house on fire. If she was honest, she also knew that she was very attracted to her. It wasn't a new feeling. She'd had a few dalliances with women over the years. However, she had put them down to youthful high spirits, alcohol, drugs and experimentation. Yet there was a nagging feeling that, if anything, her attraction to women was growing stronger and more prevalent as the years went on.

'Right everybody, if we can settle down,' Brooks boomed as he went into the centre of the room. His voice jolted Ruth out of her train of thought. He looked around the room for her and Lucy. 'Lucy, Ruth, now that we've closed down some of the lines of enquiry, where are we at with the murder of Hamzar Mujic?'

Ruth looked over at Lucy and gave a knowing nod. They had agreed to run a routine robbery case on the surface to keep Brooks, and anyone else who took an interest, quiet. They would then pursue their own clandestine investigation into Simo Petrovic.

'Still waiting for the forensics to come back, guv,' Lucy said.

Ruth looked up at him and said, 'We've run the prints, but we didn't get a match.'

'There was some valuable jewellery taken from Hamzar Mujic's flat, guv. Looks like robbery was the motive after all,' Lucy explained.

It was a blatant lie. There was no jewellery missing from Mujic's flat, but they needed to create a smokescreen to hide what they were up to.

'Robbery's a bit of a handbrake turn from KGB hitmen isn't it, ladies?' said Gaughran, shaking his head sarcastically.

Ruth watched as Lucy put on a forced smile and gave Gaughran the finger.

'Not helpful, Tim ... What about the daughter?' Brooks asked.

Lucy shook her head. 'She didn't know anything.'

Ruth looked up and shrugged. 'The door was forced open. The neighbour heard shouting and a struggle. Jewellery was taken from his flat. The fentanyl is a bit of a weird one, but we're pretty sure that some kind of robbery was the motive rather than anything more sinister than that.'

Brooks nodded and couldn't hide the fact that he looked visibly relieved that Ruth and Lucy were now towing the line. 'Good. Talk to robbery and see if we've got any local burglaries with a similar MO.'

Lucy looked over at Ruth and smiled – *job done.*

A few minutes later the briefing was over, and the CID officers went back to their desks or headed out.

Ruth looked up from her desk and saw Lucy approaching. 'Get your coat.'

'Why? Where are we going?' Ruth asked.

Lucy headed for the door. 'Cobham.'

CHAPTER 17

Having navigated the Wandsworth one-way system, Lucy and Ruth soon found themselves on an open stretch of the A3, heading south out of London towards Cobham in Surrey. As far as Ruth was concerned, Surrey had always been a very affluent county, home to bankers and stockbrokers. When she was younger, people would mock its inhabitants by pronouncing the county *Sorry,* mimicking their cut-glass English accents.

Having taken the turning towards the village of Cobham, they drove along a road that was lined with a series of huge mansions.

'Like bloody Beverly Hills down here, isn't it?' Lucy said.

'Yeah, I wouldn't mind a house like one of these. I think Cliff Richard lives over there.'

Lucy rolled her eyes. 'Please don't tell me you like Cliff Richard too?'

'Not really. My Mum did though, especially around that whole *Wired for Sound* and *Devil Woman* time.'

Lucy pointed to a sign that said *St George's Estate.* 'Yeah, well more importantly, Ringo Starr and John Lennon both had houses up there. I think Ringo is still there.'

Ruth chuckled. 'It really is Beverly Hills!'

A moment later they arrived in the middle of Cobham village, which was just as twee and middle class as Ruth had expected it to be. They parked up outside the post office and got out.

They walked inside and headed over to the counter where a middle-aged woman was busy sorting out some packages.

Ruth got out her warrant card. 'DC Hunter and DC Henry. I wonder if you could help us with our enquiries. We are looking for someone and we wondered if you had seen him in here?'

Lucy showed her the photograph of Petrovic. The woman picked up her glasses from the counter and put them on. 'Sorry, I can't see much without these.' She peered at the image. 'Erm ... no, sorry. I don't recognise that man. Jack?'

An older man came over, looked at the photograph, and shook his head. 'No. I've never seen him in here.'

Ruth looked at Lucy – *back to square one.*

They spent the next ten minutes going from shop to shop but no one in the village had seen anyone who looked remotely like Petrovic.

Getting back into the car, Ruth and Lucy sat for a moment. Ruth was feeling annoyed. She had already flagged up that coming to Cobham was a waste of time with only the postmark to go on.

'We're never going to find him, are we?' Lucy said despondently.

'I really don't know, Lucy,' Ruth answered, unable to hide her frustration.

'It's the only lead we had,' Lucy snapped.

Ruth tutted. 'I'm well aware of that. But it's a two hour round trip for nothing.'

Before Lucy could say anything else, Ruth's phone rang.

It was DC Hassan. 'Syed?'

'Ruth. One of the people you were looking for. Safet Dudic?'

'Yeah?'

'Got an address for him from the electoral register. He lives in Stoneleigh. 35 Hatton Close.'

'Thanks Syed.' Even though Hassan spent a lot of time with Gaughran, Ruth knew his heart was actually in the right place.

'What's that?' Lucy asked, still sounding irritated from their little tiff.

'We've got an address for Safet Dudic ... Where's Stoneleigh?'

'About fifteen minutes from here,' Lucy said brightly. 'And you said this was a wasted journey.'

Ruth rolled her eyes.

AS THEY PARKED IN THE leafy suburban close, Ruth looked at the detached houses, well-tended gardens, and new cars on the driveways. Stoneleigh was a different world to the streets of SE19 where she and Lucy spent most of their time.

'Nice place,' she remarked as they got out of the car.

'That's Surrey for you, if you can afford it,' Lucy said, and then gestured to the house that had been identified. 'This is it.'

They walked up to the front door and knocked. A few seconds later, a smiling middle-aged woman with a tea towel draped over her shoulder answered.

Ruth and Lucy showed her their warrant cards and identified themselves.

'We're looking for Safet Dudic? We understand that he lives here?' Ruth asked.

The woman nodded but her face fell. 'Yes, he does. What's he done now?' She spoke with the trace of an accent.

Ruth and Lucy looked at each other with a frown. Not the reaction they were expecting.

I don't think we've got the right Safet Dudic.

'As far as we know, he hasn't done anything. We just wanted to talk to him as part of an ongoing investigation,' Lucy explained.

'Sorry, please come in,' the woman said, ushering them into the hallway. 'Safet? Safet? Can you come down here please?'

There were an awkward few seconds before a sixteen-year-old boy with jet black spiky hair came very gingerly down the stairs. His eyes widened when he saw Ruth and Lucy standing in the hallway.

'Safet Dudic?' Lucy asked, and then looked at the woman. 'Erm, we were expecting someone a lot older.'

'He looks young for his age, but he has just turned sixteen,' the woman said while glaring at her son.

'Our investigation centres on events back in Bosnia, possibly four or five years ago,' Ruth explained, trying to be as vague as possible. 'I think we might have got the wrong Safet Dudic.'

The woman shook her head. 'Oh, you must be talking about my father. Sorry. Of course, they have the same name. He came to live with us four years ago when he moved over here.'

Ruth looked at Lucy – *That makes more sense.*

'Does he still live here?' Lucy asked.

'Yes. We have an annexe. I'll take you through. Sorry, my son has been in trouble with the police a couple of times. My father is seventy and he goes nowhere,' the woman explained with a nervous laugh as she took Ruth and Lucy through a hallway and showed them into the annexe.

'It's fine. Don't worry. Easy mistake to make. How long have you been in the UK, Mrs ....?' Ruth asked giving her a kind smile.

'Tatiana ... I came here to study and met my husband at University. That was about twenty years ago. We got married and stayed. My father was very happy in Bosnia until the war and ...' she said and began to look a little choked. 'Sorry ...'

'It's fine. We realise it's a very emotive subject,' Lucy said.

Tatiana gestured for them to go into a living room. 'Dad? Dad? There are some people here to speak to you.'

A few moments later, a small man with a grey moustache and cardigan shuffled in and looked at them. 'Visitors? I don't know anyone.'

Tatiana looked at Ruth and Lucy and said under her breath, 'He gets a bit confused ... Dad, these two ladies are police officers. They just want to ask you a couple of questions. Is that okay?'

Safet nodded, gestured to the sofa and smiled. 'Of course, of course. I'm not in trouble, am I?'

He looked at them with a twinkle in his eye and then lowered himself carefully into a large armchair opposite the sofa. Tatiana gave them a little wave as she left them to it.

'No, no. Nothing like that, Mr Dudic,' Ruth laughed, as she and Lucy sat down on the sofa.

'We're looking into the death of a man called Hamzar Mujic,' said Lucy.

Safet frowned in disbelief. 'Hamzar is dead?'

'I'm afraid so. Did you know him?' Ruth asked gently.

Safet was clearly upset by the news and nodded. 'Yes, yes. Of course. Of course, I did. We grew up together in the same village, the same school. I'm sorry to hear that ... Was he ill?'

'No ... We believe that Hamzar may have been murdered,' Lucy said gently.

Safet's face drained of colour. 'Murdered? No, that cannot be right. He was an old man. Who would want to murder him?' he asked as he shifted uncomfortably in his chair.

'That's why we wanted to speak to you,' Ruth explained.

'Me? How would I know?'

Ruth watched as his eyes roamed the room and his brain worked overtime trying to comprehend the news.

'You said you and Hamzar were friends,' Lucy said.

'Yes. But I had not seen him for nearly two years. My health has been poor. We spoke on the telephone maybe six months ago, but not since then.'

Is he trying to distance himself from Hamzar for some reason?

Something about Safet's manner didn't sit right with Ruth. He had rapidly gone from being upset to highly anxious.

'You really don't have any idea about who might have wanted to harm him?' Ruth asked.

Safet's face was pale, and the muscles around his eyes began to twitch. 'No. The man didn't have an enemy in the world.'

Ruth looked over at Lucy. Something was wrong. They allowed Safet to compose himself a little.

'We're here today because we found your name in Hamzar's diary, along with his own name and two others,' Ruth explained.

'You don't think I had something to do with his death?' Safet mumbled anxiously.

'No, nothing like that. There was another man on the list. Mersad Advic?' Lucy said.

Safet nodded his head. 'Yes, Mersad. Like Hamzar, we all grew up together. But I haven't seen him since I arrived in England.'

Is what he's telling us the truth? He seems to be hiding something.

'There's no easy way to say this Mr Dudic ...' Ruth said, '... but I'm afraid Mersad is also dead. We're treating his death as suspicious.'

Safet inhaled deeply. He looked visibly shaken. 'Oh, this is terrible.'

'Yes, it is.' Ruth looked over at Lucy – they were both thinking the same thing. Safet was utterly terrified, rather than sad or shocked. They were very different emotions and hard to hide.

'Is everything okay, Mr Dudic?' Ruth asked.

He shook his head and shifted uncomfortably in the chair. 'No, no. You have told me that two very old friends of mine have been killed. It is so horrible.'

Maybe that was it. Maybe it was just shock? But he was definitely hiding something from them.

'The last name on the list was a woman, Katerina Selimovic?' Lucy said. 'Do you know her?'

Safet nodded and asked in a virtual whisper, 'Please ... tell me she is okay?'

'As far as we know. Is she someone you know?' Lucy asked.

'Yes. I have known Katerina just as long as the others.'

'And have you seen her recently?' Ruth asked.

'Yes. Maybe a month ago,' he mumbled.

'Do you have an address for her?' Lucy asked.

'Yes. She lives in London. Mortlake.'

There was another name on the same page of that diary. Do you recognise the name Simo Petrovic?' Lucy asked.

'Yes. Of course,' Safet said with almost no reaction.

He didn't even flinch. He knew we were going to ask him about Petrovic.

'Why do you know that name?' Ruth asked.

'I think that you know what kind of man he was. But I have no desire to talk about that,' he said dismissively.

'Would it surprise you if we told you that Hamzar was convinced he saw Simo Petrovic in London three weeks ago?' Lucy asked.

'What? That's ridiculous!' Safet snorted.

'Why is that ridiculous?' Lucy asked.

He shook his head. 'Simo Petrovic killed himself like the coward he was. He is buried in Bosnia. How can he be walking around London?'

I can't tell if he's telling the truth or if he knew that Hamzar believed he had seen Petrovic.

'Hamzar made no mention of this to you?' Lucy asked.

'No. Of course not. I would have told him that he was mad.'

Ruth leaned forward and looked at Safet. 'Mr Dudic, before we go, I really want you to think if there is anything you want to tell us.'

'No. I have told you everything.'

'Anything you tell us is in the strictest confidence. And if you felt you were in any danger ...' Lucy said.

'Danger? This is ridiculous,' Safet said without making eye contact. He pushed himself up out of his armchair. 'Now, I am feeling very tired ... My daughter will give you Katerina's address.'

He's definitely rattled.

Ruth took a card from her jacket and handed it to him. 'Mr Dudic, if you remember anything, or if on second thoughts there's something you want to tell us, please give me a ring.'

'Thank you,' Safet said gesturing to the card, 'but you're better off giving that to my daughter.'

Ruth nodded.

RUTH AND LUCY JOINED the A3 and headed north towards London. They had said very little about their conversation with Safet Dudic. Ruth was digesting what he had told them. Why was he lying to them? Did he know about Hamzar Mujic's sighting of Simo Petrovic?

They stopped at some traffic lights. Ruth gazed up at the sky that was darkening with clouds. She wished it wouldn't rain. She was hoping to take Ella up to the swings on Clapham Common after nursery. Ella had only asked where 'Daddy' was a couple of times. Ruth explained that he was just staying with a friend. Ella shrugged. She was used to Dan's nocturnal life and so his disappearance from their lives hadn't struck her as anything particularly new.

'Dudic knew, didn't he?' Lucy said, breaking Ruth's train of thought.

'About Petrovic?'

'Yeah. He wasn't surprised by the news that Hamzar Mujic had seen him.'

'Not one bit. And he was terrified by the time we left.'

'I've seen grief and shock before. But that wasn't it. He was shit scared.'

'Scared that he is going to be next?' Lucy suggested.

Ruth shrugged. 'Possibly. But why not tell us what he knows?'

'Maybe he doesn't trust the police? From what I remember, the Bosnian police were mainly Serbian. They were implicated in war crimes against Muslim civilians.'

'That would explain it,' Ruth said.

'We have four ageing Bosnian Muslims who grew up in the same village. They're all in touch with each other to varying degrees. What happens when Mujic sees Petrovic at Waterloo?' Lucy asked.

Glancing into the wing mirror, Ruth noticed a black BMW behind them. It pulled out for a few seconds as it tried to overtake them.

'He rings them all. He tells them who he's seen. This is the man that ruined their lives and murdered their friends and family,' Ruth said. She glanced back and saw that the BMW was still very close behind.

'What's with the BMW behind us? she asked.

'God knows. I thought it was a boy racer with a small knob.'

Ruth smiled. 'Usually is ... You think they decided to do something with this information about Petrovic?'

Lucy nodded. 'Yes. Maybe they decided that they don't trust the police with it, so they're going to contact a journalist?'

'That doesn't explain the missing papers from Mujic's flat. The stuff that had been ripped from the board,' Ruth said. 'He was working on something that someone didn't want us to see.' She looked over at Lucy. 'They were tracking Petrovic down themselves and they going to murder him.'

'Except Petrovic and his cronies found out and decided to kill them all first.'

Ruth raised an eyebrow. 'Slight problem with our theory.'

'Which is ...?'

'How does Petrovic find out that these ageing vigilantes are planning for his death?'

'No idea. Maybe they asked the wrong person or went to the wrong place?' Lucy glared in her rear-view mirror. 'Bloody idiot! It's a single-lane, you dickhead.'

Ruth frowned as she looked again in the wing mirror.

'Problem?' she asked.

'I don't know. This BMW has been behind us since we passed the turning to Chessington,' Lucy said quietly.

She sounds a bit spooked.

'Yeah, I just noticed it trying to overtake us.' Ruth leant down to look in the wing mirror again. At that distance, she couldn't see the driver or whether anyone else was in the car. 'What do you think?'

'I don't know.'

'Pull them over?' Ruth asked.

'Not yet. I can't be arsed with the paperwork.'

The road opened up onto a slip road that then joined the three lanes of the A3.

Lucy took her hand from the steering wheel and placed it onto the gear stick.

'I think we'll see how determined this dickhead is to piss us off,' she said, and dropped the car down a gear.

Ruth felt the two-litre engine kick in, and the acceleration pushed her back in her seat.

'All right, Damon Hill, be careful!'

'Hey, you've seen me pursuit drive before,' Lucy protested.

'Exactly ... be careful.'

Lucy revved the engine. 'You mean like this?'

Suddenly, she pulled the Astra out into the middle lane of the by-pass.

Ruth felt herself jolted in her seat. 'Yes, exactly like that.'

'Are they following us? I can't see,' Lucy said anxiously.

Ruth spun around. The black BMW had overtaken a lorry and had now followed them into the middle lane.

'They're right behind us again!' Ruth said in a tremulous voice.

'Shit! This is the wrong way round isn't it?'

'You mean we chase criminals, we don't get chased?' Ruth started to feel the tension in her stomach.

'What do you want, you dickheads?' Lucy yelled as she glared into the rear-view mirror.

It was starting to worry Ruth. Her palms were starting to feel sweaty.

Are we actually being chased?

'I can't see the driver, can you?' she asked.

'No. I think the windscreen is tinted because I can't see anything.'

'Isn't that illegal?'

'Very.'

'Can you see the plate then?' Ruth asked.

'Not really,' Lucy said, 'but I think it's foreign.'

Ruth clicked the Tetra radio. 'Control from alpha zero. We have a suspect vehicle tailing us. Northbound on the A3, about ten miles from Kingston Upon Thames. I'm going to need back up and a PNC check.'

'Alpha zero, received. Standing by,' the CAD, Computer Aided Dispatch, operator said.

Lucy was staring in the rear-view mirror. 'Right, sunshine, I've had enough of your stupid little games now,' she growled as she took the car up to ninety. Then to just below a hundred.

'Careful,' Ruth said under her breath. She had never been a fan of speed.

They hit a bend. Ruth felt herself being pushed hard towards the passenger door. She gripped the seat and grimaced. They flew past a road sign. The car edged over a hundred miles an hour.

The BMW was closer than ever.

'I can see some of the plate now,' Lucy said.

'I think it might be a bit late for that.'

Ruth glanced in the wing mirror. The black BMW was only about twenty yards behind.

Fuck! This is not good.

'What the bloody hell do they want?' she said.

'Maybe they want to scare us.'

'Well, they're doing a bloody good job.'

'Plate is just numbers. Three numbers, then another three,' Lucy said.

I'm not interested. I just want to get out of the car in one piece, thank you.

They hurtled around a long bend. Ruth felt the Astra's back tyres skid. They were going too fast.

'Lucy ...' Ruth said in a cautionary tone.

'What?' Lucy barked at her.

Ruth glanced back again. There couldn't have been more than three or four feet between the cars.

I do not want to die today.

'They're going to go into the back of us or ram us off the road!' Ruth said nervously.

'Hang on!'

'Why?' Ruth said with a gulp.

'Just hang on! No one is ramming us off the road today!'

Lucy swerved the car left into the middle lane. She then started to brake hard, but not hard enough to skid out of control.

Bloody hell!

Ruth clung on for dear life as the smell of burning rubber filled the car.

For a moment, she closed her eyes.

The manoeuvre had the desired effect. The BMW had continued its speed and was now a good two hundred yards ahead of them.

Slowing more, Lucy pulled the car right over into the inside lane.

'They're not slowing down,' she remarked.

Ruth took a breath as she watched the BMW continue to race away around the bend and out of sight.

'Thank God,' Ruth sighed.

'Bastards!'

Ruth's heart was pounding. 'What the bloody hell was that all about?'

'No idea. Wankers.'

'Did the plate have a D in the middle of the six numbers?' Ruth asked.

'I don't know, why?'

'I've just remembered what that means.'

'Which is?'

'It's a diplomatic plate. Three numbers, a letter D, then three more numbers. Did you see the first three numbers?'

'No, why?' Lucy asked.

'It's the country code.'

'Why are we being hounded by a car with diplomatic plates?'

'No idea.'

As Lucy picked up to a normal speed, Ruth felt her pulse beginning to slow.

'You think that was connected?' she asked after a few minutes.

'To Petrovic? I don't know. But if someone was trying to warn us off, they can go and fuck themselves,' Lucy said with a determined look on her face.

CHAPTER 18

Having drunk half a bottle of wine to take the anxious edge off the day, Ruth lay down next to Ella on her bed. The evening was warm, and Ella's bedroom was cosy and dimly lit. She began to read her *The Tiger Who Came to Tea* by Judith Kerr. She loved the story and remembered reading it to her younger brother when he was little. It was so simple, yet she found the mother and daughter's trusting nature - and the fact that they allowed the tiger to wreak havoc in their house - disturbing. Maybe it was just the kind of mood she was in.

When she got to the part about the family going out for a tea of sausages and chips, and then ice cream, Ella looked at her.

'Can we have that Mummy?' she asked.

'You don't like sausages,' Ruth said gently. Ella was extremely fussy when it came to food. Ruth was often jealous when she heard what other mothers had managed to get their children to eat. It made her feel inadequate.

'I do. I like sausages, silly.'

'Okay. So, you want sausages, chips, and then ice cream for tea tomorrow?' Ruth asked with a smile.

'And ketchup.'

Ruth pulled a face. 'Eww. You want ketchup on your ice cream?'

Ella scowled at her. 'Mummy!'

'Sorry. How about *Green Eggs And Ham*?' Ruth asked. They both loved Dr Seuss books.

For the next ten minutes, Ruth read through the surreal rhymes from the book and by the time she had stopped reading, Ella had fallen asleep. For a while, Ruth just watched her. Her tiny hands on the pink pillow. Her chest moving up and down with the slightest of movement.

Gazing up at the ceiling, Ruth watched the tiny pink lights that moved gently, interweaving with each other hypnotically. She drifted off to sleep.

Suddenly, she was aware of a noise as she came out of her dream. The sound of a key in the front door. It must be Dan. He still had a few boxes of records to collect and, unfortunately, she had forgotten to take his key from him.

Maybe I should just stay here and pretend to be asleep. I really don't have the energy for a row.

The noise at the front door continued. It sounded as if someone was trying to jiggle a key, but it wouldn't fit into the lock. She knew what it was. When Dan was drunk or stoned, he had a habit of trying a variety of keys in the front door until he found the right one. Depending on what state he was in, it sometimes took him ages.

Fuck him! I'm not letting him in. Especially if he's off his head.

The noise continued.

Ruth found herself becoming increasingly irritated. She leapt up from the bed. Pacing out into the hallway, she went to the front door.

She could see Dan's shadowy figure behind the frosted glass.

'Why can't you just remember to use the right key?' Ruth called out loudly in total exasperation.

The noise stopped.

'If I let you in, I want you to take your stuff and go. I'm not prepared to discuss anything with you. It's too late.' She put her hand on the lock.

Then something about the shadowy figure behind the glass made her stop.

That doesn't look like Dan. Much taller.

Ruth's heart was in her mouth.

Suddenly, the figure disappeared.

There was the distinct sound of footsteps walking away.

Then nothing.

She waited, holding her breath.

Who the hell was that?

Her pulse started to race.

She waited another minute.

Spotting a screwdriver that she had left when putting up the hall mirror, she grabbed it.

Anyone comes at me, and this goes into their eye!

She listened again.

Nothing.

Opening the door, she prepared to stab anyone who was out there.

There was no one.

What the hell is going on?

A strong wind rattled the leaves and branches on the tree which towered above the pavement.

Ruth looked into the darkness of the front patio. The streetlight cast long shadows across the front of the house.

I'm officially spooked.

She walked down the path, glancing left and right. There was no one to be seen.

Was that Dan?

She went back to the door and looked at the Yale lock that was just about level with her chin. Peering closer, she spotted something. One of the screws that had held the lock in place was gone, and the other was half out as if someone had been unscrewing it.

Ruth's stomach lurched.

Someone had tried to get into her flat.

With her heart starting to beat heavily, she took a breath.

Surely, she would have noticed before if the screw from the lock on her front door had gone.

Now in a panic, she remembered that when she'd taken Ella to bed she hadn't locked the door that leads from the kitchen out to the back garden.

Slamming the front door behind her, she sprinted through the flat to the kitchen. She reached the glass door and locked it quickly.

Staring out into the darkness, she tried to see if there was anything or anyone out there.

It was too dark.

Feeling shaken, she pulled the curtains, making sure there were no gaps. She took her phone and rang Dan's number.

'Hi Ruth,' he said in a slightly suspicious tone.

'Hi Dan. Where are you?'

'Erm, Camden. Why? Is there a problem? Is it Ella?' he asked.

'No, no. It's nothing. Honestly. I'm just moving stuff around the flat and wanted to know when you were going to come and get the rest of your records?'

'Oh, right. I'll pick them up tomorrow. Is that it?'

'Yes. There's something wrong with the lock so I'll have to let you in. Come after five.'

'Fine. I'll see you then.'

Ruth hung up and sat down on the sofa. She was starting to feel incredibly scared about what had just happened.

Brooks and Lucy lay breathless in bed at her home. Pulling the sheet up around her, Lucy sat up against the pillows.

Brooks swung his legs out of the bed and made his way across the bedroom.

'You know, you've got a really tight arse for an old man,' Lucy said with a grin.

'I'm not old,' he protested.

'Forty-five is officially kicking on a bit, Harry,' she joked, as she watched him grab a towel and wrap it around his waist like a skirt.

'Do you want a drink? I was going to have water but now I quite fancy a vodka and something.'

'Ooh. Vodka and something sounds good. If you drink too many then you'll have to stay here,' Lucy said hopefully. She really did wish that she could wake up next to him just once.

She watched him leave the room, then got up and put on a green patterned kimono. She had decided to come clean. She had told him earlier about the incident with the BMW. Brooks didn't like the sound of it and said he would have a quiet word with traffic to see if they could track down the BMW for him.

'Where do you keep the vodka?' he called from the kitchen.

'In the freezer,' Lucy said as she joined him. She put her hands on his hips for a second. 'You don't have to cover up for me, Harry. I'm happy for you to wander around my flat as free as a bird.'

He pointed to the windows. 'Yeah, but I don't want anyone else getting an eyeful. They might get jealous.'

Lucy laughed. 'Oh, would they? Don't worry, I don't get many people sneaking around the house, peeping in at my windows.'

'Glad to hear it,' he said as he poured out the iced vodkas and handed one to her.

Lucy took a sip of her vodka, opened the back door, and stepped out onto her patio. The air was still warm and full of the perfume of spring blossom. Above, the moon was bright, its beams spilling across the garden in a blueish hue.

'This is nice,' Lucy said taking in more fresh air.

Brooks took a few steps across the garden. 'We'll have to do it alfresco next time.'

'You kinky bugger.'

He looked over towards the patio doors. 'That's a shame. You've smashed that flowerpot I bought you.'

Lucy frowned. 'No. I haven't.'

He walked over and crouched down on the patio. Lucy joined him and saw that the pot was on its side and now lay in pieces.

'Yeah, well I definitely didn't do that,' she said, feeling a little spooked.

'Are you sure?' he asked as he continued to look.

'Of course I'm sure, Harry! I haven't got bloody dementia, have I? Maybe it was a cat or a fox.'

'Only if the cat or fox wears size ten boots,' he said, pointing to a footprint on the soil that had spilled onto the patio from the pot.

'Bloody hell!' Lucy explained. She felt her pulse start to quicken.

'Not only was someone creeping around out here, but they also didn't even bother to hide the fact,' he said as he got up.

Even though it was spring, the breeze was chilly and Lucy shivered. 'What does that mean?'

'It means that either they don't care that you know they were here. Or they actually want you to know,' he said in a serious tone.

'I don't like the sound of that,' Lucy said under her breath.

'You need to pack a bag.'

'Why? Where am I going?'

'I don't know yet. But you're not staying here anymore.'

'I'll be fine tonight. It's really late so I'll go to my sister's tomorrow.'

Brooks nodded and pulled her towards him. 'Make sure you do. And lock everything after I leave.'

CHAPTER 19

Ruth looked up from where she was standing on Balham Hill. She remembered when the Deco building across the road had been a cinema before they turned it into a bingo hall in the 1980s. She recalled her dad telling her that he had gone there with his mates to see Elvis Presley in *King Creole* in 1957. He must have been in his early teens. She had seen the photos of her dad dressed as a teddy boy. Black lacquered quiff, long Edwardian jacket, drainpipe trousers, and brothel-creeper shoes. He'd told her that some of the south London teddy boy gangs, also known as cosh boys, were *bloody hooligans*. They had ripped apart a cinema in Elephant and Castle while watching the rock'n'roll film *Blackboard Jungle*, and had fought with the police outside. Eventually, Ruth's dad had been banned from going out at night after a Clapham gang of teddy boys called The Plough Boys had knifed and killed a boy by the bandstand up on Clapham Common. Even though it was near-ly fifty years ago, Ruth thought of the parallels. Teenage boys still hung out in gangs and killed each other today.

A car pulled over and the driver beeped its horn. It was Lucy. She was picking her up and they were heading up to Kensington to collect the toxicology report on Mersad Avdic, and to talk to CID. Of course, they had to change their ap-proach now so there would be no mention of Simo Petrovic to anyone.

Ruth got in and put on her seatbelt.

'Bloody hell. You looked miles away when I pulled over,' Lucy said as she pulled out into the traffic.

'I was just thinking about my dad being a teddy boy back in the 50s.'

'Eww. Big greasy quiffs. My cousin was a mod back in the day. Had the scooter, all the mirrors, big parka coat. Big group of them used to go down to Brighton and fight all the rockers.'

'We weren't even born then,' Ruth mumbled and then looked over at Lucy. 'I think someone had a go at my front door lock last night.'

'What? Are you sure?'

'I heard what I thought was someone trying to put a key in the lock. I saw a figure through the glass. When I went outside, one of the lock's screws had gone and the other was half out. Like it had been unscrewed.'

'Bloody hell. Have you reported it?'

'Who to?'

'Why didn't you ring me for starters, you daft sod?'

'I thought I was imagining things.'

'You need to tell Brooks,' Lucy said.

Ruth frowned. 'I can't tell Brooks. We're not meant to be anywhere near Petrovic.'

Lucy looked at her and pulled a face. 'Actually, Brooks knows everything. He's looking into Petrovic too. He thinks there's something very dodgy going on.'

'What? How come you know that, and I don't?' Ruth asked, feeling slightly angry.

'He didn't want you to know. Thought it might compromise you if you knew that he was disobeying direct orders from the Yard.'

Ruth was annoyed. 'Nice to be kept in the bloody loop. Why are you suddenly his bloody favourite, especially after your row the other day?'

'Sorry. I was just working late, and he told me.'

'Why have you told me now then?' Ruth asked, aware that she was sounding a little petulant.

'Someone has been snooping around my garden. They kicked over a flowerpot and left a dirty great footprint. Now you've told me that someone's had a go at your locks. After the wacky racers on the A3 yesterday, I suggest that someone is trying to put the frighteners on us. And Brooks needs to be kept in the loop on everything.'

Ruth nodded. It was starting to sound like their investigation was ruffling a few feathers.

HALF AN HOUR LATER, Ruth and Lucy were sitting in a side office in Kensington CID. DS Kevin Hart walked in with a fax, put it on the table, and sat down.

'Tox report for you ladies,' he said. Hart wore an ill-fitting grey suit and, with his moustache and fidgety manner, Ruth thought he seemed more like a car salesman.

'Anything come up?' she asked.

'Same as your bloke. Lethal levels of fentanyl.'

Now that confirms Petrovic killed both Mujic and Advic – no question.

'Same MO,' Ruth said.

'You got any ideas about motive?' Hart asked.

Ruth glanced at Lucy. 'We've got a load of missing jewellery.'

'Robbery then,' he said nodding.

Hart frowned, trying to make sense of it. 'Maybe our killer took stuff from Avdic's flat. It's hard to tell. He was just a pensioner so he couldn't have put up much of a struggle. Instead of banging him on the head and nicking his stuff, someone injected him in the neck and killed him. Why?'

Lucy shrugged. 'It's a mystery at the moment.'

Hart nodded. 'But both victims came from Bosnia and they were friends?'

'Yes. But we can't see any link. They were just two old men from Bosnia. And they were friends,' Ruth said.

'Does the name Simo Petrovic mean anything to you?' Hart asked.

Oh shit!

Lucy looked over at Ruth. 'Simo Petrovic? No, I don't think so. Why?'

'One of my officers was looking through some of the books from his flat. At the front of one of them was written *Simo Petrovic 16th April 1997.* The book's in Serb-Croat so I don't know what it's about.'

Ruth shrugged. 'Sorry. Name doesn't ring a bell.'

'I did some digging around on this Petrovic,' Hart added.

Oh great. Sherlock bloody Holmes. Just what we need.

'Find anything?' Lucy asked.

'The Butcher of Mount Strigova. That's what they called him. He ordered the deaths of loads of Muslim civilians in Bosnia. A right evil bastard by all accounts.'

Ruth was starting to worry about where Hart was going with all this. They did not want him to come to the same conclusion as they had, that Petrovic was behind Advic's and Mujic's murders. That would make everything a thousand times more complicated.

'I think I remember reading about that somewhere,' Lucy said nodding. Ruth could see that she was getting tense.

'I don't think it's relevant though,' Hart said.

'Oh, why not?' Ruth asked, with some sense of relief.

'Simo Petrovic shot himself in the head a couple of years ago. He's buried in Bosnia,' he explained.

'Oh right. No, I don't suppose it is relevant then,' Lucy said.

'I mean it's not likely that he's going to be wandering around London or anything,' Hart said with a smile.

Lucy gathered her papers into her file and stood up. 'Right. Well, thanks for your help Kevin. Not sure where we go from here.'

'I'll let you know if we come up with anything,' he said as he went over to the door to show them out.

'And we'll keep you posted if we come across anything,' Ruth added as they left.

RUTH AND LUCY PARKED up in a residential street in Mortlake, West London. It was the address that Safet Dudic had given them for Katerina Selimovic.

A car slowed down beside them for a second, but before Ruth could see inside it had speeded up and gone.

Who the hell was that?

Walking up to the tall Victorian terraced house, Ruth looked around carefully.

'I know this sounds paranoid, but I keep thinking that we're being watched,' she said.

Lucy rang the doorbell. 'No, I keep thinking the same. I'm sure we're not, but the last twenty-four hours have been a bit spooky.'

After a few seconds, an attractive woman in her 50s answered the door.

'Katerina Selimovic?' Lucy asked showing her warrant card.

Katerina smiled and gestured for them to go inside. 'Come in. Come in. Safet said that you would be coming to see me.'

'Sorry. We were in the area, so we thought we'd see if you were in,' Lucy explained.

'Thank you,' Ruth said as she followed Lucy inside.

The flat was tastefully decorated, if a little old-fashioned for Ruth's taste. The walls in the hallway had several beautiful photographs of landscapes. Ruth stopped to look.

Katerina pointed to them. 'My sister took those. She's an excellent photographer.'

'She is ... Where is that?' Ruth asked.

'The Loire Valley, northern France.'

'Looks beautiful.'

'The most beautiful place I've ever seen. Why don't you come and sit down?' Katerina said as she led them to a small but attractively-furnished living room.

Ruth could smell something as soon as she walked into the room. At first, she thought it was strong cigarettes. *No, that's the smell of cigar smoke. And Katerina doesn't seem the kind of woman who would smoke cigars!*

'I'm not sure how much Safet told you,' Lucy said as she and Ruth sat down on the plush sofa.

'He told me the terrible news about Advic and Hamzar,' Katerina said sadly.

'Their names were on a list that we found in a journal in Hamzar's flat. Your name, and Safet's, were on there too. Four names. Do you know why you were on that list?' Ruth asked gently.

'We were all friends. We all grew up together in the same village in Bosnia,' Katerina explained. 'It is so sad. We only saw them a few months ago.'

Ruth looked over at Lucy – *that doesn't tally with what Safet told us yesterday.*

She then heard a faint noise which sounded like a door closing – it could have been next door. Victorian terraces weren't the best when it came to soundproofing.

'When you say 'we', I assume that you are referring to yourself and Safet?' Lucy asked.

Katerina nodded. 'Yes. All four of us got together once or twice a year. I wish it was more but we're all getting old. And now ...'

Ruth could see that Katerina was getting teary and gave her an empathetic nod.

'Safet led us to believe that he didn't see much of Advic in recent years,' Lucy said, trying to lead Katerina in to contradicting his account from the day before.

Katerina raised an eyebrow. 'Why would he say that?'

Lucy shook her head. 'I've no idea. Do you know why he might have told us that?'

'No, I am afraid not. Safet is a very private man. He doesn't like talking about his personal business to anyone.'

Ruth gazed over at some photos that were spread over a long, teak, 50s-style sideboard.

'Mind if I have a look?' she asked, indicating the photos.

'No, of course not.'

As Ruth got up, she heard a faint sound from above – *Someone is upstairs.*

'Does the name Simo Petrovic mean anything to you?' Lucy asked.

Katerina visibly tensed. 'Yes.'

'Hamzar claimed that he had seen Simo Petrovic a few weeks ago in London. Did he tell you that?'

'Yes. He rang me to tell me.'

'What did you say?'

Katerina shifted uncomfortably in her chair. 'I told him that he was an old fool and not to go around telling people.'

'Why was that?' Ruth asked as she peered at the black and white photos of family events, which she assumed had taken place back in Bosnia. A wedding, a family picnic, and a christening.

'That man is dead. He killed himself because he was a coward. I have seen a photograph of his grave in Bosnia. How could he be here?'

Ruth spotted a small, ceramic ashtray which had been pushed out of sight behind a photograph at the end of the sideboard. The dark brown butt of a cigar and ash were inside. Beside it was an old Panama hat.

There's someone else here, Ruth thought.

'And you hadn't met up with Hamzar, Advic, or Safet since Hamzar claimed to have seen Petrovic?' Lucy asked.

'No. I wish I had seen Hamzar and Advic recently ...' Katerina said quietly.

After a few seconds, Ruth came and sat back down. 'And you live here alone, do you Katerina?'

Ruth saw Lucy glance over at her – they were on the same page.

'Yes. Just me.'

'And you don't have anyone staying here with you?' Ruth asked.

Katerina looked uncomfortable. 'No, of course not.'

Ruth waited for the pressure to build a little and then looked up at the ceiling. 'No one here visiting you for the day?'

Katerina shook her head with a frown. 'No, no. No one.'

Lucy leaned forward. 'You know if you feel that you are in any kind of danger, you can tell us.'

'Why would I be in danger? I'm just an old woman.'

Ruth handed Katerina her card. 'If you change your mind, or if there's anything else you want to tell us, please give me a ring.'

RUTH AND LUCY WERE making their way across London to have a meeting with Claire Gold, the human rights lawyer that Shiori had suggested.

'Did you get the impression there was someone upstairs?' Lucy asked after a few minutes of silence.

'Yes. Did you?'

'Definitely. The cigar smoke was a bit of a giveaway.'

'Plus a cigar butt hidden away in an ashtray on the sideboard.'

'Maybe she just had her lover hidden away up there?' Lucy suggested.

'Maybe. She was definitely spooked when we asked about Petrovic.'

Lucy raised an eyebrow. 'Everyone seems spooked when we mention Petrovic.'

'Should we be worried that there was someone upstairs?'

'Yes. But we don't have enough for a warrant. We could pop back later?' Lucy replied as she parked outside the lawyers' offices in West London.

Getting out of the car, Ruth looked up at the office blocks that dominated this part of London. The pavements were full of smartly-dressed professionals drinking takeaway coffees and talking on their phones.

Ruth and Lucy went inside, showed their warrant cards, and were shown to the fifteenth floor where they waited in a large office with glass windows that gave them an amazing view north over London.

'Better than the view from Peckham CID,' Lucy said. 'Any sightings of Dan?'

Ruth shook her head. 'He's got a few more things to pick up. Frankly, it's nice without him there.'

'Hey, less washing, cleaning and cooking.'

The door opened and a tall woman in her 30s strode in. She was carrying a folder of papers.

'Hi, hi. I'm Claire,' she said as she shook their hands and sat down at the table. 'Have you been offered coffee or something to drink?'

'We're fine, thanks,' Lucy said.

'And which one of you is Shiori's friend?' Claire asked.

Ruth smiled. 'Guilty.'

Claire took a few moments, sat back in her chair, and then looked at them.

'If what I've been told is true, then you are sitting on something that is potentially incredibly damaging and explosive,' Claire said opening the folder. 'If I go over the information that Shiori gave me, you can fill in the blanks. Okay?'

She seems uber calm and confident.

Ruth and Lucy nodded.

'There have been two murders. Mersad Advic and Hamzar Mujic. Both men were Bosnian Muslims and living in London. They were friends. There were no signs of robbery at either of the murders, so the motive is unclear. They were both poisoned by an injection of fentanyl which is highly unusual. Hamzar Mujic had claimed that he saw a Serbian war criminal called Simo Petrovic at Waterloo station three weeks ago. Home Office records show that the Bosnian government officially confirmed that Simo Petrovic committed suicide in Bosnia and was buried there. However, there is CCTV footage from Waterloo, from the date mentioned by Mr Mujic, that shows a man bearing a very striking resemblance to Simo Petrovic entering Waterloo station ... How am I doing?' Claire asked looking up from her folder.

'Pretty good. There's not much more than that. We have a theory that Simo Petrovic is now going by the name Oliver Stankovic. He had a plane ticket booked on a flight to Germany a couple of days ago but didn't use it,' Lucy explained.

'And we know that an Oliver Stankovic was being sent post to an address in Hammersmith. MI5 have that property under surveillance, but we have no idea why,' Ruth added.

'Shiori mentioned that there might be some other Bosnians involved?' Claire asked, clicking her pen to take notes.

'Hamzar Mujic's final entry in his diary had a list of four names. His own, Mersad Advic, Safet Dudic and Katerina Selimovic. We've been to see the last two in the last twenty-four hours. They claim to know nothing more than Hamzar Mujic's claim to have seen Petrovic. Both of them thought his claim was ridiculous,' Ruth said.

'Did you believe them?'

'We're not sure. Both of them were hiding something. It may be that they are scared. Two people on that list have been murdered and it could be they're frightened that they might be next,' Lucy said.

'Do you think they are in danger?'

Lucy answered, 'Not to the point where we can do anything about it. It's difficult if they're lying to us.'

'And you have had a visit from the Home Office to ask you not to pursue any investigation into the theory that Simo Petrovic is alive, in London, and had something to do with these murders?'

Ruth nodded. 'We were told by them, and our DCI, to drop it as a line of enquiry. We assumed that it was something to do with the election.'

'We guessed that news of a wanted Serbian war criminal living it up in London wouldn't be good PR for the current government,' Lucy added.

'Yes, that does sound like a very credible theory. Hard to prove of course. But I actually believe that the motivation behind this isn't just the coming election.' Claire delved into her folder and pulled out a photograph. It showed a robust-looking man in his 60s with swept-back grey hair. 'This man is Colonel Matija Tankovic. He was Simo Petrovic's right-hand man in their division of the Serbian army. He is also on the Hague Tribunal's wanted list for war crimes. Tankovic managed to escape to the UK, change his identity, and set himself up in the oil business. You've heard of Natell?'

'The oil company?' Ruth asked. It was one of the only oil companies she had ever heard of.

'Yes. Tankovic brokered a deal between Natell and Yugopetrol to supply oil once sanctions from the west were lifted. Natell made millions from that contract and it made Tankovic a very wealthy man. He still acts as a consultant.'

'Sorry, but how does this relate to our investigation?' Lucy asked.

'This is where it starts to get a little bit complicated, but bear with me.' Claire took out another photograph. It was of a well-dressed man in his 70s. Ruth was certain she had seen him somewhere before. 'Sir George McEwan. Gained a life peerage last year and now sits in the House of Lords.'

Ruth nodded. 'Yeah, I recognise him.'

'McEwan sits on the board of Natell Oil. Which means he has stock in the company. However, he was also made aware of how and when the sanctions on Bosnian oil would be lifted by the Foreign Office.'

Lucy looked up and frowned. 'Which is a major conflict of interest.'

Claire pulled a face. 'Actually, it's a criminal act.'

'Oh my God, that's appalling,' Ruth said. 'He was a member of the government. Why did no one notice?'

'By the time the deal was completed, McEwan had secured a peerage and was out of harm's way,' Claire explained. 'Now comes the clincher. Under his new name of Nikolic, Tankovic made a donation of half a million pounds to the Conservative Party eighteen months ago.'

'Jesus!' Lucy said, her eyes widening.

Ruth shook her head. 'What? They took money from Tankovic?'

'They thought he was Oliver Nikolic, and they didn't do a huge amount of checking into his background. However, six months ago they did some proper digging around and discovered Nikolic's true identity.'

'Shit. Why didn't they do anything about it?' Ruth asked.

'They couldn't admit that they had taken party funds from a Serbian war criminal. It would mean that every investigative journalist worth their salt would look at everything that Tankovic had done, including the deal for Natell Oil.'

'Bloody hell. There was us thinking that the Home Office was scared that we would find Petrovic because having an undetected Serbian war criminal would damage their election chances,' Lucy growled. 'The Home Office don't want us to search for Petrovic because that would lead us to Tankovic as well.'

'Possibly, yes,' Claire said.

'What's stopping all this coming out?' Ruth asked.

'We need to find a newspaper with the balls to run the story. And the finances for the lawyers to make sure the government doesn't wrap the whole thing up in litigation, red tape and political bullshit,' Claire explained.

'Have you found one?' Lucy asked.

'Not yet.'

'What about Petrovic?' she added.

'Oh, he's in London. And he's doing Tankovic's dirty work for him.'

'Two innocent men were murdered but we can't investigate it because no one wants Tankovic's identity to be revealed. That's disgusting!' Ruth said, feeling the anger welling inside her.

'If this story ever sees the light of day, it's very damaging for everyone involved. And it could bring down the current leadership of the party, whether or not they win this election.'

'What do we do now?' Lucy asked.

'I will let you know how things proceed,' Claire said.

'Thank you for your time,' Ruth said getting up to go.

'Oh, and one more thing. Watch your backs. The men you're looking for are incredibly dangerous.'

TANKOVIC BUZZED DOWN the window at the back of his Jaguar. It was a mild spring day and the air was warm against his face. Normally he would have been happy on such a day. However, his inability to halt, or at least hamper, the police investigation into Advic and Mujic's deaths was becoming more than an irritation. His whole way of life, and that of his closest friend, was being seriously jeopardised. And what a life it was. He had an enormous house in Holland Park that his beautiful Russian wife, Annika, had transformed into a luxurious palace. He called her his *kroshka*. The literal English translation was 'a crumb', but it essentially meant 'little one.' He wasn't about to give all that up, and live out his days in prison, without a fight.

He watched as the unmarked police Astra pulled into the car park at Peckham police station.

'Pull forward a little please,' a voice next to him said. It was Simo Petrovic.

The driver moved the car forward slowly so that they could look through the fence and see the car park properly.

There was silence in the car. Tankovic watched the Astra pull into a parking space and stop. Then the two female police officers got out and, deep in conversation, headed into the police station.

'And that is them?' Petrovic asked.

'Yes. Fucking *gabors* ...' Tankovic said as he looked down at a surveillance photograph he had of the two officers. *Gabors* was Serbian slang for ugly women. 'DC Ruth Hunter and DC Lucy Henry.'

'You have their addresses yet?' Petrovic asked, sitting forward to look closely at the photograph.

'Yes. And we have already started to apply a little pressure.'

'Clearly not enough though?' Petrovic said sharply as he took a cigarette and lit it. 'And the woman they spoke to this morning?'

'Claire Gold. She is an American human rights lawyer,' Tankovic said. 'She used to work for Amnesty International.'

'Amnesty? That's all we need. Why would they go to her?'

Tankovic shrugged. 'I suspect their superiors do not believe them and think they are wasting their time. I had hoped they would have been dissuaded from continuing by now.'

'I thought you spoke to your sources at Whitehall and they were going to make all this go away.'

'They said they had made themselves very clear.'

Petrovic shook his head. 'Not clear enough. And the Embassy?'

'There is no one left from the old days. I am a stranger there now. It's all changed,' Tankovic said.

He watched as Petrovic sat back in the plush leather seat, took a lungful of smoke, and blew it in a stream out of the window. 'The visits to Safet Dudic and Katerina Selimovic are a worrying development.'

'It can be dealt with.'

'I'm not sure it's going to be enough now. It's gone too far. These bloody *kurvas*!' Petrovic snapped as he spat out of the window. *Kurvas* was slang for whores.

'Don't worry. By this time tomorrow, these officers won't dare give us any more trouble. I promise you.'

CHAPTER 20

B y the time Lucy got home, the daylight was beginning to fade. Her head was still reeling from the ramifications of their meeting with Claire Gold. She couldn't believe where the investigation into Hamzar Mujic's murder had led them. She had worked in CID in south London for over fifteen years and had never encountered anything like it. War criminals, assassinations, and political corruption. It was the stuff of films.

Taking her handbag from the car, she remembered that Brooks was swinging by in about an hour for *a chat* before she went to stay at her sister's flat. The thought of going to bed with him gave her a little tingle. She would have a shower as soon as she got inside, tidy up the flat, and make it look vaguely romantic.

As she neared the door of the flat, she reached inside her handbag for her keys. Suddenly, she sensed that someone was approaching. She glanced up and saw a tall, shaven-headed man wearing a bomber jacket coming her way.

I don't like the look of him.

She froze for a moment, making no eye contact. It was dangerous to run and open the door, only to be shoved inside by a would-be attacker. She had heard about that MO too many times before from female victims of sexual attack and rape.

Why has he stopped? This doesn't feel right.

With her pulse starting to quicken and tension in her stomach, Lucy turned, looked at the man and asked, with her best police officer smile, 'Can I help you?'

'I'm looking for Mrs Lucy Henry,' he said in an accent that sounded distinctly Eastern European to her.

'Okay. That's me. What do you want?' she asked, feeling vulnerable and nervous. She glanced over his shoulder but could see that there was no one else around.

'We have a couple of mutual friends.'

'Do we?'

What the hell is he talking about?

'Yes. And they have asked me to have a chat with you about something you are working on at the moment.'

'I can't discuss any ongoing investigation that I'm working on with anyone,' Lucy said, trying to work out exactly what she was going to do should the man try to attack her.

He shrugged. 'Maybe we should go inside your flat for a chat. It is not very discreet out here.'

Are you fucking kidding me?

Lucy raised an eyebrow. 'I'm an experienced police officer. And it would be very stupid of me to go into my flat with a strange man whom I have never met before, don't you agree?'

She glanced down the street again, and then back over her shoulder. Still no one.

'You seem a little nervous?'

'Do I? I'm not used to being accosted outside my home by strange men,' she snapped.

He smiled. 'There's that word again. 'Strange'. I assure you, I am not strange.'

'You think this is funny? Is this how you get your kicks, intimidating women?' Lucy growled at him.

I wish I had some kind of weapon so I could knock him out.

'If I have frightened you, then I am sorry. I just have a message that I have been asked to deliver to you. That is all,' he said with a shrug.

Her heart was racing. 'Well could you get on with it?'

The man took two steps closer.

Lucy put the house keys in between her fingers to form a weapon.

If he comes for me then I'm going to stick the key in his eye.

The man spoke in a hushed voice. 'My friends understand that you are looking for someone. This person has no desire to be found. He has many friends, and they want you to understand how dangerous it is to keep up this search. They want to make that very, very clear to you.'

At that moment, the front door to the next-door house opened. A young man came out carrying a mountain bike. It was Mikey. He had moved in about six months ago, but she knew him to say hello to.

'Hi Lucy,' Mikey said as he struggled to manoeuvre the mountain bike out of the door. 'You okay?'

Lucy gestured to the man in the bomber jacket. 'This gentleman was looking for someone. He's got the wrong address.'

She walked rapidly to the front door with her keys, turning to look first at the man and then at Mikey.

The man nodded. 'Thanks for your help.' He turned and sauntered away down the road.

Lucy watched him go for a few seconds and then glanced over at Mikey. 'Have a nice bike ride.'

'Cheers, I will. Love it when the evenings start to draw out, don't you?' he asked as he swung his leg over the saddle.

'Yeah,' she replied as she pushed the key into the lock, but she didn't register what he had said. Her hand was still trembling.

As soon as she was inside, she pushed the door shut quickly. She locked it, put on the chain, and then marched around the flat closing all the curtains.

AS RUTH WHEELED ELLA in her pushchair across the final section of Clapham Common, she glanced over at a couple of football games that were being played. She thought of her dad, who everyone said had been a decent footballer in his day. He claimed to have been on the books at Chelsea as a schoolboy, although no one else in the family could remember that. But that was her dad. Never let the truth get in the way of a good story.

They had just spent an hour at the swings and playground. As Ruth passed the entrance to Clapham Common underground station, she felt the gust of warm air that swept out through the ticket office every time a train pulled into the platforms below. Someone told her the evocative smell was the particular grease they used on the rails.

Turning right at the top of Balham Hill, she could hear Ella singing to herself while kicking her legs up and down.

Oh my God. Could she be any cuter?

As she approached her flat, Ruth reached into her pocket for the front door keys. All she wanted to do now was have a shower, a big glass of wine, and flop in front of the television.

As she moved the pushchair out of the way to get to the door, she noticed that it was already open. It was resting against the doorframe – but it was definitely open.

I know I locked it this morning. Didn't I?

Ruth wondered if Dan had let himself in to collect his final boxes of records and had left it open by mistake. She wouldn't put it past him.

Then she had a darker thought.

The rattling of the lock the night before and the missing screw.

She moved the pushchair to one side and looked down at Ella. 'Mummy's just going to go inside for a second. Just stay there.'

Pushing the door open very slowly, she listened carefully.

Nothing.

She took a step inside. And then another.

From where she stood now, she could see down through the flat to the kitchen area at the back.

Oh my God!

Everything had been turned upside down.

We've been burgled.

Moving slowly through the flat, while glancing back at Ella in the pushchair, she saw that the flat had been totally ransacked.

I can't believe it! Bastards!

She stopped again. Was anyone still in there?

'Hello? I'm a police officer. Is there anyone there? Hello?' she called out.

Nothing.

She glanced back to check that Ella was still by the front door.

Creeping slowly forward, she went into the kitchen area. The place looked like a bomb had gone off.

Then she realised that someone was lying on the floor.

She flinched and jumped back in shock.

'Oh my God!' she shouted.

As her eyes moved up the body, she could see it was Dan. He was unconscious – or worse.

She crouched over him quickly and checked that he was still breathing. He was.

Thank God!

There was a large, nasty gash on his temple.

He must have disturbed whoever wrecked the flat and they attacked him.

Moving his sleeve up, she felt for his pulse and found it.

She got up, ran to the door, and pulled Ella inside. Grabbing the phone, she dialled 999.

'Yeah, I need an ambulance as quickly as possible.'

CHAPTER 21

Lucy was on her third glass of wine by the time Brooks knocked on the door. At least the booze had stopped her feeling jittery.

Going to the door, she took a deep breath. 'Who is it?'

'Who do you think it is? Jack the Ripper?' came a voice.

It's Harry. Thank God.

She took the chain off, unlocked the Chubb lock and then opened the door.

'Bloody hell, Luce. What's going on?' Brooks asked.

'Just come in, will you?' Lucy said as she hastily ushered him inside before closing and locking the door behind him.

'Am I missing something here?'

Lucy took another deep breath. 'As I got home tonight, a man approached me and made a threat.' She had been in many dangerous situations as a copper in London, but a threat on her own doorstep felt very personal and had really rattled her.

'What? Are you bloody kidding me?' Brooks said, getting angry.

'It was all very polite. He sounded Eastern European. He said that continuing to try and find the person I'm looking for was going to be very dangerous.'

'Right, I'm taking you to your sister's immediately.'

Lucy nodded. 'I'll get my stuff.'

'At some point, I'll have to go and talk to the Chief Super. That time might be now,' he said as he followed her through the flat.

'Do you trust him?' Lucy asked.

Brooks thought for a moment and scratched his nose. She could tell he was on edge. 'He's very belt and braces, and I want to protect you and Ruth as much as I can.'

'Give me another twenty-four hours to find this bastard, Harry. Please.'

'No. It's not safe anymore.'

Lucy went to him and put her arms around his waist.

He looked directly at her. 'This case has really got to you, hasn't it?'

She squeezed her arms around him and pulled him closer. 'Yeah. Twenty-four hours.'

'What's going to be different this time tomorrow?'

'Petrovic knows we're closing in. If he's desperate enough to have someone threaten me on my doorstep, then he's going to do something stupid. He's going to make a mistake. And then we've got him.'

'You sound very confident about that.'

Lucy frowned. 'I thought you said I was a bloody good copper.'

'You are, but I don't want you or Ruth to get hurt before we sort this out.'

'Anyway, you can stay with me tonight,' she said, reaching up and kissing his neck. 'My sister's in York on a business trip.'

Brooks smiled sadly. 'You know I can't, Luce. I would love to but ...'

'I know. I just like making you feel guilty.' Lucy moved back from him and nodded. 'So, twenty-four hours, Harry. Come on.'

He put his hands up defensively. 'Okay, okay. Just get your stuff together.'

Lucy pulled a mock upset face. 'Oh ... are you not taking me to bed before we go?'

'Aren't I?' he said uncertainly.

'Yes, you bloody are.' She took him by the hand and led him to the bedroom.

BY THE TIME THE PARAMEDICS had arrived, Dan had regained consciousness. While he was being taken to St George's Hospital, Ruth gave a statement to a uniformed officer. She then had to arrange for someone to come and sit with Ella so she could go to the hospital to check on Dan. Mrs Bateman, her elderly neighbour from upstairs, said she was more than happy to babysit for a while, and although she was very forgetful, Ruth didn't have much choice.

As Mrs Bateman sat and watched the telly and ate biscuits, Ruth spent a few minutes tidying up the flat and trying to ascertain if anything was missing. Nothing of any value had been stolen. The television, CD player, jewellery, and even some cash in the kitchen had not been touched. It hadn't been a robbery. Whoever had broken in was looking for something specific, and Ruth could only conclude that it was related to the Simo Petrovic case. It might have also served as a warning for her to back off. It had certainly unnerved her.

It was nearly two hours after Ruth had discovered Dan. She parked up in St George's car park and dialled Lucy's number.

'Ruth? Everything okay?' Lucy asked immediately.

She doesn't sound herself.

'Erm, not really. Where are you?'

'I just got to my sister's. What's happened?' Lucy asked with concern.

'Someone trashed my flat. They knocked Dan unconscious.'

'Oh my God. How is he?'

'I'm outside the hospital now, just about to go in and see him, but I rang earlier for news. He's fully regained consciousness and he's not in any danger. I guess he'll just have a whopping headache.'

'Maybe he deserves one,' Lucy said sarcastically. 'How bad's the flat?'

'Nothing obvious was stolen. They left valuables and cash so they must have been looking for something else ... unless it was some kind of warning.'

'Which is why I'm at my sister's already.'

'Why, what's happened?'

'A delightful man doorstepped me and told me that it was dangerous for us to keep looking for his friend.'

'Bloody hell. Did he hurt you?'

'No, no. But he scared the shit out of me.'

'Did you tell Brooks?'

'Yes. Have you told him about your break-in and Dan?'

'Not yet. I'll ring him from here once I've checked on Dan.'

'Okay. I'll see you in the morning. And you and Ella need to stay somewhere else tonight,' Lucy said.

'Yeah. I'll sort something out.'

Ruth ended the call and walked across the car park, feeling very uneasy. It seemed that both she and Lucy had been targeted tonight. Petrovic, and possibly Tankovic, were clearly now willing to take risks to protect their new identities. Threatening police officers and breaking into their flats were incredibly bold moves by anyone's standards. Ruth had Ella's safety to consider and she needed to think about staying somewhere else for a few days.

Making her way through the ground floor of the hospital, she started to scan the signs for Warwick Ward. Dan had been moved from the Medical Assessment Unit to a regular ward over an hour ago.

Having found the ward entrance, Ruth made her way to the nurses' station and asked for him. Even though there was part of her that hated Dan for the way he had behaved in recent weeks, she also felt a little guilty. If she and Lucy hadn't decided to pursue Petrovic, no one would have broken into her flat and knocked him unconscious.

As she approached the double doors into the ward itself, Ruth spotted Dan in the corner. His head was heavily bandaged, and he was linked up to a drip. Beside him was a woman in her 20s who was holding his hand.

Oh my God. Are you kidding me?

Watching for a few more seconds, Ruth was left in no doubt that this was the woman he was having an affair with. Although she hadn't told Dan that she was coming to visit, she couldn't believe what she was seeing.

Taking a breath, Ruth could feel a tear in her eye.

Fucking bastard!

She wandered over to the coffee machine while she weighed up what to do next. Go in and confront them? It wasn't her style.

She popped a pound coin into the machine and selected a latte. After a few strange noises and gurgles, the machine stopped.

Where's my fucking coffee?

Ruth gave it a kick out of total frustration. 'For God's sake!'

'I've lost a small fortune in these bloody things,' said a female voice behind her.

Ruth turned to see it was the woman who had been sitting with Dan.

Oh great.

'Right. That's a bit of a pain.'

'My nan was in this hospital last year. The nurses might make you a tea if you ask nicely,' the woman explained with a smile. She had an Australian accent.

Now what do I do?

'Haven't we met before?' Ruth said, raising an eyebrow.

The woman gave her a quizzical look. 'Have we? Sorry, I...'

Ruth held out her hand. 'I'm Ruth. Must have been at some club or something.'

'Yeah, well I was probably off my head. Angela,' she said as she shook hands.

'Are you visiting your nan again?'

'No. She's fine. Just a friend. He was attacked but he's going to be okay,' Angela said.

'Oh no. That's sounds awful.'

'Yeah, that's south London for you. I come from a tiny little place outside Melbourne where you can leave your doors open and cars unlocked,' she said with a shrug.

'That sounds nice,' Ruth said.

'Yeah, it is. Do you happen to know where the nearest toilets are?' Angela asked.

'Out here, turn right and head back towards the staircase,' Ruth said gesturing.

'Thanks. Nice to see you again, Ruth,' Angela said and walked away.

Bloody hell!

Ruth took a breath, walked into the ward, and headed for Dan's bed.

He looked up and his eyes widened.

'Ruth. Hi, errrm ... I didn't know you were coming to visit me tonight. I thought you'd text me or something,' Dan said, squirming.

He's such a prick.

Ruth was enjoying how uncomfortable her presence was making him feel. 'We are still married, Dan. You're the father of our daughter and you were assaulted in our flat. Why would I not come to see you?'

'Thanks for coming. I'm just really tired. It's all the painkillers.'

'Sounds like you want me to go?'

'Oh no, it's not that. I think I'm just going to sleep that's all,' he said, shifting awkwardly and looking over her shoulder.

Yes. I wonder when Angela is coming back.

Ruth looked behind her, and then looked at Dan. 'She seemed nice.'

'Who?'

'Angela.'

'Angela? Who's Angela?'

'You know Angela. Attractive, slim. Australian. Comes from a little place near Melbourne. She was sitting here about ten minutes ago holding your hand. You must remember that, Dan? Unless you've got amnesia?' Ruth said sardonically.

Dan closed his eyes for a few seconds. 'I ... I'm sorry ...'

'Don't worry. I'm not going to make a scene. I'm not even surprised. It just confirms to me that you are a lying, cheating, emotionally-stunted prick, that's all,' she said as she got up. 'I actually feel sorry for Angela.'

She turned and walked out of the ward without looking back.

CHAPTER 22

Sipping from her lukewarm coffee, Ruth shuffled through the mountain of paperwork that was growing on her desk. She was aware that for the last hour she had done little *other* than shuffle. She couldn't get the discovery of Dan's affair out of her head. Every time she managed to preoccupy herself with something work-related, a few seconds later the thundering realisation that her husband had been cheating on her came rushing into her head like an oncoming train.

The sound of laughter came from where Hassan and Gaughran were sitting. Ruth looked over and saw Hassan talking quietly to Gaughran. They didn't know she was listening.

'Why do I have to ask them?' Hassan asked Gaughran.

'Because they're a pair of Dorises,' was the reply. 'Doris' was a derogatory term used in the Met for women police officers.

Utter dickheads.

Hassan approached, looking decidedly awkward.

Here we go.

'Ruth, we wonder if you and Lucy could help us with something?' he asked.

Ruth raised an eyebrow. 'What's that then?'

'Old lady in the flats in Adams Court claims she was sexually assaulted. We wondered if you could talk to her.'

'Oh right. What's her name ... Doris?' Ruth asked dryly.

Hassan glanced over at Gaughran who snorted with laughter.

'Eh? Oh no,' Hassan said with a frown.

'You know what, part of me would love to watch you two toddlers squirm with embarrassment taking down her statement. But in reality, the idea of subjecting that poor woman to you two is such a horrible thought that me and Lucy will deal with it.'

'Thanks, Ruth,' he said, looking relieved.

'Syed?' Ruth said very quietly.

He came a little closer. 'Yeah?'

'Don't let Tim drag you down to his level. Seriously.'

Hassan nodded with a look of embarrassment and went back to his desk.

For a few seconds, Ruth's thoughts went back to Dan. How had she allowed this affair to happen? As a copper, she knew that her instinct was 99% right about the investigations that she'd worked on. Why hadn't she trusted the same instinct when it came to Dan? Deep down she knew that she'd deceived herself that he wasn't having an affair. Maybe she just couldn't deal with the rejection. Maybe she hoped it would somehow go away. She kicked herself for not confronting him months, or even years, ago and throwing him out.

As her mind then turned to Ella, that beautiful, innocent little girl who would have to grow up without the constant, reassuring presence of her father, Ruth felt quite overwhelmed. She closed her eyes for a moment and took a deep breath, but she couldn't stop a tear from welling in her eye.

'Ruth?' a voice said. She looked up to see Lucy approaching.

'Yeah?' Ruth replied, wiping her eyes.

'Phone call from Surrey Police. There's been an incident involving Safet Dudic.'

LUCY AND RUTH RACED down the A3 with the blues and twos blaring. Lucy zipped in and out of the traffic and within twenty minutes they had arrived at Stoneleigh High Street. The only information they had been given was that the victim was called Safet Dudic and that he had Ruth's police information card in his pocket, which is why Surrey Police force had called her.

As they parked up, Ruth could see that the street had been taped off by uniformed officers. The blue lights of the ambulance and patrol cars threw a rhythmic light over the rubberneckers, the term police officers used to describe the inquisitive onlookers who came to gawp at whatever had happened.

Ruth and Lucy headed for the officer who was clearly running a scene log. They showed him their warrant cards and explained they were from Peckham CID.

'Are you the first responder?' Ruth asked. The young PC looked pale and a little bit shaken. She had seen it before in young officers.

The PC nodded. 'Yes, ma'am.'

'Can you tell us what happened, constable?' Lucy asked.

The PC pointed to the newsagent's on the corner. 'According to witnesses, the victim came out of the shop over there and headed for the zebra crossing. As he was crossing, a car came out of nowhere, hit him, and drove off. He was dead when I arrived.'

'Anyone get a look at the driver or the car?'

The PC looked down at his notebook. 'A Mrs Kate Pullinger over there said that she thought it was kids in a small blue car, but the man who runs the off licence was sure that the car was expensive-looking and black. That's it at the moment, ma'am.'

Ruth gave him an empathetic smile. 'Thank you, constable. Don't worry. I remember seeing my first few RTAs. They really shook me. Fortunately, in this job you do get used to it.'

The PC nodded but was still visibly shaken.

As Ruth got closer to where the ambulance was parked, she saw the outline of the body under a grey blanket.

Lucy stopped and looked at her. 'Poor bugger.'

'There's no way that Dudic wasn't targeted is there?' Ruth said gesturing to his body.

'You know what I think of coincidences.'

A uniformed sergeant noticed their presence and came over.

'One of you ladies DI Hunter?' he asked.

Ruth didn't like his tone. It sounded patronising and he used the word *ladies* as if he was asking them if they wanted a drink in a nightclub.

'That's me, sarge,' she said.

'Victim had your card on him. Did you know him?'

'We interviewed him in connection with a murder enquiry we're running out of Peckham nick,' Ruth explained.

The sergeant paused in thought for a moment. 'You think the two are connected?'

'Possibly,' she said. She wasn't about to give too much away.

'I've got an eyewitness who claims she got a good look at the driver and the car. Driver was a middle-aged man with a shaved head. The car was big, black, and expensive-looking. She didn't know for certain, but it could have been a Jaguar.'

'Not your average hit and run then?' Lucy said.

Out of the corner of her eye, Ruth noticed something that was out of place. One of the victim's feet, in a dark Nike Air trainer, was partially visible.

'Lucy,' she said under her breath, giving her a nudge and indicating the trainer.

Lucy frowned and then said with some urgency, 'Come on.'

Walking quickly over to the body, they showed their warrant cards to the paramedics who stepped aside for a moment.

Ruth lifted the blanket back to reveal the victim's face – it was Dudic's 16-year-old grandson.

It's the wrong Safet Dudic.

Ruth looked at Lucy.

'Shit! So, where's the old man?'

They turned quickly and ran back to the car.

CHAPTER 23

Five minutes later, Lucy and Ruth screeched to a halt outside the Dudics' home. A patrol car was a few seconds behind them.

Ruth unclipped her seat belt, threw open the car door and sprinted towards the front door. Not only did she know that Safet Dudic Senior was now in great danger, or worse, but she also had to break it to Mrs Dudic that her son had been killed in a hit and run.

Hammering on the door, Ruth looked at Lucy who was peering in through the windows. She glanced over at the driveway.

'No car on the drive,' Ruth said. Her adrenaline was starting to pump.

What if they've killed Dudic already?

She put her ear to the door – nothing. 'I don't think there's anyone in.'

Lucy spotted two uniformed police officers striding up the driveway. 'Constables, please stay at the roadside to make sure no one comes in or out. We don't think Mrs Dudic is in. See if there's any other way of getting hold of her.'

Ruth looked up at the front of the house. 'How are we going to get in?'

197

'Round the back?' Lucy suggested. She gestured to a seven-foot high solid wooden side gate that was padlocked. 'Through there.'

'And how are we going to get over that?'

'We're not.' Lucy took a small run up and booted the gate with the sole of her boot. The lock broke noisily as the gate flew open with a bang. She turned to Ruth and winked.

'Oh, okay. Well that's definitely easier,' Ruth said dryly.

They moved quickly into the large, well-tended back garden. On the far side was the annexe which Ruth knew was where Safet Dudic lived. Spotting a half-open door, she went over and looked in cautiously.

'Mr Dudic?' she called. 'It's Detective Constable Hunter. We spoke to you yesterday.'

Lucy peered through one of the windows. 'Shit! The place has been wrecked,' Lucy yelled.

Taking out her extendable baton, Ruth proceeded cautiously in through the door. If the annexe had been trashed, or Dudic attacked, the intruders might still be in there.

Lucy was now behind her with her own baton drawn and ready for action.

Ruth could feel her pulse thudding in her neck. She took a deep breath and readied herself for whatever or whoever was inside.

'Mr Dudic? We're coming in now. Okay?' she called out as she and Lucy proceeded carefully along the passageway that led to the rooms of the annexe.

They stopped for a moment and listened.

Nothing.

Ruth looked at Lucy with a well-rehearsed gesture to ask if she had heard anything. Lucy shook her head.

Walking into the living room, Ruth saw that the place had been turned upside down. She thought of her own flat that had been left in the same state the day before.

Bastards!

'Alpha Zero to Dispatch, are you receiving, over?' Lucy said into her radio.

'Dispatch receiving Alpha Zero, go ahead,' came the response.

'We're going to need SOCOs as soon as possible and a uniformed patrol to secure our scene of crime, over.'

'Alpha Zero, received. Will advise, over.'

Lucy crouched down to inspect the objects and papers that were littered all over the floor.

'I'll check the other rooms,' Ruth said quietly as she went slowly through the rest of the annexe.

There was a small bedroom. The mattress had been thrown against the wall and the wardrobe emptied. Off the room was a bathroom with cupboards opened and the shower curtain pulled across the bath.

'Anything?' Lucy called out.

'No ... Where the hell is Dudic then?'

'If no one's in, maybe he went out with his daughter?'

Ruth turned and headed back towards the living room. 'I really hope so.'

'I've found something,' Lucy called.

Ruth entered the room and went over to Lucy, who handed her a photograph. It showed Dudic, Katerina, Mujic and Advic all sitting at a restaurant table. They were smiling and raising their glasses.

'Do we know when that was taken?' Ruth asked.

Lucy flipped over the photo and saw a printed date. 'Three weeks ago.'

'Not only was Dudic lying about how often he saw the others, but Katerina also said she hadn't seen them for months.'

'Why lie to us? There's nothing criminal about meeting up with friends,' Lucy said.

'Exactly ... unless you're planning to do something criminal,' Ruth suggested.

'The fact that they both lied about it suggests they had something to hide. Whatever they were doing scared them both.'

'Mujic sees Petrovic at Waterloo just over three weeks ago and tells the others. They decide to meet,' Ruth said gesturing to the photo. 'They have lunch and agree to do something about Petrovic. Expose him or kill him. They can't admit to meeting up because they know what they've chosen to do, and they're scared.'

Lucy nodded. 'Still doesn't explain how Petrovic knew who they were and what they were planning on doing.'

Ruth shrugged. 'It's a small community in London. Someone heard something.'

There was a noise from somewhere in the annexe. It was either a movement or a groan.

'What the bloody hell was that?' Ruth asked, suddenly feeling tense.

'Someone in here?' Lucy asked.

'I thought I'd checked,' Ruth said, gripping her baton again as they made their way back towards the bedroom.

She got to the bathroom first.

It sounded like the noise had come from there.

She glanced in the mirror and spotted something she hadn't seen the first time.

The reflection of a bloody smear across the white tiles of the wall behind the shower curtain.

Oh my God!

'In here,' Ruth said quietly. Bracing herself, she pulled back the shower curtain slowly.

A man's body, drenched in blood, was laying in the bath. Lifeless grey eyes, wide open with fear, were staring up at her.

It was Safet Dudic.

Lucy took a step back. 'Jesus Christ!'

'Bastards!' Ruth said looking at his blood-soaked clothes and hair. His throat had been cut from ear to ear.

Lucy looked at Ruth. 'Katerina Selimovic ...'

'You think they'll go after her next?' Ruth said, but she already knew the answer to that.

'Yes. Of course.'

CHAPTER 24

Ten minutes later, Ruth and Lucy were hammering up the A3 towards London, weaving in and out of the traffic.

Ruth clicked her Tetra radio, 'Alpha Zero to Dispatch, Alpha Zero to Dispatch, do you read me, over?'

'Alpha Zero, this is Dispatch reading you, go ahead, over,' came a voice.

'Possible incident at 24 Crown Gardens, Mortlake. Occupant's name is Katerina Selimovic. Repeat, Katerina Selimovic. I'm going to need two patrol cars and an ARV on stand-by, over,' Ruth said. ARV stood for Armed Response Vehicle. After what they had seen at Safet Dudic's home, they weren't going to take any risks.

There were a few seconds of silence as the CAD operator checked the availability of nearby marked patrol cars.

'Alpha Zero from Dispatch. I have one patrol car en route. ETA is ten minutes, over.'

'Dispatch from Alpha Zero, out,' Ruth said, looking over at Lucy and then at the road ahead. 'You going via the Lower Richmond Road?'

Lucy nodded. 'Yep. Putney Hill is a nightmare this time of day.'

'Good shout. We might even beat the woodentops there,' Ruth said as Lucy undertook three cars and then pulled back into the outer lane. Ruth gripped her seat. 'If we get there alive.'

'Do you want to drive?' Lucy asked raising an eyebrow.

'Bit touchy,' Ruth said. She put her left hand up to the grab handle above the passenger door and held it tightly as they zig-zagged through the traffic again.

The blues and twos were on full. As Ruth looked up, she could see the traffic in the outer lane indicating left and pulling over.

As they turned into the right-hand filter to Roehampton Lane, Ruth felt the back tyres skid a little.

I am now officially scared by Lucy's driving.

Crossing the southbound lanes of the A3, Ruth saw a huge articulated lorry coming across their path.

'Lucy?' she said under her breath.

'Shit!' Lucy growled as she stamped on the brakes.

The car skidded but kept moving forward.

This is not good!

'Jesus!' Lucy said as she flinched.

The car stopped.

The lorry came thundering past with about an inch between it and the front of their car.

Lucy blew out her cheeks. 'Now that was fucking close!'

'Too close.'

Before Ruth had time to process what had happened, and think about just how close they had come to being killed, Lucy had slammed her foot on the accelerator. The wheels squealed as they tore off down Roehampton Lane.

A minute later, they swung left onto Lower Richmond Road, snaking in and out of the traffic as cars pulled over for them. Taking a right, they were soon screeching to a halt outside Katerina Selimovic's house.

Leaping out of the car, Ruth scanned the road for anything suspicious. Nothing out of the ordinary as far as she could see.

'Anything?' Lucy asked.

'Clear,' Ruth replied.

They dashed across the road. There was no sign of the patrol car yet.

I pray that we're not too late.

Ruth knocked loudly on the door while Lucy went to the ground floor windows and peered in. It was all too similar to their visit to Dudic's house an hour earlier. And look how that turned out.

Come on! Come on!

Ruth looked anxiously over at Lucy. 'Anything?'

'Nope. Nothing.'

'Shit!'

Maybe we're too late?

Ruth knocked again – this time more urgently. Then she crouched down and pushed open the letterbox. 'Mrs Selimovic? It's the police. Can you open the door please?'

Ducking lower, Ruth squinted through the letterbox into the hallway. Nothing.

Then she heard a noise. She put her hand up to signal to Lucy that she had heard something.

They both moved back cautiously from the front door.

'Someone in there?' Lucy said in a virtual whisper.

Ruth nodded.

Suddenly, she heard a voice. 'I'm coming ... I'm coming.'

Ruth looked at Lucy – *Bloody hell! That's a relief.*

The door opened. Katerina looked at them in puzzlement. 'What is with all this fuss?'

'Can we come in?' Ruth asked in a tone that left her no option.

'If you must,' Katerina said irritably as she ushered them in.

How are we going to tell her that another of her friends has been killed?

They followed her to the living room where Katerina sat down on a large, jade-green armchair.

'We have some bad news I'm afraid,' Lucy said gently.

Katerina looked up at them nervously. 'Safet?'

For a moment, Ruth and Lucy said nothing – but the silence told Katerina everything she needed to know.

'I'm afraid so. I'm so sorry,' Ruth said.

Katerina shook her head. 'I don't understand. We all came here because we thought it was safe.' She took a tissue from the sleeve of her cardigan and dabbed her eyes.

'We are really sorry. We also think that you are in a great deal of danger,' Lucy explained.

'Me? No. I cannot believe that,' Katerina said as she sniffed. She looked shaken and confused.

Ruth and Lucy went and sat down on the sofa.

'Katerina, we need you to tell us the truth. We know that you met Safet, Hamzar and Mersad a few weeks ago. Just after Hamzar saw Simo Petrovic at Waterloo,' Lucy said.

Katerina looked at them but said nothing.

'Can you tell us what you talked about when you met?' Ruth asked softly.

There were a few more seconds of silence.

'Please ...' Lucy said.

'What do you want me to say? That we agreed to track down that man?' Katerina asked.

'Did you? Did you agree that you would try to find Petrovic?' Ruth asked.

Katerina waited for a moment and then nodded slowly.

'And did you find him, Katerina? Do you know where he is?' Lucy asked.

Katerina shook her head.

Their attention was drawn to a noise outside.

What the hell was that?

Lucy looked over at Ruth with concern.

'Uniform?' Ruth suggested, getting up and heading for the window that was obscured by net curtains.

'What was that noise?' Katerina asked anxiously as she got up from the chair.

Ruth spotted a dark figure through the opaque material.

The figure stopped, turned, and looked directly at her.

They were wearing a balaclava.

Jesus Christ!

CRACK!

A bullet splintered the window.

Ruth instinctively flinched and ducked.

Dashing across the room, she dived towards Katerina and, in a rugby tackle, threw her to the floor.

CRACK!

Ruth glanced up at the window.

Another bullet came through the glass which shattered noisily.

'Jesus!' Lucy shouted. 'Keep down!'

Aware that she was on top of Katerina, Ruth rolled off onto the carpet and looked over at her. Katerina groaned through trembling lips.

Glancing towards the window, Ruth could see that the figure had now gone.

'Katerina? Are you all right?' she asked.

'Alpha Zero to Dispatch, Code Zero, I repeat Code Zero. Officers under fire at target address. Require AFO now!' Lucy shouted into the radio.

'What happened?' Katerina mumbled under her breath. Blood was trickling from her mouth.

Oh God! Has she been shot?

'Are you okay?' Ruth asked, moving closer towards Katerina.

There was no response.

RUTH AND LUCY HAD BEEN in St George's Hospital for an hour. Katerina had regained consciousness in the ambulance on the way in. From what the paramedics told them, she was just suffering from a split lip, cuts and bruises, and shock.

Ruth looked up to see a young doctor heading their way with notes in hand.

'How's our patient?' Lucy asked.

'She's going to be fine. Nothing more than a few bumps. She's in shock so I have sedated her. I'd like to keep her in overnight for observation, but I can't see why she can't go home tomorrow morning.'

'Thanks,' Ruth said.

The doctor frowned as he looked at Lucy. She had two cuts on her face. 'Are you okay?'

Lucy pointed to her face. 'What, this? I just cut myself shaving.'

The doctor gave her a sardonic smile. 'I understand that Mrs Selimovic will need some kind of protection?'

Ruth nodded. 'Yeah. We're going to have to post an armed officer on her door, I'm afraid.'

He shrugged. 'We're a South London hospital. It's not the first time. Bit scary for some of the other patients though.'

Ruth watched the doctor walk away and noticed Lucy checking him out.

'Hmm ... I would,' Lucy said, raising an eyebrow and tipping her head towards the doctor as he went.

'Lucy! We both just nearly got killed, for God's sake!'

'I know. I think all that adrenaline has made me horny.'

'And that's way too much information, thanks all the same,' Ruth said with a smile as she shook her head.

Ruth glanced up at the television that was mounted to the wall. The BBC News was on.

'Christ, the election is in a couple of days, isn't it?' she said as she watched footage of Tony Blair shaking the hands of the general public.

Lucy looked at the television. 'I can't stand him,' she said.

'Well he's going to increase our budgets and probably give you a pay rise.' She thought that's what she had read in the New Labour manifesto.

Brooks came marching into the ward. Next to him was a tall, thick-set firearms officer in a black uniform with a large pistol holstered on his hip.

'Bloody hell! Are you two all right?' Brooks asked.

'Yes thanks, guv,' Ruth answered.

'Where is she?' Brooks asked of Katerina.

Lucy indicated the corridor. 'The single room down there. She's sedated but she'll be discharged tomorrow morning.'

Brooks looked downcast. 'I've arranged for her to go to a safe house while we sort out this mess.' Ruth could see he wasn't happy.

He looked at the officer and gestured down the corridor. 'Officer, if you go and grab a chair outside her room, I'll be with you in a minute.'

As the officer made himself scarce, Brooks gave them both a withering look. 'I gave you twenty-four hours and it nearly got you both killed.'

'What happens now, guv?' Ruth asked, trying to appease him.

'What happens now? I'm taking everything we've got to the Chief Super tomorrow. Whatever is going on, it's far too dangerous for us to deal with on our own.'

'You do know we're *this* close to finding and nicking Petrovic,' Lucy said, using her fingers to demonstrate.

'I don't care. Whoever is protecting him and this Tankovic chap are happy to kill people. You are not going to get yourself killed for this, Lucy.' Brooks took a breath – he was getting worked up.

'We understand, boss. It's just hard to hand this over to someone else now,' Ruth said meekly.

'Well that's what's happening, Ruth. Where are you staying tonight?' he asked.

'I've got a friend, Shiori. She's putting me and Ella up for a bit.'

'Good.' He turned to Lucy. 'And you're at your sister's?'

'Yes, guv. She's going to her boyfriend's tonight, so I've got her flat to myself.'

Brooks looked at them both. 'Please, please be careful. No unnecessary risks. Keep a low profile for the next twenty-four hours until I can sort this out.'

CHAPTER 25

Ruth walked up Battersea Rise with Ella singing and chattering in her pushchair. She had been to buy Ella some new 'princess' pyjamas as they were staying with Shiori in her swish, four-bedroomed Victorian house in Clapham. That's the type of house you can afford if you have a husband who works in finance, she presumed. Even though the circumstances of her asking to stay were frightening, there was also part of her that got a little tingle at the thought of staying over at Shiori's home. She knew it was all fantasy in her head, but it made her feel better – so she didn't care.

An hour earlier, Ruth had received a text from Dan to say that he was now out of hospital and that he would like to see Ella in the next few days. Maybe he could take her to the swings. There was no mention of Angela, or the fact that she had caught him with another woman by his bedside. She could feel her body tense as she thought of it now. The next thing is that he'll be moving with Angela to Australia. Even though it would deprive Ella of a father figure as she grew up, there was part of Ruth that felt relieved at the thought of Dan being thousands of miles away.

As she headed for the multi-storey car park in Clapham Junction, her mind wandered fleetingly to the image of Safet Dudic's blood-stained face in the bath. His darkened opaque eyes showing that all life had gone. At that moment, a red London bus slowed at the adjacent bus stop and its air brakes hissed loudly. It made Ruth flinch.

God. I really am quite jumpy.

Having paid for the parking ticket, Ruth went to get the lift to the fifth floor of the multi-storey. Yellow tape across the doors signalled that it was out of order.

Bloody great. Five flights of stairs with a pushchair and a toddler.

Folding up the pushchair, Ruth leant down to Ella. 'Ella, we've got to go up all the stairs to the top. Is that going to be okay?'

Ella nodded. 'Yep.'

'Good girl,' Ruth said, guiding her with her free hand and tucking the pushchair under her other arm.

This is going to be fun, she thought ironically.

Ella started going up the stairs one by one, then stopped for a moment and took one step back down.

It's going to take a while.

'Do you need a hand?' said a voice.

Ruth looked back to see a tall man with a shaved head, and wearing a bomber jacket. He had some kind of accent, but she couldn't place it.

I don't like the look of him one bit.

Instantly, Ruth could feel herself tense. She felt incredibly vulnerable on the stairs with Ella and no one else around.

She looked at the man and shook her head. 'No, it's fine thanks.'

The man raised his eyebrow and smiled. 'Really? I've got a son about her age. I know what it's like.'

'Thanks, but we're okay,' Ruth said, feeling increasingly uneasy.

'Come on. My wife and son are waiting for me in the car. She'd never forgive me if I didn't help you,' he said as he gestured for her to hand him the pushchair.

He isn't going to take no for an answer. Maybe I'm just being paranoid.

Glancing down at his hand, she saw that he had a ring on his wedding finger.

'That's very kind of you,' Ruth said as she handed him the pushchair to carry.

'That's the problem with London. If you offer to help someone, they think you're some kind of weirdo,' he chortled as they began to make their way up the stairs slowly.

'That's very true,' Ruth said with a smile, and scooped Ella up into her arms. 'Probably a bit quicker if I carry you, young lady.'

'What floor are you on?' the man asked.

'Fifth, unfortunately.'

'Us too,' he laughed, as if the coincidence was hilarious.

To be fair, he doesn't strike me as a Serbian hitman.

Ruth glanced at a door on the stairwell. They had now reached the third floor.

'You're from London?' he asked.

'Born and bred. I'm guessing from your accent that you're not?'

'Me? No, no. I'm from a tiny little village in Herzegovina.'

Ruth frowned and tried to remember where that was. She didn't want to appear ignorant.

'You'll have to remind where that is,' she said with an embarrassed smile.

'In the Balkans.'

'So, it's near Bosnia?' As soon as she'd spoken the words she realised that this was way too much of a coincidence.

He glanced quickly at her. 'Actually, it's part of Bosnia.'

Shit! I don't believe in coincidences.

Ruth's pulse started to quicken rapidly as she drew in a breath.

Looking up the stairs, she could see that the next door read *Floor 5*. They were only five or six stairs away. If he was going to attack her, then it was going to be now.

'I love the way you dress Ella. The little Adidas trainers. Very cute,' the man said as he looked directly at her.

Oh my God! He knows her name.

Ruth felt sick.

She could hardly get her breath.

'What do you want?' she asked, aware that her voice was trembling.

'Want? I'm just helping you and Ella up the stairs,' he said with a shrug.

'Stop saying her name!'

As they reached the top step, the man opened the door for the fifth floor and gestured for her and Ella to go through first.

What is he going to do with us?

'It's all right thanks,' Ruth snapped.

The man smirked. 'I insist.'

'Someone waiting for us out there?' Ruth asked, trying to hide her fear.

'Believe me, if I wanted to harm you and your daughter, I would have done it by now,' he replied casually.

Ruth went through the door out to where the cars were parked in rows.

It was silent.

Taking a deep breath, she quickly scanned the area, hoping to see someone else around.

There was no one.

The man came over and put the pushchair down by her feet.

The sound of a car engine broke the silence.

A large black BMW loomed into view with its headlights glaring.

The car pulled up beside them.

Ruth held her breath – *I'll kill them if they come anywhere near Ella.*

The driver, with a dark beard, wound down the window. He said something in another language that Ruth didn't understand.

Oh my God. What are they going to do?

The other man moved towards Ruth.

She flinched away.

'Nice to meet you, Ruth,' he said, and then put his hand to Ella's face and ran his finger gently down her cheek.

Ruth held her breath.

An elderly couple came out of the exit behind them. They were chatting loudly as they headed for the ticket machine.

The man looked over at the couple and then directly at Ruth.

'Next time, I'll be taking Ella with me. Understand?'

He walked around the car, got in, and it pulled away with a loud screech of its tyres.

CHAPTER 26

Lucy went into the living room at her sister's flat with two cans of beer. Brooks was sitting on the sofa surrounded by some of the papers and documents that had been recovered from the murder victims' homes.

'Here you go. Get that down your Gregory,' Lucy said with a grin. Gregory, short for the actor Gregory Peck, cockney rhyming slang for neck.

'Gregory? I haven't heard that for years,' Brooks chortled as he swigged from the can.

As Lucy sat down, she could hear a song by the band Simply Red.

'Oh my God! Did you put this crap on?' she groaned.

'Hey, it's in your sister's record collection,' he said defensively.

'Yeah, well she's got terrible musical taste. The only decent albums she's got are the CDs I buy her.'

Brooks frowned. 'CDs? What's wrong with records?'

'Bloody hell, Grandad. CDs are digital. No scratches, any track at the push of a button.' Lucy rolled her eyes as she went over to her sister's fancy stereo. She worked in television doing something called 'development', so she could afford a CD player. Lucy took an Ocean Colour Scene CD and placed it into the CD tray. She loved how the tray just slid smoothly back in-

217

to the stereo and began to play track one immediately. Records were a pain in the arse.

'And what's this racket?' Brooks asked with a mischievous smile. She knew he was playing up to the whole middle-aged-man persona. And he looked so attractive when he smiled at her.

'Ocean Colour Scene. You won't know them.'

'You do know that all this Britpop crap just sounds like a load of Beatles' B-sides,' he said mockingly.

Lucy ignored him and gestured to the paperwork. 'Found anything yet Detective Chief Inspector?'

'Nothing interesting. Just a couple of maps in the stuff you got from Safet Dudic's place.'

'Maps of what?'

'London and Surrey ... Nothing from Mujic's diary that might narrow down where Petrovic might be hiding?'

Lucy went over to her folder and fished out the translation document. 'Last entry we have is this page. We have the four names written on the left - Advic, Selimovic, Dudic and Mujic. Simo Petrovic's name is written here with a word in capitals and underlined that translates as 'kill'. Then the name Ben Fleet, also in capitals, scribbled at the top.'

'Anything come up for Ben Fleet?' Brooks asked.

'Nothing on the PNC. There's a retired schoolteacher in Aberdeen, an accountant in Bristol, a schoolboy in Norfolk ... Nothing that helps us.'

'You had the address in Hammersmith but the place is empty,' Brooks said, thinking out loud. 'And there are spooks watching it.'

'We had a false name too, and the post that came from a Surrey postmark,' Lucy added.

'What about the footage from Waterloo? Any idea where Petrovic had come from? Platform numbers?'

Lucy shook her head. 'Nothing. Except that Waterloo serves trains to Surrey and then to the South West.'

It's like looking for the proverbial needle in a haystack.

Brooks frowned for a second and then looked at her. 'The name Ben Fleet. How was that written in the diary?'

'What d'you mean?'

'Was it written as two names distinctly separated? Or could the two words have actually been one word?' he asked.

What the bloody hell is he talking about?

'Harry, you knob, you're not making any bloody sense,' Lucy said getting exasperated.

'I worked a case donkey's years ago. A snout of mine was killed in Brixton. He had this betting slip on him which had loads of scribbled writing on it. It had a name, *Peter Lee*, written on it, and then the words *white house*. We asked around but no one had ever heard of a Peter Lee and he had no previous. When I dug around, it turned out that my snout, and the bloke that murdered him, came from a place in Durham called Peterlee. Peterlee White House was a community centre where this murderer worked. It wasn't someone's name, it was a place.'

'Did you nick him?' Lucy asked.

'He died in prison.'

'So, it could be Benfleet? I've never heard of it.' When Lucy said it out loud, it didn't sound like a place name.

'Got a London A-Z?' Brooks asked.

Lucy went to the bookshelf, took a tatty A5 copy of the London A-Z street guide, and tossed it over to him. 'Here you go.'

This is a total waste of time.

Brooks looked inside and thumbed through a few pages. 'There is a place called Benfleet but it's near Canvey Island in Essex.'

Lucy shrugged despondently. 'Harry, we're not going to find him. Petrovic could be anywhere. He might not even be in the country.'

Brooks looked at her for a moment. 'This case really means a lot to you, doesn't it Luce?'

She nodded. The thought of Petrovic getting away made her feel tearful. Maybe it was just that she was exhausted and rattled by the events of recent days.

'Yeah. I'm just too close to it,' she whispered.

Brooks nodded, got up, and gave her a hug. 'We all get cases like that.'

Lucy squeezed him, feeling his muscular torso in her arms.

Why can't he be here every night?

She watched him taking the London A-Z back towards the bookshelf. He flicked through the index as he went, then suddenly paused.

'You okay?' she asked.

'I've found two Benfleet Roads. One is in Finchley ...'

'Put it down, Harry. We're wasting our time.'

He looked over at her and raised his eyebrow. '... and the other is in Cobham.'

Oh my God!

'What? Are you kidding me?' Lucy raced over to look. She saw where his finger was pointing on the map and there it was.

She looked up at him. 'I love you Harry Brooks.'

He smiled at her. 'I love you too.'

Lucy was now feeling overwhelmed. 'No. I mean I *really* love you.'

'What's changed? I thought you wanted everything to be footloose and fancy free?'

'I just say that to protect myself,' she said with a shrug.

Brooks took her in his arms. 'I wasn't going to say anything but ...'

'What?' Lucy asked. Her mind was running away as she wondered what he was going to say.

'I'm going to leave Karen. I can't be there anymore. It's making us both miserable. What do you think?'

'What do I think?' Lucy said with her heart fluttering. She pulled him down to her and kissed him hard. 'I think it's a crazy but brilliant idea.'

DRAGGING HARD ON A cigarette, Ruth stood by the fireplace in Shiori's Clapham home. It was tastefully decorated with dark leather furniture, rugs, and floor-to-ceiling bookcases.

Shiori came in with two large glasses of wine and handed her one. 'Here you go, you poor thing.'

Ruth had told her all about the incident at the car park. It had really shaken her.

'Ella okay?' Ruth asked as she stubbed out the cigarette. It was her second in about fifteen minutes.

'She's fine. They're asleep holding hands. Sooo cute,' Shiori said and then gestured to the sofa. 'Come and sit down.'

Ruth nodded and went and sat on the plush sofa. 'I'm so sorry to impose on you like this.'

'Don't be daft. It's lovely to have company. Stay as long as you need. Once Koyuki has gone to bed, I'm normally here on my own.' She moved some of the cushions and sat back. 'I had a phone call from Claire Gold.'

'Any news?'

'She has an experienced investigative journalist who is interested in the story, but they need their Editor to come on board. She's meeting with them tonight.'

'That's great news. Thank you,' Ruth said as she sipped her wine.

'They might need to talk to you and Lucy at some point.'

'Of course. I'm not sure that we're ready to go on record yet. But as unnamed sources, we're more than happy to meet.'

'Great. I'll let her know.'

Ruth spotted a photograph above the fireplace of Shiori, Koyuki and a man who she assumed was Shiori's ex-husband. He was handsome in a preppy kind of way.

'Happy families, eh?' Shiori said sardonically.

'How did we get it so wrong?' Ruth asked.

Shiori kicked off her shoes. 'And then that horrible question, why weren't we enough?'

'That's not a great place for me to go to at the moment. I have an awful feeling that Dan is going to run off with this Australian girl and move to the other side of the world.'

'Would that be such a bad thing?'

Ruth shrugged. 'I don't know. Ella wouldn't have a dad. But how much would she see of Dan anyway now he's moved out? He doesn't seem interested.'

'Koyuki hasn't seen her dad for nearly four months now. They adapt.'

'Hey, we could be in exactly the same situation in a few months,' Ruth said.

Shiori laughed. 'Two hot single mums with cheating, arsehole ex-husbands thousands of miles away.'

Ruth smiled and raised her glass. 'To hot single mums.'

Shiori lifted her glass and clinked Ruth's. They looked at each other for a moment. 'Amen to that, sister.'

Ruth drained her wine. As she leaned forward to put it down on the small side table her hand visibly shook.

God, I'm still really quite shaky.

Shiori frowned. 'Your hands are shaking. Are you okay?'

Ruth nodded, but she wasn't.

For a moment, she tried to compose herself, but it was too hard. 'I ... I really thought he was going to take Ella.' As Ruth said the words and thought of her daughter, she felt the tears well in her eyes. 'Sorry ... I ...'

Shiori shifted closer to her on the sofa and put a comforting hand on her shoulder. 'Don't apologise, silly. It must have been terrifying.'

Ruth blinked and wiped the tears from her face. 'Yeah. I've seen all sorts of terrible things. But when he came over and put his hand to her face ...' Ruth took a deep breath. Her lips began to tremble, and she felt completely overwhelmed.

Shiori put her arms out and pulled Ruth towards her. 'Hey, it's okay. Ella's here. And she's safe. You're safe. You don't need to worry.'

It feels so nice to be hugged and held, Ruth thought.

'Thank you,' she said quietly.

As they moved apart, Ruth looked into Shiori's eyes. They held each other's gaze and didn't say anything.

What are we doing?

They instinctively moved towards each other and, very slowly, they kissed. Softly at first, and then a little harder.

Shiori moved back, her eyes moving furtively around the room. 'Sorry, I ... God, I'm really sorry.'

'It's okay. Don't worry,' Ruth said reassuringly. The kiss had felt exactly right in that moment.

'Wow. Did *not* see that coming ...' Shiori looked flustered as she got up from the sofa. 'I think I'll go and check on the girls and then have a bath.'

Ruth smiled affectionately. 'Okay.' She could tell that Shiori was completely freaked out.

'Do you need anything?' Shiori asked as she went to the door.

Ruth shook her head. 'No. I'm fine thanks.'

CHAPTER 27

As Ruth drove her and Lucy through the heavy traffic towards St George's Hospital, she was preoccupied by the events of the previous evening. The incident with Petrovic's thug in Clapham Junction. Seeing Ella so vulnerable. And then the awkward kiss with Shiori. Had she completely misread the signals that Shiori was giving out? Had she just mistaken a growing friendship for something more? She didn't even know who had kissed who. It had seemed to have happened quite naturally. Or was that just how Ruth remembered it? Her instinct told her that there was something between her and Shiori other than friendship. As a copper, she relied on her instinct day in and day out. However, she found it far harder to trust when it came to matters of the heart.

'You're away with the fairies this morning,' Lucy commented as they approached the hospital.

'Just tired. I'm worried about Ella after yesterday.'

'Where is she today?'

'Shiori offered to look after her today at her house. I don't want to take the risk of her going to nursery.' She didn't know whether she had been followed and if Petrovic and his cronies knew her every move.

'Bastards. Brooks wants us to hand over everything we've got to take it upstairs,' Lucy grumbled.

'Yeah, well I don't think I can do this anymore. Not now they've threatened Ella. Nothing is worth any harm coming to her,' Ruth said, starting to feel emotional as she thought back to the man stroking Ella's cheek in the multi-storey car park.

'No, of course not. I just wanted to look that wanker Petrovic in the eye when I nicked him. We've worked our tits off on this case and now someone else is going to collar him.'

Ruth nodded. She understood that Lucy wanted to get justice for the people that Petrovic had murdered in the last ten days, as well as those back in Bosnia.

As Ruth parked, her instinct was to look in the rear-view mirror to make sure they hadn't been followed. She couldn't see anything.

They walked across the car park into the hospital, and made their way to the ward where Katerina was recuperating. A doctor confirmed that she'd had a good night and was now fit enough to leave.

Walking down the corridor, Lucy glanced over at Ruth. 'Brooks wants us to take Katerina back to the station. Witness Protection will take her to a nearby safe house.'

Ruth nodded. 'You know what? For once, the idea of drinking coffee and doing lots of paperwork for a few days seems like a bit of relief.'

'Yeah. You're not wrong there,' Lucy said but then her expression changed.

'You all right?' Ruth asked.

Lucy looked at her. 'Where's the armed officer?'

Ruth looked at the chair outside Katerina's single room. It was empty.

Oh God!

'Shit!' Lucy broke into a run.

Ruth followed, dreading to think about what they might find.

Flinging the door open, Lucy looked back at Ruth.

The room was empty. And so was the bed.

'Where the bloody hell is she?' Lucy thundered.

Ruth's mind spun with all the different scenarios. Had Katerina been kidnapped? Where the hell was the armed officer?

Then she spotted Katerina come wandering down the corridor accompanied by the officer.

Well, that's a bloody relief!

'Christ, you scared us Katerina,' Lucy said letting out a sigh.

'I needed to stretch my legs, and this young gentleman was kind enough to escort me.'

'Okay, well we need you to get your things together,' Ruth said gently.

Katerina nodded and then gestured into her room. 'I have something that I need to tell you.'

Ruth and Lucy glanced at each other – *what's she talking about?*

They followed her into the room and closed the door.

'Everything okay?' Ruth asked her.

Katerina went over to the bed, sat down, and looked at them for a few seconds.

Okay. The suspense is killing me, Ruth thought.

'I can help you to find Simo Petrovic,' she said quietly.

'What?' Lucy said, her eyes widening.

Did she say what I just thought she said?

'I didn't want to tell you before. I was too scared,' Katerina admitted.

'How can you do that?' Ruth asked.

'I have a friend. He contacted me yesterday morning and told me he had found out where Simo Petrovic is hiding.'

'Did he say where?' Lucy asked.

Katerina shook her head. 'No. He didn't want to say it over the phone. He is very frightened.'

'Will he talk to us?' Ruth asked.

Katerina nodded. 'If I come with you, he might do.'

'Where are we going?' Lucy asked.

'Cobham. It's in Surrey.'

They knew exactly where it was.

'Benfleet Road?' Lucy asked. She had told Ruth earlier about her discovery that Ben Fleet was the name of a road, not a person.

Katerina looked confused. 'How do you know that?'

'Your friend, Hamzar, wrote it in his diary,' Ruth explained. 'We thought it was a person's name.'

'And if we take you to Cobham, we can talk to your friend?' Lucy asked.

'Yes. We must stop this man ... before he harms anyone else,' Katerina said as she got up from the bed. 'We must stop him today.'

BY THE TIME THEY REACHED the car, Ruth had made it clear that she wasn't happy about them swanning off to Surrey with a key witness. They helped Katerina into the back seat of the car.

'If you've got something to say, just say it Ruth,' Lucy snapped.

'We need to run this past Brooks.'

'Brooks won't let us go. He'll tell us to wait, or hand it on to someone else.'

'Maybe that isn't a bad thing. Every step of this investigation seems to have led us to another dead body.'

'You don't bloody get it, do you Ruth? Petrovic is *our* collar. And we've got a chance to get him today,' Lucy growled.

'And we're going after him on our own, are we?'

'No. We get the address where Petrovic is hiding out, liaise with local police to provide backup, and go and nick him.'

'I bloody hope it's that easy, Lucy,' Ruth said as she got into the car.

'I can drop you in Peckham if you want?' Lucy sneered.

'Don't be stupid.'

Ruth had no choice. Lucy was her partner and her friend, but she had a feeling that it wasn't going to be as straightforward as Lucy had pitched it to her.

Five minutes later, they had pulled out of the hospital car park and were heading towards the Wandsworth one-way system where they would join the A3 and head south to Cobham.

There was a tense silence in the car. Ruth reached for a cigarette and then turned to offer one to Katerina.

'I have my own, thank you.' Katerina reached into her handbag and pulled out a filterless brand of cigarettes that Ruth had never heard of.

'Here you go,' Ruth said as she passed Katerina the lighter.

Looking out at the South London suburbs, Ruth took a long deep drag on her cigarette. She felt apprehensive.

'In my country, we don't have any women as police officers,' Katerina said.

'No? There still aren't that many in London,' Ruth said with a smile. 'Or at least, there aren't enough.'

'You read Hamzar's diary?' Katerina asked.

'Yes, we had it translated so we could read it,' Lucy explained.

Katerina nodded as she thought about what Lucy had said. 'Then you know that we saw things that no one should ever see.'

Ruth nodded solemnly. 'Yes. It was very upsetting to read. You were with Hamzar in Keraterm, is that right?'

'Yes. We were taken to the old tile factory. The women slept in the canteen and kitchens. I looked after Hamzar's daughter for a while. The men slept by the machines on the floor, sharing blankets.'

'Did you stay there?' Lucy asked.

Katerina took a few seconds before she answered. 'No. A few of the women were taken elsewhere. And I ...' She stopped talking, took a drag of her cigarette and looked out of the window. 'I was taken somewhere else. That's all.'

Ruth could tell that it wasn't something Katerina found easy to talk about, and she wasn't about to push her on it. She looked up and saw that Lucy was taking the exit from the A3 that led to Cobham.

A moment or two later, they turned into a small side road, Benfleet Road.

'This is it?' Lucy asked.

Ruth turned and saw Katerina staring intently at the houses as Lucy slowed the car.

'Yes. It is on the right. Just here,' Katerina said, pointing to one of the small newly-built houses.

Lucy parked the car and they all got out.

For a moment, Ruth was distracted by the sky. Its baby-blue hue was dotted with wispy clouds that resembled pulled candyfloss. It was one of those spring days when that kiss of coldness somehow intensifies the warm rays of the sun. However, the tension in her stomach warned her that something about this trip was making her feel uneasy.

'This the one?' Lucy said, pointing to the painted door with the number 27 on it.

'Yes, yes,' Katerina said. 'He said he would be in all day.'

Lucy gave the door a decent knock, and a moment later a bearded man in his sixties partially opened the door.

'Katerina?' the man said with a friendly smile.

'We must talk to you. We must put an end to all this,' Katerina said looking at him.

He nodded, looked around nervously, and then opened the door fully and beckoned them in.

As the front door closed behind them, Ruth was struck by the lack of furniture and possessions inside. She had assumed that they were walking into the man's home, but the house was just a shell.

What the hell is going on here?

Suddenly, Ruth felt the hard jab of something metallic at the base of her skull.

Please don't tell me that's a gun.

'Don't move and don't turn around,' said a man's voice in a thick accent.

Glancing at Katerina, Ruth saw that her face and whole demeanour had changed. She was no longer the frightened old lady that she had seemed to be all day.

Oh shit. We've just walked into a trap.

CHAPTER 28

Ruth looked over at Lucy who was clearly more angry than frightened. Having had their radios, phones, and handcuffs taken, they had been marched at gunpoint into a small room by the man who had threatened Ruth and Ella the previous day in the car park. The door had been locked from the outside. Having established there was no way to escape, they had no choice but to sit on the floor.

'How did we not see that coming?' Lucy said, shaking her head.

Ruth didn't think it was the right time to mention that she'd had an uneasy feeling about this trip. She was starting to feel panicked. It had been demonstrated in the last week that Simo Petrovic, and those who sought to protect him, had no regard for human life. There was no reason to think that wouldn't extend to British female police officers.

'I don't understand. Katerina Selimovic suffered at the hands of Petrovic. She has known the men that he killed all her life. She was meant to be their friend,' Ruth said thinking out loud. It was hard for her to make any sense of it.

'Maybe she was blackmailed into setting us up?' Lucy suggested.

'Once we were inside this house, she didn't act like someone who was being blackmailed,' Ruth pointed out.

Before they could say anything else, there was a metallic click as the door was unlocked from the outside.

As it opened, Ruth shifted awkwardly on the floor.

What the hell are they going to do with us?

The man who had forced them into the room at gunpoint came in. Behind him were two figures - Katerina Selimovic and a man with a large frame who was in the shadows.

As they moved into the room, Ruth instantly recognised the man.

Simo Petrovic.

A chill ran up Ruth's spine. She had been in the presence of murderers before, but never one who had taken such pleasure from killing so many.

She looked up at Katerina and shook her head. 'What are you doing?'

'Be quiet!' Katerina snapped.

'This man destroyed your friends, your family and your village.'

Katerina gave her a withering look. 'You wouldn't understand.'

'Try us,' said Lucy.

'He also chose me over all the others to save. Simo had his pick of all of those women – but he chose me.'

Is she really saying that? What kind of twisted logic is that?

'What are you talking about?' Ruth asked.

'He saved me and my family. You have no idea what that means,' Katerina sneered.

'When Hamzar Mujic contacted you to say that he had seen this monster at Waterloo station, you already knew he was here?' Lucy pointed to Petrovic.

Katerina snorted. 'Here? Don't you get it? Simo is with me. We are together.'

Ruth couldn't understand how Katerina had chosen to be with this cruel psychopath and allow her friends to be murdered. Was it some warped version of the Stockholm syndrome? Some kind of twisted love that had developed between captor and captive?

'Get up,' Petrovic barked.

'Are we going somewhere?' Lucy asked sarcastically.

Petrovic didn't answer but looked at the man. 'Zivko.'

Zivko moved forward and gave Ruth's feet a kick. 'Get up!' he growled.

'Manners,' Lucy said with a sneer.

With her stomach now tense from anxiety, Ruth put her hands onto the dusty floor and got to her feet. With a sigh of reluctance, Lucy did the same.

Lucy stared at Petrovic. 'You do know that our DCI is going to be here any minute now?'

'I doubt that very much. In fact I'd be surprised if he even knew that you were here,' he replied coldly.

He's right. No one knows we're here.

Zivko waved their handcuffs at them. 'Put these on each other.'

'Are you taking the piss?' Ruth asked rhetorically.

Zivko gave her a scathing look – he was deadly serious.

'And if we don't?' Lucy asked.

Zivko looked over to Petrovic for a moment.

CRACK!

He fired a bullet into the floor beside Lucy's foot. Within the confines of the room, the sound of the gun was deafening. Ruth flinched.

Jesus Christ! You had to ask, didn't you?

'Then I will shoot you both,' Zivko said quietly.

Ruth grabbed the handcuffs from him. She turned to Lucy, opened them up, and clicked them closed around her wrists.

'Be gentle,' Lucy said under her breath.

Not the time for jokes, Lucy.

As Ruth secured her own handcuffs, she was very relieved that they hadn't insisted that they put them behind their backs. It was far less restrictive and more comfortable to have them in front. She also knew that if they had any chance of escape, they would need the use of their arms in front of them, not behind.

Petrovic looked at them. 'Out this way.'

Zivko gestured towards the door with his gun.

Ruth followed Lucy out of the room and through the empty house to a side door.

Two large black cars were parked to the rear of the house – a Mercedes and a Jaguar. Zivko ushered Ruth and Lucy into the back of the Mercedes at gunpoint before getting into the driver's seat.

Petrovic and Katerina got into the Jaguar.

Both cars pulled away, and ten minutes later they were on the A3 heading south towards Portsmouth.

CHAPTER 29

G azing out of the car window, Ruth watched the country-side zipping by. Where were they going? What were their captors going to do with them? She knew that they were unlikely to drag two detectives around with them for very long. Petrovic had murdered several people in recent days to protect his identity. Two police officers weren't going to make any difference to him. She had to conclude that they were going to kill her and Lucy in a remote area.

Her thoughts couldn't help but turn to Ella. She would be happily playing with Koyuki with no idea of what was happening to her mother. The thought of her daughter's innocence made her feel both frightened and angry.

I'm not going to let this fucker take us into a field somewhere and shoot us. I'm not going to leave Ella on her own.

Glancing up ahead, she saw that Petrovic's Jaguar was about five hundred yards ahead of them.

Looking over to Lucy, she knew they were both thinking of ways to escape and get away. However, Zivko was armed and they were handcuffed. What were the options? And then she thought of something.

She glanced down at the side of the driver's seat.

Zivko wasn't wearing a seatbelt. Why would he? He was a Serbian hitman with a gun. Wearing a seatbelt didn't really fit his mindset. But it gave Ruth an idea.

She nudged Lucy with her elbow to indicate that she needed to communicate something to her urgently. Now that she had Lucy's attention, Ruth very slowly moved her hands up to the rear seatbelt. Taking the seatbelt strap in her hand, she started to pull it very gradually across her body an inch at a time so as not to alert Zivko that she was doing anything.

Gesturing with her head, Ruth signalled to Lucy to do the same. After a few minutes, Ruth had managed to ease the seatbelt strap diagonally across her body. With the metal buckle now in her right hand, she pushed it down very slowly into the locking clip until she heard it click into position.

She held her breath. *Did Zivko hear that?*

For a second, she froze, not daring to move. They had to get this right. It might be their only way to escape.

Glancing right, she saw that Lucy had also managed to pull her seatbelt into position across her body. She was now lowering the buckle into its locking clip.

Ruth coughed quietly as Lucy clicked it into position.

Lucy looked at Ruth and raised an eyebrow as if to say *Now what?*

Ruth knew she needed to find exactly the right moment. If she got it wrong, Zivko could turn and shoot them.

Having passed Guildford, she could see that the road was now far less busy and had gone down to a single lane. However, they were still travelling at 60 mph and an accident at that speed could kill them all.

Then she saw it.

Roadworks up ahead, and a temporary set of traffic lights currently at red. That meant Zivko would have to reduce speed and stop, as long as they stayed on red. It also meant that his speed would be lower as they pulled away from the lights.

As the car slowed to a halt, Ruth looked at Lucy to signal that she was about to do something.

After a few seconds the lights turned green. Zivko revved the engine and they pulled away. Ruth looked ahead and realised that Petrovic's Jaguar was nowhere to be seen. They would have to deal with him later. First thing was to get out of this bloody car.

With her eyes locked on her side of the road, Ruth felt the car starting to speed up. She knew what she was looking for, but time was running out.

Come on. Come on.

As they rounded a corner, Ruth saw a line of large trees up ahead, set back about thirty yards from the road.

Bingo! That's perfect.

Glancing back, she could also see that there were no cars behind them. Even better. She didn't want anyone ploughing into the back of them.

Two hundred yards to go.

She braced herself, her eyes darting between the approaching trees and Zivko's hands on the steering wheel.

A hundred yards.

Here we go. Let's bloody do this.

Fifty yards.

Twenty.

Ruth launched herself forwards, grabbed the steering wheel in both hands, and twisted it hard to the left.

Zivko let out an undecipherable yell.

Ruth looked out. The car was now hurtling towards the trees.

She pushed herself backwards into the rear seat and braced herself for impact.

'Hold on, Lucy!' she yelled.

BANG!

The sound of metal tearing and glass smashing.

The car had ploughed headlong into the trunk of one of the trees.

With the impact, Ruth was thrown forward hard against her seatbelt before bouncing back into her seat.

The back of her head hit the headrest hard.

Bloody hell. That hurt!

Then the searing burn of the seatbelt which had cut into her left shoulder.

'Jesus Christ!' Lucy shouted.

For a moment, Ruth just sat there breathing deeply.

As she shook her head, she glanced at the driver's seat.

It was empty.

Only a few broken fragments of the windscreen remained, and blood was dripping from the window trim.

'Are you okay?' Ruth asked turning to Lucy.

'For fuck's sake, Ruth. Are you trying to kill us?' Lucy exclaimed, and then she looked at the empty driver's seat, the remains of the windscreen, and the blood that was pooling on the dashboard. 'Did you know he wasn't wearing a seatbelt?'

Ruth nodded. 'Why did you think I told you to put yours on?'

'You're a clever fucker, DC Hunter, I'll give you that,' Lucy said with a laugh of shock.

'Come on,' Ruth said as she took off her seatbelt, opened the door, and got out.

She moved to the front of the car, twisted and smashed beyond all recognition, and looked around.

Twenty yards away, Zivko lay flat on the ground. He wasn't moving.

Ruth cautiously approached him. From the unnatural shape of his body and lack of movement, she knew he was dead. His face was a bloody, uneven grid of cuts and gashes.

'Clunk, click, every trip,' Lucy quipped.

'Never mind the jokes, we need to find a key for the handcuffs. My wrists are killing me,' Ruth said as they crouched over him.

Lucy pulled the gun from his jacket. 'I might hold onto this. You never know ...'

Ruth pushed her hand into his blood-soaked trouser pocket. She felt the shape of the handcuff key and pulled it out.

She manoeuvred the key into the lock of her handcuffs, unclipped them, and then freed Lucy from hers.

'Jesus, that's better,' Lucy said, rubbing her wrists. 'How did you know we weren't going to get killed in that crash?'

'I didn't,' Ruth admitted.

'Fair enough. He was going to shoot us anyway. Where's Petrovic?'

Ruth shrugged. 'We lost them at the traffic lights.'

'Shit!' Lucy said, and then Ruth watched her storm into the middle of the road, take out her warrant card, and flag down the next car.

What the bloody hell is she doing?

'Lucy?' Ruth yelled. Her shoulder was still stinging, and her mind was in a whirl.

'What?' Lucy asked, as she guided the oncoming car into the side of the road. It was a brand new Audi, with a red number plate in the window to signify that it was being test driven.

'Where the bloody hell are we going?' Ruth asked.

'After Petrovic.'

Ruth strolled over to where Lucy had stopped the car. 'We've lost him. We don't know where he's going.'

'I do,' Lucy said as she went over to the driver's window. 'DC Henry. I'm sorry sir but I'm going to have to commandeer your vehicle.'

'What? But I'm test driving it. It's not even my car,' the driver protested in a very middle-class accent.

Ruth watched as the furious car dealer got out of the passenger door and glared at her.

'You can't do this! I need to speak to my head office,' he uttered in disbelief.

Ruth had no choice but to back Lucy up. She flashed her warrant card at him. 'Sorry, sir, but this is a matter of life and death. And we do have the legal power to commandeer this car.'

'Right sir, out we get. Quickly please, and stand to the side of the road,' Lucy snapped at the driver.

'This is ridiculous!' he said as he reluctantly got out.

Lucy replaced him in the driver's seat. As Ruth tried to get into the car, the dealer stood in front of her to block her way. 'I don't think this is even legal,' he said angrily. 'How do I know you're real police officers?'

Get out of my way you dickhead!

Ruth held her warrant card about six inches from his face. 'There. You've got my name. If you don't get out of my way, I will nick you for obstruction.'

The man stood back. Ruth got into the car and, before she had even closed the door, Lucy had sped away.

'Jesus, Lucy!' Ruth exclaimed, trying to get her breath back.

'I know. We've lucked out getting our hands on this Audi. It'll go like the fucking clappers,' she said.

'Where the bloody hell are we going?' Ruth asked.

'Portsmouth.'

'What? Why? Did you bang your bloody head back there?'

'We were following Petrovic down the A3 which leads to Portsmouth.'

'So what? They could be going anywhere.'

Lucy shook her head. 'No - they need to get out of the country. And what do we know about Katerina Selimovic?'

Ruth thought for a moment. 'She has a sister in northern France.'

'And which port runs ferries closest to the Loire Valley?'

'At a guess, I'm saying Portsmouth.'

'Yep. The Loire Valley is a three-hour drive from Cherbourg.'

CHAPTER 30

A n hour later, Lucy and Ruth pulled into Portsmouth Ferry Terminal. There was only one more ferry that day and it didn't leave until 7pm, which was in just over an hour's time. Ruth had rung Shiori to explain some of what had happened, but she had kept it as vague as possible. They had now informed Brooks of what they were doing, and had asked Hampshire Constabulary to provide two uniformed units as backup in case Petrovic and Katerina were indeed trying to escape to France.

As they made their way towards the Customs and Immigration Office, Ruth looked up into the greying sky. Two gulls dived and flapped overhead, their loud rhythmic squawking was loud and unsettling. The air was thick with diesel fumes and the smell of the sea.

Arriving at the office, Ruth and Lucy showed their warrant cards and were directed to Gary Baker, Head of Operations.

Baker sat in a small, untidy office eating a sausage sandwich and nursing a huge mug of tea. 'I understand that you ladies are down from the Met. To what do we owe the pleasure?'

Ruth wasn't sure if he was being sarcastic or just irritating.

'We've got two murder suspects that we think are going to board the last ferry out of here to Cherbourg,' Lucy explained.

'You can have a look at the passenger lists,' Baker suggested, putting down his sandwich and wiping his hands on his trousers.

'They'll be in a car,' Ruth said.

Baker went to his computer. 'Got the registration?'

Ruth and Lucy looked at each other. In the confusion and stress of their kidnapping, Ruth had only looked at the registration of Petrovic's Jaguar a few times.

Ruth looked pensive. 'Hmm ... I know it's a P registration Jaguar.'

'That narrows it down,' Baker gibed.

Is he being sarcastic or is it that everything he says sounds barbed?

Baker hit the printer and a moment later it whirred into action. Getting up from his desk, he hitched his trousers over his midriff and retrieved the printout.

'That's the passenger and vehicle list for tonight's ferry,' Baker said as he handed them over.

Ruth smiled. 'Thanks.' She was still in a bit of daze from the kidnap, the crash, and Zivko's death. On top of that, she had Ella to think about - even though she knew that with Shiori she was in good hands.

'I guess we're looking for Oliver Stankovic?' Ruth asked.

'I don't think that even he has the balls to travel as Simo Petrovic,' Lucy said as they both scoured the lists.

She ran her finger slowly down the vehicle list. There were no Jaguars listed, and very few P registrations. Maybe Petrovic and Selimovic weren't on the ferry. Maybe they had gone to a different port? They could even be flying from a smaller airport such as Southampton.

'Anything?' Lucy asked.

'Nope. Nothing even close,' Ruth admitted. 'You?'

Lucy shook her head. 'No, nothing. Not a Serbian sounding name in sight.'

Baker looked over from his desk. 'At the risk of making things difficult, there will be some last-minute foot passengers who don't appear on that list.'

Lucy and Ruth looked at each other – that *did* make it more difficult.

'How far is Southampton from here?' Lucy asked.

'Half an hour's drive,' Baker replied.

'And if you're travelling from London on the A3, is it easy to get to?'

'Piece of piss. You just come off onto the M27.'

Lucy let out an audible sigh. 'Maybe we just got the wrong ferry terminal.'

'There's only one ferry a day to France from Southampton, and that takes eleven hours to Brittany. If I was your suspects trying to get out of the country, I'd be going from here,' Baker said, glancing at his watch. 'If you want to observe everyone getting on, you'd better hurry up. Passenger boarding starts in five minutes.'

'Thanks for your help,' Ruth said.

'Hope you catch the bastards,' Baker said, as they left his office and headed out towards the dockside.

Ruth was feeling emotional and exhausted. 'I'm starting to think this is a waste of time.'

'We were so bloody close to him,' Lucy said in a frustrated tone.

'Yeah, but we were also bloody close to getting killed.'

They made their way quickly over to the foot passenger entrance for the 7pm ferry, and identified themselves to the ticket collectors and immigration officers.

For the next ten minutes, they watched the stream of passengers queuing and showing their tickets and passports before boarding. However, there was no sign of Petrovic or Selimovic.

As the queue shortened, Lucy gave an exasperated sigh. 'We can't let him get away after all that bloody hard work. If he gets to Europe, he'll probably disappear forever.'

Ruth knew that was true, and she shared Lucy's determination to bring Petrovic to justice. However, she also felt at breaking point after the events of the day.

'We're running out of passengers,' Ruth said quietly.

'Don't you want to find him?' Lucy snapped.

Ruth decided to ignore Lucy's comment. They were both tired, and nerves were starting to fray.

As the queue reduced to a single file, Ruth knew that the chances of finding them now were diminishing fast.

Gazing up at the ferry, Ruth wondered if they had just got it wrong. There were no names or vehicles matching the passenger or vehicle lists. They could have decided to go from another port on the south coast. It had been a long shot at best.

Out of the corner of her eye, Ruth spotted a man leaning with his back against the ferry's guardrail. It seemed odd to her that, although he was extremely well-dressed, he was wearing a very old Panama hat. For a moment, she wondered where she had seen the hat before.

Then it clicked.

Katerina Selimovic's flat.

Bloody hell.

The man moved out sight, but it could have been Petrovic.

Am I just seeing things?

'You okay?' Lucy asked. She had clearly spotted Ruth's changed expression. Ruth was staring up to see if the man she thought was Petrovic would return to where she could see him.

'Up there,' Ruth said pointing.

'What am I looking at?' Lucy asked putting her hand over her eyes to block out the fading sunlight.

Then suddenly, in the same place where the man had been standing, a woman looked over the rails. She was wearing sunglasses, but even from a distance Ruth recognised her.

Shit! Katerina Selimovic!

'They're on the ferry!' Ruth cried out.

'What?'

'Come on!' Ruth took Lucy by the arm and they both broke into a run.

As they sprinted over to the ferry, Ruth noticed that there were no more passengers to get on, and the check-in point was now closed.

They showed their warrant cards and boarded.

A deep, thunderous blast of a horn sounded.

Ruth glanced over at movement on the dockside as one of the enormous steel mooring chains began to be wound in noisily.

She glanced at Lucy. 'Looks like we're going to France.'

CHAPTER 31

Ruth and Lucy had been searching the ferry for over twenty minutes but hadn't seen any sign yet of Simo Petrovic or Katerina Selimovic. They walked back through the huge lounge and bar on the upper deck. With 1,500 passengers on board, their search wouldn't be easy.

'And you're sure it was her?' Lucy asked.

Ruth gave her a scornful look. 'Come on. If we keep circling, we'll find them.'

Lucy nodded and went over to the central concourse where there was a deck plan of the ferry. 'We've been everywhere, haven't we?'

By now, Ruth was starting to doubt what she had seen.

'Where would you go if you wanted to keep out of sight on a cross-channel ferry?' Ruth asked.

Lucy scoured the map for a few seconds and then pointed to a small rectangle on the lower deck marked *Cinema*. 'It's dark, no one walking around. I'd hide in there.'

'As good a place as any,' Ruth agreed.

They turned and headed for the central stairwell where they could access the lower decks.

'At least we know he hasn't got a gun,' Ruth said as they clattered down the stairs at speed. There was no way of getting a gun through the metal detectors at the gates.

At the bottom of the stairs, they ran straight ahead towards the cinema. They then slowed as they reached the doors where a ticket collector sat.

'Police officers. We think there might be two suspects inside here,' Lucy whispered as she showed her warrant card and gestured into the cinema.

'Call security and tell them to wait for us here,' Ruth said quietly.

'Okay ...' the ticket collector stammered, looking terrified.

Feeling the tension in her stomach, Ruth opened one of the doors very slowly. A loud noise of sound effects and an orchestral score came from inside the cinema. Some kind of sci-fi film was being shown.

At least it's loud enough to cover the sound of us coming in, Ruth thought.

Moving forward into the darkened cinema, Ruth could see that they had entered halfway down the room, with the screen to their left. Scanning the audience, it was difficult to see much. The lights and flashes from the screen meant that the members of the audience were only visible for a second or two before being plunged back into obscurity.

They gradually made their way towards the screen at the front.

It was difficult for them to disguise the fact that they were scanning the audience and looking for someone.

Suddenly, two figures rose from their seats on the other side of the auditorium. They headed towards the green light of the nearest exit.

Ruth nudged Lucy and pointed.

As they squinted and began to move, Ruth recognised them.

Petrovic and Katerina. Got you, you bastards!

'Over there!' she yelled, tapping Lucy's shoulder.

They broke into a run and, a few seconds later, Ruth smashed through the exit doors with Lucy just behind her.

They looked left and then right.

Nothing.

'Where are they?' Lucy shrieked.

Ruth saw Petrovic and Katerina heading back towards the stairwell.

'There!' she said, and they set off again.

By the time they got to the stairs, Petrovic and Katerina had disappeared again. However, Ruth could hear the sound of running feet above them.

'Up this way!'

Leaping up the steps, two by two, Ruth felt the muscles in her thighs begin to burn.

Jesus, this is starting to really hurt.

Reaching the middle deck, she glanced both ways. Nothing.

The sound of running feet came again from above.

'Come on,' Lucy urged, as she took over the lead.

Dragging in air, they arrived on the upper deck. Glancing around, there was no sign of them, but there was a door about ten yards away that led outside.

Lucy ran to it, opened it, and Ruth followed.

The wind whipped around their faces as they ran down the deck towards the stern.

They spotted Petrovic and Katerina up ahead.

He was dragging her by the hand as other passengers jumped out of their way with irate glances.

Ruth and Lucy followed after them.

'OUT OF THE WAY! POLICE!' Lucy yelled.

The fugitives had now reached the end of the deck.

Right! Now they're trapped!

However, Petrovic and Katerina climbed rather awkwardly over the safety rail onto the final ten-foot of deck beyond. Nothing now protected them from a fifty-foot drop into the white, swirling depths of the English Channel.

Lucy and Ruth stopped at the rail, breathing heavily.

'What are you doing?' Lucy yelled at them both before climbing over the rail.

Nearby passengers were looking on in shock.

'Stay where you are!' Katerina shouted at Lucy, before moving backwards away from Petrovic.

Oh God, if she slips now, she's going into the sea.

'What's this all about Katerina?' Lucy asked, raising her voice over the noise of the wind.

Petrovic hadn't moved a muscle. He just glared at Lucy.

Katerina shook her head. 'You wouldn't understand.'

'This man is a monster. He killed women and children from your village,' Lucy shouted in disbelief.

'Simo picked me. Of all the women in that camp, he picked me to be with. Because he loved me and I loved him,' said Katerina, trying to explain.

'But you betrayed your friends here in London, and now they're dead.'

'They were never my friends. I knew that one day there would be rumours that Simo was alive, and they would want to take revenge. I decided to keep them close by in case that day ever came ... and it did.'

Katerina glanced backwards and saw that the heels of her shoes were now only a foot from the edge.

'Okay. You're right. I don't understand, but I don't want you to die,' Lucy said as she pointed to the sea.

Ruth very slowly climbed over the rail. The slight rolling of the deck, and the battering wind, made it feel very precarious.

Katerina shrugged. 'What is the choice?'

'You can't believe that jumping off there is the only choice you have?' Lucy asked.

'I will spend my life in prison. So will Simo, and I don't want to live without him,' Katerina said as she turned to Petrovic. 'I don't want to be without you.'

He nodded. 'I understand,' he said quietly.

With that, Katerina turned and prepared to jump into the sea below.

'NO!' Lucy said, making a dive to stop her.

It was too late.

Katerina had already stepped out into the abyss and was falling feet first into the icy sea below.

Oh my God!

By now, several of the ferry's security officers had arrived and were moving passengers back and out of the way.

Lucy looked at Petrovic. 'What about you? Are you going to jump?'

Petrovic shook his head and said quietly, 'No.'

Ruth watched as Lucy grabbed Petrovic's arms and handcuffed them behind his back. 'Simo Petrovic, I am arresting you on suspicion of the murders of Mersad Advic, Hamzar Mujic and Safet Dudic. You do not have to say anything, but it may harm your defence if you do not mention, when questioned, something which you later rely on in court. Anything you do say may be given in evidence.'

Bloody hell! We got him! We bloody well got him, Ruth thought triumphantly to herself.

Lucy pushed Petrovic forward and the security officers helped him over the railings.

Ruth looked at Lucy with a mixture of relief, joy, and utter exhaustion that they had managed to actually track Petrovic down and arrest him. She thought it was never going to happen.

She turned to the security officers. 'Tell the Captain that he needs to stop the ferry. Someone's jumped overboard.'

'They won't have survived the drop,' one of them said gravely.

'In that case we need to give the coastguard our position so they can retrieve the body, and you're going to need to turn the ferry around. We have arrested that man and he needs to go into British custody as soon as possible.'

As Lucy and Ruth escorted Petrovic along the now empty deck, he looked at them.

'You do know that I'm going nowhere,' he said.

'Shut up and keep walking,' Lucy growled.

'Your star witness has just jumped into the sea. Everything else is circumstantial. And I have very powerful friends with very deep pockets. The worst that will happen to me is that I will be sent back to Bosnia where I will be greeted as a hero,' Petrovic said arrogantly.

Ruth looked at him. 'You'll be standing trial as a war criminal and you will die in prison.'

'No. That will never happen. You wait and see,' he smirked.

Lucy gave Ruth a worried look as they exited the upper deck.

CHAPTER 32

It was nearly midnight by the time Ruth and Lucy had got back to Peckham nick, processed Petrovic into custody, and debriefed Brooks. As their DCI, Brooks had nearly had a heart attack when they described their day. However, he had admitted that bringing a known war criminal to justice was an incredible piece of police work. He had no idea what the Home Office or MI5 were going to say, but he didn't care.

'Where is he?' Brooks asked, as he closed the blinds in his office.

'In a holding cell downstairs,' Lucy said.

'Who did you book him in as?'

'Oliver Stankovic,' Lucy smirked.

'Yeah, he didn't find that particularly funny,' Ruth said dryly.

It would have been foolish to use his real name until they knew the 'lie of the land' when it came to the Met's top brass, the Home Office and MI5.

Ruth sensed that even though they had Petrovic in custody downstairs, Lucy was still worried. 'Something he said has really got to me. He said he would never serve any time in a prison, because his friends were too powerful and too rich to let that happen.'

Ruth tried to reassure her. 'Don't worry. He's just bullshitting. Trying to get to you.'

Brooks nodded. 'He'll be on a plane to The Hague in a few days and then he'll rot in jail for the rest of his life.'

'I just have a horrible feeling that's not going to happen,' Lucy said, sounding a little choked.

Ruth put a comforting hand on Lucy's arm. 'Come on, Lucy. We're both tired, and we've been through hell in the last few days. But we got him. We got Petrovic. And without your persistence and bloody brilliant detective work, he would still be out there.'

'She's right Lucy. You might have nearly cost me and yourselves our jobs, and been a monumental pain in the arse, but you brought him in. And that means hundreds of people will get justice.'

Lucy smiled at Brooks' compliment, but Ruth could see that she was still fearful that Petrovic might somehow escape prosecution.

LUCY STOOD UNDER THE hot stream of water trying to shower away the stresses of what had been a physical and emotional rollercoaster of a day. She had downed half a bottle of wine as soon as she got in and was now feeling a pleasant warmth and numbness. As she rubbed in the shower gel, she noticed that her whole body seemed to ache.

Did all that chaos happen in just a few hours? she thought for a moment, as if the events of the day had been a bad dream.

Letting the water bounce off her face, she took a deep breath of steamy air. In her memory, the car crash in which Zivko had been killed seemed to have happened a few days ago.

His broken, bloody face sat in her mind's eye for a moment, but she felt no remorse that he had died.

She dried her hair with a towel, and put on thick, winter pyjamas and a dressing gown. Even though it was a warm spring evening, she felt cold and shivery. She poured herself another glass of wine and switched on the television.

She sat back to watch an old sitcom for a while, but she couldn't concentrate. What she really wanted was for Harry to be by her side. She wondered if he really meant his promise to leave his wife. They had never had children because she had a medical condition that prevented her from getting pregnant. Harry blamed her terrible temper and mood swings on that fact. Not having children meant there would be less emotional damage if he left her, but it was uncomfortable for Lucy to think about being the cause of someone else's pain.

She poured more wine and looked in the fridge. She wasn't hungry and nothing in there seemed to entice her anyway. The sensible thing would be for her to go to bed and get a decent night's sleep. However, she wasn't tired. She was too wired from the day, and adrenaline was still coursing through her veins.

As she slumped back into the sofa and changed the channels on the television, she spotted the large photo album on the shelf. She went and grabbed it. There were some lovely photos at the front of the album of her and her sister as toddlers, and one of her sitting with her mum and the family dog, Honey.

Turning another page, she saw a photograph of her and her dad. She instantly took a breath seeing him looking out at her. His dark hair, twinkling eyes, and infectious smile. He had been stationed at the British Army base in Westfalen in the

North Rhine area of West Germany. She was probably about seven or eight when they had moved out there. As she looked at her dad's tattooed arm wrapped protectively around her, she felt tears well in her eyes. She wished he was still alive now. What she would give to sit and talk to him right at that moment. The pain of grief twisted her heart as more tears came.

The noise of her phone startled her.

'Hello?' she said, answering the phone.

'Lucy, it's Ruth. I just wanted to ring to see if you're okay?' Ruth asked gently.

'Yeah, I'm fine,' she replied, aware that her voice was still full of emotion.

'You don't sound fine.'

'It's nothing. I just found a photograph of my dad and it upset me.'

'Oh, sorry. After today, I just wanted to check in. Are you back at home?'

'Yeah. While Petrovic was in hiding, we were a target to stop us looking for him. Now he's in custody and Zivko is dead, I don't think we're in danger any longer.' It hadn't stopped her locking everything up and closing the curtains though.

'I thought the same. I just wanted to check you were okay?'

'Thanks. I'll be fine. Maybe looking through an old photo album wasn't the best idea after a few glasses of wine and the day we've had,' Lucy said as she sniffed.

'I've seen the photo you've got by your desk, but you don't really talk about your dad,' Ruth said.

I don't want to talk about him now.

Lucy was aware that she had never told Ruth that her father was dead. It was too painful to talk about.

'No. It's complicated. Long story. I'll tell you about it one day ... I can't sleep, can you?' Lucy said, keen to change the subject.

'No. My brain's racing. I'm just watching stuff about the election.'

'That will send you to sleep,' Lucy joked.

'When I collected Ella, Shiori told me she'd had a message from Claire Gold. It's possible that the newspaper story about Tankovic and party funding will be released tomorrow.'

'Tomorrow? I think you mean today. Look at your watch Ruth, it's one o'clock in the morning. It's election day.' Lucy said. *That doesn't make any sense.*

'One o'clock already? Blimey, I've lost all track of time. Anyway, it's the perfect day to bury a story like that. Everyone will be caught up in the election and will be busy voting anyway. There might be some resignations of civil servants and ministers of the Home Office. A few stories on pages four or five of the national papers, and then it will disappear.'

'Bastards. How can anyone let that happen?' Lucy said, feeling angry.

'Money, politics, power. Unfortunately, I think stuff like this goes unnoticed all the time.'

'What about Petrovic being brought to justice?' Lucy said anxiously.

'We did everything we could to find him and bring him in. Whatever happens to him now is out of our hands.'

The thought of that made Lucy very uneasy. *Maybe that isn't good enough for me.*

'I'll see you in a few hours,' Lucy said. 'Thanks for ringing.'

CHAPTER 33

E ven though Brooks had told Ruth and Lucy not to come in until the afternoon, Ruth had got up early, voted at the nearby polling station, and made her way into CID by 9am. The amount of paperwork that needed filling in after the chase, and subsequent arrest, of Petrovic was daunting. She also had to speak to various high-ranking officers in the next two days to report on yesterday's sequence of events. Although the Police Complaints Authority weren't yet involved, preparations had to be made in case there was some kind of enquiry.

Feeling the need for a caffeine hit before starting work on the mundane tasks she faced, Ruth went to the canteen to grab a coffee. As she returned to the CID room, she saw that Gaughran and Hassan were engaged in furtive conversation.

'Where have you two been the last few days? Getting your hair done?' Gaughran joked.

'Yeah, something like that,' Ruth said. She didn't have the energy to react to Gaughran.

Hassan approached with a more serious expression. 'Something going on?'

'What do you mean?' Ruth asked as she busied herself at her desk.

'Brooks is acting strangely. You two disappeared. Lots of hushed conversations,' he said under his breath.

'Nothing to report I'm afraid, Syed.'

Hassan nodded over at Gaughran. 'Tim thinks it's to do with that old man, Hamzar Mujic, who was murdered in Comeragh Gardens.'

'Does he now?' Ruth said in a tone that made it clear she wasn't going to tell him anything.

As Hassan wandered away, Ruth looked over at Lucy's desk. Her computer was on, but her jacket wasn't over the back of her chair – which suggested she had gone out.

Wonder where she's gone?

'You guys see Lucy this morning?' she called over to Hassan and Gaughran, bracing herself for another infantile joke.

'Came in early. Then said to tell Brooks she was popping out for a bit,' Hassan said with a shrug.

'When was that?' Ruth asked.

'An hour ago.'

Ruth nodded and went back to sorting out her paperwork.

Twenty minutes later, after a cigarette break, Ruth went over to Lucy's desk. They worked as partners, so it was very unusual for her to be out of the office without Ruth knowing where she was. After the events of the last few days, Ruth began to feel uneasy.

She sat down at Lucy's desk, and looked around to see if there were any clues as to where she had gone. The photograph of Lucy's father, dressed in his military uniform, had been moved from where it normally sat by the computer screen. It had been placed in the middle of the desk. A small note pad to one side had a scribble in Lucy's handwriting – *Brookwood.*

Looking again at the photograph of Lucy's father, she could see that printed at the bottom was *Sergeant Mark Henry,*

4th Regiment Royal Artillery. As she picked the photo up for a closer look, the light from above made the colours in the image stand out a little.

Is he wearing a blue beret? Ruth wondered. *I didn't know British soldiers ever wore blue berets. It looks strange.*

Squinting at the camouflage jacket that Mark Henry was wearing, she noticed a square of blue material on the arm. She recognised the symbol in the centre of the square.

Isn't that the emblem of the United Nations?

Then she saw the words *United Nations – Nations Unies* which confirmed her suspicions. It also brought a more worrying thought.

Weren't British troops used as part of the UN Peacekeeping force during the Balkan War?

Ruth was confused.

If Lucy's father had been part of that force, then wouldn't she have mentioned it to me at some point? Why would she not *have mentioned it?*

Grabbing the phone, Ruth went through the main Met police switchboard and got through to the headquarters of the 4th Regiment Royal Artillery in Osnabrück, Germany.

'Good morning, this is Detective Constable Ruth Hunter from the Metropolitan Police in London. I'm running a murder investigation and I need to confirm a couple of facts about your regiment,' Ruth explained.

'Can you tell me the nature of your enquiry?' the woman at the other end of the phone asked.

'I wanted to check whether your regiment was part of the United Nations Peacekeeping force in the Balkans a few years ago?'

'Yes, that's right. Several units from our regiment were part of the UN Peacekeeping force during the Balkan conflict,' she replied.

Ruth's heart dropped. *Why didn't Lucy mention that her father had been in Bosnia? It doesn't make any sense. We've spent the past ten days investigating murders directly linked to that war.*

'I also need some information about a soldier in your regiment. Sergeant Mark Henry.' She wasn't even sure if Lucy's father was still a soldier.

'I'm going to put you through to our Commanding Officer, Lieutenant Colonel Brannings. Could you hold the line please?'

'Of course,' Ruth said. She wasn't sure if asking about Mark Henry was an issue.

A few seconds later, a man's voice came onto the line. 'Detective Constable Hunter? Is that right?'

'Yes,' Ruth said.

'I'm currently Commanding Officer for the 4th Artillery. I understand that you're making an enquiry about Sergeant Mark Henry,' Brannings said.

'Yes, that's right. In fact, I'm not even sure if he's still part of your regiment.'

There were a few seconds of silence. 'I'm not sure I understand. Can you tell me the nature of your enquiry?' he asked.

Why is he being so cagey about this?

'I get the feeling that there's an issue with regards to Sergeant Mark Henry, Colonel?'

'The only issue, Detective Constable, is that Sergeant Mark Henry was killed five years ago.'

What the bloody hell is going on?

'I see. I'm so sorry to hear that. And that was when he was part of the UN Peacekeeping force?' Ruth said, making a guess.

'I'm afraid so. Could you tell me what this is all about?' Brannings asked, clearly losing patience.

'Could you tell me where Sergeant Henry is buried, please?' Ruth asked.

'Yes, he's buried at the British Military Cemetery in Surrey,' Brannings said. 'Brookwood.'

Glancing over at Lucy's pad, she looked again at the scribbled word *Brookwood*. With a growing sense of unease, she wondered what on earth Lucy was doing?

LUCY PUSHED DOWN ON the accelerator and watched as the speedometer hit 70mph. Glancing to the right, she saw the familiar sights of the Surrey countryside as the London suburbs gave way to open fields.

A few minutes later, a white building that used to house the San Domenico restaurant loomed into view. Lucy remembered that her uncle had told her various stories about the restaurant in its heyday in the 70s and 80s. It was a favourite of stars such as Tom Jones, Cliff Richard, Eric Clapton, and even the racing driver Ayrton Senna. However, since its closure in 1990, there had been rumours that it was being used as a government safe house, or a meeting place for the London-based Italian mafia.

'I've told you already, this isn't the way to central London,' came a gruff male voice from the back of the car.

Looking quickly in the rear-view mirror, Lucy could tell that Petrovic was feeling concerned.

He should be concerned, she thought.

'Just sit back and enjoy the countryside,' Lucy said.

Petrovic struggled in the back. However, his hands were handcuffed behind him and the doors were locked – he was going nowhere.

It had been forty minutes since Lucy had been to the custody suite at Peckham police station. She had known Smithy, the Duty Sergeant, for years. She explained that Petrovic needed to be transferred to Wandsworth Prison while they waited for the appropriate judge to decide whether or not he should be extradited to The Hague to face trial over his war crimes. She had assured Smithy that Ruth was accompanying her the journey. The Met had a policy of a minimum of two officers to escort any prisoner within London.

Lucy signed the paperwork, marched Petrovic down to her car, and drove out of Peckham nick without a hitch. Thankfully, there had been no one around to ask her what she was doing.

'Where are we going?' Petrovic growled from the back.

'Magical mystery tour,' she answered sarcastically.

Watching him squirm made her feel happy. She wanted him to suffer and to feel scared. She hated the very sight of him, and today was the day she would be able to get some sense of closure over what had happened to her father. A beautiful man who had joined the army through a sense of duty and to serve his country. A man who had gone to Bosnia to help innocent civilians escape a brutal, hideous war - but had never returned.

'You'll lose your job if any harm comes to me,' Petrovic warned her.

'I assure you there is no 'if' about it,' she snapped at him.

She watched Petrovic frown as he processed what she had said.

'If you turn around now, you can hand me over to the appropriate people in your government and no one will be the wiser,' he said. He was starting to sound scared.

'I need to take you somewhere.'

'Where? Where are you taking me?' he thundered.

I'm really getting under his skin, Lucy thought with delight.

'We're going to a little place in Brookwood. I want you to meet someone.'

CHAPTER 34

With a growing sense of unease, Ruth had trawled Peckham nick in her search for Lucy, but she was nowhere to be found. The word Brookwood scribbled on Lucy's pad, the information about her father, and the photograph, indicated that she might be planning a trip to visit her father's grave. There was nothing particularly unusual in that. However, Ruth's instinct told her that there was more to it. All through the case, Lucy had been driven in her quest to find and capture Petrovic. Why? Was it just a sense that she was also getting justice for her father?

As Ruth turned into the corridor to head back to the CID office, she saw Brooks coming the other way.

'What are you doing in Ruth?' he asked in a paternal way.

'Have you seen Lucy, guv?' she asked, unable to mask her anxiety.

'An hour ago, maybe. Have you lost her?' Brooks joked.

'Where did you see her, guv?'

Brooks frowned and then gestured. 'Heading towards the back staircase. I assumed she was going to the canteen.'

'Or the custody suite?' Ruth said thinking out loud.

'Possibly. Everything all right?' Brooks asked looking puzzled.

'I'm sure it's fine, guv,' Ruth said, registering that she didn't want to say anything else until she knew what was going on.

'Let me know when you find her,' Brooks said.

As soon as Brooks had disappeared out of sight, Ruth broke into a run and headed down the corridor that led to the back staircase of the station.

She pounded down the stairs at speed, then made her way into the custody suite. It was quiet and empty, apart from Smithy who was leaning on the reception desk, sipping tea as he did some paperwork.

'That was quick. I thought the traffic would have been murder,' he said.

What the bloody hell is he talking about?

'What traffic?' Ruth said, trying to keep her breath steady.

'Here to Wandsworth and back. It's always bad,' Smithy said with a smile as he glanced down at his watch. 'Actually, how the bloody hell did you travel - by helicopter?'

'Smithy, what are you talking about?' Ruth asked, her stomach starting to clench with nerves.

'Lucy came down here about an hour ago. She signed out your prisoner, the Serbian chap. She said you and her were taking him over to Wandsworth Prison,' he said, and then pointed to the transfer sheets. 'She signed the paperwork.'

Oh shit! This is not good.

'Oh right. I didn't go. She took another officer,' Ruth said calmy, trying to cover her total panic. 'Sorry about the confusion.'

'Yeah, I was gonna say,' he laughed. 'You looking for someone down here?'

'No, it's all right. Just having one of those days,' she answered with a forced smile.

'Rumour has it you and Luce have had one of those weeks,' Smithy said with a knowing raise of his eyebrow.

'You could say that,' Ruth said, but her mind was already on what the hell Lucy was doing with Petrovic. She'd had a sinking feeling since starting to put together everything she had found out about Lucy's father.

I've got a horrible feeling about this.

For a moment, she wondered where Lucy might be heading with Petrovic. Then it came to her. It made perfect sense.

Brookwood.

HAVING STOPPED AT A shop to pick up a bottle of Navy rum, which had been her father's favourite drink, Lucy slowed the car. Then she saw a sign at the side of the road – *Brookwood Military Cemetery and Memorial.*

'What is this place?' Petrovic asked as they drove slowly into the entrance.

'Shut up!' Lucy yelled as she took a swig of the rum. If she was going to do this, then she needed some Dutch courage.

Spotting the car park, she drove to the furthest end where there were virtually no cars parked. She turned off the ignition and sat pensively for a moment. The alcohol had made her head fuzzy, but it had also taken the edge off her nerves.

Glancing in the rear-view mirror again at Petrovic, her anger and fury grew.

Fuck you and the misery you inflicted on all those innocent people. You robbed me of my dad. You deserve to die. And this is the perfect place, she thought to herself.

'This is a military cemetery,' Petrovic said with a puzzled look on his face.

'I told you to shut up!' Lucy bellowed as she took another mouthful of the rum.

'You do know that you don't have what it takes to kill me,' Petrovic sneered at her from the back seat.

'We'll see about that,' Lucy snarled, aware that her words were now a little slurred.

Better stop drinking or I'm going to mess this up, she thought to herself. It was a question of balance. Drink enough to have the balls to kill Petrovic but not so much that you're incapacitated.

Lucy reached across to the glove compartment, and took out the six-inch kitchen knife she had brought from home. The metal handle was cold against her palm. She then grabbed the bottle of rum and started to get out of the car.

'You're a little, drunken whore. And you don't have the guts to use that,' Petrovic scoffed.

Lucy turned and glared at him for a moment. She felt no fear as she met his eyes. 'If you don't stop talking, I'm going to cut out your fucking tongue.'

She saw Petrovic react.

He's not sure if I've completely lost the plot or not. He looks scared.

Opening the back door, Lucy glanced around the car park. The place was deserted now.

Good. Let's get this done.

'Get out!' Lucy barked.

'I'm not going anywhere,' Petrovic said giving her a scornful look.

Lucy gestured with the knife. 'I said get out!'

Petrovic smirked at her. 'I don't think so.'

With a quick movement, Lucy jabbed the knife into the flesh of his left thigh. She felt the blade penetrate about two inches before she pulled it out.

Petrovic yelled with pain. 'My God!'

'Get out of the car,' Lucy said through gritted teeth.

'Are you mad?'

'Very. So, for the last time – get ... out ... of ... the ... car.'

Petrovic gasped with the pain and then looked at her.

Lucy raised her arm as if to stab him again.

'All right! All right!' he groaned as he manoeuvred out of the car and stood up.

Lucy went behind him and pushed him in the back. 'Come on.'

Petrovic stumbled and then began to limp forward towards the path that led to the graveyard.

As they turned the corner, Lucy saw the huge stone plinth with the words *Their Name Liveth Forevermore* carved into it. It had been over two years since she had been to her father's grave. She found it too painful.

Beyond that were perfectly symmetrical rows of white gravestones of soldiers that had died in both World Wars, Korea, Ireland, The Gulf and of course, Bosnia.

Lucy remembered the emotion she had felt at her father's military funeral when she had first seen the endless lines of graves.

'You realise that I am no different to the men that are buried here?' Petrovic said.

Lucy took another swig of the rum. She knew that in the next ten minutes she was going to have to murder Petrovic.

'I was a soldier in a war. No different to these men.'

How dare he say that!

'You are nothing like these men,' Lucy snarled as she shoved him forward again.

'You are not naïve enough to think that the British army doesn't commit atrocities, are you? In Ireland? In Kenya against the Mau Mau?'

'Shut up!'

'The Germans did not invent concentration camps. It was the British army in the Boer War.'

Lucy wasn't listening anymore. She was scouring the graves for the place where her father rested.

As if on cue, clouds moved away from the sun, and bright shafts of light descended on the tended lawns of the cemetery.

And then she saw it.

A white grave in the sunlight, no different to the 8,000 others in lines across the cemetery.

Sergeant Mark Henry, 4th Regiment Royal Artillery

1st October 1950 – 19th February 1993

Her father's neat, well-tended grave glowed in the sunshine. The Commonwealth War Graves Commission made sure all British soldiers' graves were well maintained.

'Sit down,' Lucy snapped as she kicked Petrovic in the leg.

'This is your father?' he asked as he tried his best to sit on the grass a few feet from the grave.

'Yes. This is who I brought you to meet today.' Lucy took another swig of the rum and felt it burn the back of her throat.

'He died in Bosnia?'

'You killed him,' Lucy said, her words slurring.

'No. I never killed anyone from the British army. Or from the UN Peacekeeping force,' Petrovic said shaking his head. 'You must be mistaken.'

'Look at the date,' Lucy snarled at him.

'Okay. I don't know what that date means. Except it was the day your father was killed.'

Tears started to roll down Lucy's face. 'On that day, you watched as a British Army troop carrier swerved to avoid a shell on the road to Kula. Then it got stuck on the road. You grabbed a high-powered rifle and fired bullet after bullet. Bullet after bullet ... One of them hit my father and killed him.'

'No ...' Petrovic said, lost in thought.

'You murdered him,' Lucy sobbed.

'That was him?' Petrovic whispered.

Lucy looked at him. He hadn't even denied it.

'I want you to apologise to him. Here and now,' Lucy said moving towards Petrovic with the knife. 'And then I'm going to kill you.'

HAMMERING DOWN THE A3 out of London, Ruth knew she needed to get to Lucy before she did something that would ruin her life forever. In the few years that they had worked together, Ruth had always seen Lucy as a little hot-headed at times – but nothing more than that. And nothing that would suggest she had the capacity for what Ruth feared she was about to do.

Trying to piece everything together, Ruth watched as the traffic parted for 'the blues and twos' that she had activated about ten minutes earlier. Time was of the essence.

However, the question did strike Ruth as she weaved in and out of the traffic. Why was Lucy's fury vented so personally on Simo Petrovic? Was it that he symbolised everything that was brutal and malevolent about the Bosnian War? There was no doubt that Petrovic was an evil monster capable of inflicting terrible cruelty on the Muslim population of Serbia. If Ruth ever felt that the death penalty was justified in the modern justice system, which she didn't, it would be for a man like Petrovic.

She looked back on Lucy's behaviour while they had been investigating Hamzar Mujic's murder and trying to track down Petrovic. It had seemed personal to Lucy all the way along. And taking Petrovic out of police custody and going to the military cemetery where her father was buried seemed *incredibly* personal.

Then, in that moment, the penny dropped.

Ruth remembered the passage from Hamzar Mujic's diary.

Petrovic hated the British and would take delight in ordering the road to Kula to be shelled. Once I saw one of the British vehicles swerve a shell and get stuck in the mud. Petrovic grabbed a high-powered rifle and began to shoot at the stationary British vehicle. He must have fired around twenty rounds. Later, it was reported on the radio that a British soldier had been killed in that vehicle. Petrovic spent the next week bragging about what a great marksman he was and how he had murdered a British dog.

Was that it? Was Lucy's father the British soldier that Petrovic had shot that day and bragged about? It had to be.

It explained everything. Lucy's unwillingness to pass the investigation over to anyone else. Her overwhelming need to find Petrovic at all costs. Then taking him out of custody, risking her own career, to take the man she knew murdered her father to his grave. It also didn't take much for Ruth to realise what Lucy intended to do with Petrovic at the cemetery.

No one knew that Ruth was heading for Brookwood. No one *could* know. Lucy would lose her job just for taking Petrovic on their little detour. However, if she could get to Lucy in time to stop her, then maybe they could cover her tracks.

As the car came screaming off the A3, Ruth picked up signs to Brookwood. If Lucy was convicted of manslaughter, her career would be over and she would spend a decade in prison. How could she think that was worth it to avenge her own father?

A sign at the side of the road – *Brookwood Military Cemetery and Memorial.*

The car tyres squealing on the road's surface. Ruth took the bend and thundered into the cemetery car park. Glancing left, she saw Lucy's car parked up.

They're here!

Ruth threw open the door. Running across the gravel, she glanced around. Nothing.

A sign pointed to the memorial and graveyard. Sprinting left, she came out by a large plinth. Beyond that, endless lines of white graves that gleamed in the spring sunshine - the final resting place of fallen British soldiers.

Then she saw them in the distance.

The figure of a man sitting on the ground beside a grave. A woman standing nearby. It was Lucy.

Oh God what is she doing? At least it looks like he's still alive, she thought.

She ran towards them, and saw Lucy look over at her and squint.

'What are you doing here?' Lucy mumbled. Her voice was slurred.

God, she is seriously drunk.

Petrovic looked up from where he was sitting. 'Can you please talk some sense into her?'

'Shut up!' Lucy said as she stumbled towards him, grabbed him by the hair, and placed the knife across his throat. 'Me and my dad have had a little drink to celebrate this little meeting.'

Ruth stepped forward. She could see that the knife was beginning to cut Petrovic's skin.

'I know why you're doing this,' Ruth said gently.

'No. No, you don't,' Lucy said, shaking her head emotionally.

'I remembered the entry in Mujic's diary. The British vehicle on the road to Kula ... the soldier that was killed inside ...' Ruth said as she looked at the name on the grave, '... I know it was your father.'

Lucy pushed the knife harder against Petrovic's neck. The skin began to split, and blood tricked down his neck. 'He murdered him. And then he laughed and bragged about it.'

'If you kill him, you'll lose everything,' Ruth said looking directly into Lucy's glassy eyes.

She's drunk too much to be logical. This is not good.

Lucy sobbed quietly as she pulled Petrovic's head back to fully expose his neck. 'If I kill him I'll be able to sleep in peace, and so will my dad.'

Oh my God. She's going to kill him!

'Lucy, please,' Ruth begged. 'I didn't know your dad, but I can't believe that he would have wanted you to spend your life in prison for doing this.'

Ruth knew she needed to find a different tack.

'Lucy!' Ruth shouted angrily. 'I don't want to have to visit you in prison. Neither does your mum or your sister. It will destroy them both. Do you want to do that to them? It's bloody selfish!'

Ruth's anger and change of tack seemed to work.

Lucy slowly relaxed the pressure on the knife.

'Why don't you give that to me, eh?' Ruth said quietly as she walked towards her.

'No. I need to kill him.'

'No, you don't. He needs to stand trial and spend the rest of his life in a horrible prison cell. Don't you get it? Every day, for years, in a single cell. That's worse than this.' Ruth said, pleading to her logic.

'Is it?' Lucy asked, her voice breaking with emotion.

'Yes, Lucy. It is worse. Much worse. I promise you. Please ...'

Taking the knife away from Petrovic's neck, Lucy's whole body began to shake as she sobbed uncontrollably. She took two steps towards Ruth, gave her the knife, and wrapped her arms around her.

'I'm sorry, I'm so sorry,' Lucy whispered through her tears.

Ruth held her tightly for a few seconds, watching as Petrovic sat forward with a groan, his eyes closed.

'You don't need to be sorry,' Ruth said. 'But I need you to be my partner, not stuck in Holloway into the next millennium.'

Lucy moved back and looked at her through glazed eyes. 'Thank you. What do we do now?'

Ruth gestured to Petrovic. 'We need to get him to Wandsworth Prison.'

Lucy nodded and then looked down at her father's grave.

'Why don't I give you a minute here with your dad,' Ruth said quietly. 'We'll be over there.'

'Yeah,' Lucy said as she wiped her tear-streaked face.

Ruth walked over to Petrovic. 'Get up,' she barked.

Petrovic looked like a broken man as he climbed slowly to his feet. He looked at her with disdain.

For a few seconds, Ruth looked over at Lucy who was crouched by her father's grave. Her lips were moving as if she was talking to him.

Ruth nudged Petrovic in the back as they headed towards the car park. 'Come on. We don't want you to miss lunch on the VP wing, eh?'

CHAPTER 35

It was mid-afternoon, and Ruth and Lucy had been with Brooks in his office for nearly twenty minutes. Ruth had plied Lucy with coffee and water to sober her up. Lucy had insisted that she didn't want to go home and be on her own after such a traumatic morning. She wanted to be at work, keeping busy. And Ruth could be there for some mutual support.

'Everything went okay getting Petrovic to Wandsworth?' Brooks asked, leaning back in his seat.

Ruth looked at Lucy for a moment – *If only he knew!*

'Yeah. No problem,' Lucy said.

'He was grumbling something about cutting himself shaving and having a sore leg, but yeah, no hitches,' Ruth said.

'According to the Home Office, he'll be in a cell in The Hague by the end of the week,' Brooks said.

Lucy glanced at Ruth. 'Good to hear. At least some of his victims will get the justice they deserve,' she said with a slight slur.

Brooks frowned and looked at them. 'You two been drinking?'

'Boozy lunch to celebrate, guv,' Lucy said.

'Well don't get nicked for drink driving on the way home, eh?' he said as he took a copy of a newspaper and tossed it over to them. 'You seen this yet?'

Ruth wondered what he was talking about. 'No, we've been a bit busy.'

'Busy getting pissed in the pub,' he laughed.

Taking the paper, Lucy looked over at him. 'What are we looking at?'

'Page 4, inside. It's the only story that's not about the election.'

Ruth watched Lucy as she opened the paper, looked at the story, and began to read. *'Dirty Money – Links between Tory Party funding, a multi-national oil company, and a Serbian war criminal. An investigation has revealed that an unnamed Serbian man, who brokered a $1.7 billion oil deal between the global oil giant Natell and Yugopetrol, donated over half a million pounds to the Conservative Party last year. The man, who cannot yet be named, is wanted by The Hague International Criminal Tribunal for the former Yugoslavia. A spokesman for the Conservative party claimed that all donors are carefully vetted before any donations can be made.'*

'That last sentence is bullshit!' Ruth said.

Lucy closed the paper and shook her head. 'What does that mean?'

'It means that very little will be done to investigate. Tankovic has not only been allowed to live freely in this country and become a very wealthy man, he is also a major donor to the current government,' Ruth said bitterly.

'I have a nasty feeling that it won't go any further. There's too much at stake for too many rich and powerful people. Talking of which, have we voted yet today, ladies?' Brooks asked, sitting forward at his desk.

Ruth nodded. 'I went before work.'

'I wasn't sure that I was going to bother,' Lucy said.

'Changed your mind?' Brooks asked.

'A lot of people have fought and died so that we can live in a democracy. Sometimes I forget that. And if I don't vote, it seems like an insult to them.'

'Wise words,' Brooks said. 'I have a suggestion - in fact, it's an order.'

'Fire away,' Ruth said.

'Get your things together. Lucy - you go and vote, and then both of you take the rest of the day off. Go and relax.'

Ruth looked at Lucy and shrugged. 'I'm knackered, aren't you?'

Lucy nodded and smiled. 'Thanks, guv. It's not true what they say. You are a good bloke.'

Brooks laughed.

Thank God. Lucy is starting to sound like her old self.

'Bloody cheek. Go on, you two. Sod off. And I don't want to see you for the rest of the day.'

Ruth and Lucy got up and headed out of the door.

HAVING GOT THEIR STUFF together, Ruth and Lucy walked out of Peckham nick together and headed for the car park. It was warm, and there was the smell of freshly cut grass from the nearby playing fields. Ruth took a deep breath and got the scent of the spring flowers that were interwoven through the wire mesh fence that surrounded the car park. Honeysuckles, primroses, and bluebells. They might have been in South

London but, for a moment, it smelled as if they were in the countryside.

They walked together for a few seconds in silence. The sun was bright enough to cast elongated shadows as they went.

'Sunglasses weather?' Lucy asked, as she gazed up at the sky.

'Definitely,' Ruth said with a smile and nod. 'You okay to drive?'

'Just about.'

They reached Lucy's car and looked at each other.

'Thank God this week is nearly over!' Ruth said with a deep sigh.

Lucy didn't immediately respond, and for a moment there was a heavy silence. 'I don't know what to say to you,' Lucy said eventually.

'You don't have to say anything.'

'Today could have gone so differently,' she said with a tear in her eye.

'It didn't though, did it? You made that man face what he had done. And now he will face justice.'

Lucy's lip trembled. 'But I was going to kill him.'

'I know Lucy, but you didn't. And it's over. We got him. And your dad would have been proud of how hard you worked to track him down,' Ruth said putting a comforting arm on Lucy's.

'Thank you,' Lucy said as she moved to hug Ruth. 'What would I do without you?'

'Works both ways. Go and vote, and then get some sleep, eh?'

Lucy pulled a face. 'I might do ... later.'

Ruth knew what Lucy was getting at. 'I thought you weren't seeing anyone. Or is this Man Boy again?'

'There is someone I see off and on,' Lucy admitted. 'But it's different.'

'You mean it's not casual?' Ruth asked, taking the piss.

Lucy thought about it for a moment. 'I don't know ... No, I don't think it is. But he is married.'

'Right. That's what they say, isn't it? All the decent men are married - or they're gay.'

Lucy laughed. 'What about you? Election night party?'

'My friend Shiori is coming over for a few drinks. I guess we'll watch the election results coming in,' Ruth said, trying not to show how she actually felt.

'You two are seeing a lot of each other?'

'We just click, that's all.'

Lucy raised an eyebrow. 'Shame she's not a bloke, eh?'

'I guess so. Think I've had enough of men for the moment.'

Lucy unlocked her car. 'Have a good evening, eh? And thank you, Ruth.'

'Drive carefully. And if everything goes as they're predicting, we can celebrate a New Labour government tomorrow.'

Lucy got into her car, waved, and closed the door.

Ruth got out her sunglasses, put them on, and turned to cross the car park to her own car.

CHAPTER 36

Lucy was slumped on the sofa looking through her family photograph album again. Even though she knew it wasn't a good idea, she was drinking vodka. Just enough to keep her numb for the rest of the day.

She turned a page and stared at the photograph of her dad. It was the one she'd seen last night. Looking at his protective, tattooed forearm around her, she remembered running her tiny hand down it. She recalled telling him it was too hairy, and that he was like a monkey. Then she remembered giggling at his silly monkey impression. Life was so precious, and it could disappear in the blink of an eye.

Sipping her vodka and wiping the tears from her face, she felt glad that she had spoken to her dad today at his graveside. She had found his death so painful and wasn't sure that she had ever allowed herself to grieve properly. In fact, she knew she'd pretended that it had never happened.

However abnormal and irrational her actions had been today, she had taken a step towards acknowledging that he was gone. At his graveside, she had told him everything that had happened and why she had brought Petrovic with her. Now that she thought about it, she knew Ruth had been right. Despite what Petrovic had done, her dad would have believed that he needed to be punished through the courts – not by her hand.

The phone rang and Lucy could see from the caller ID it was her mum.

Lucy picked up the phone but was still deep in thought. 'Mum?'

'Lucy, how are you? I tried to call you last night, but then I went out with Sandra to the bingo.'

'Did you win?'

'What do you think? Bloody waste of money but it gets me out of the house.'

'I wanted to ask you something, Mum.'

'You okay, darling? You sound a bit upset?'

'I'm all right. Long day at work, that's all.'

'I don't know how you do it. What is it? Everything okay?' Her mum now sounded concerned.

'Fine, don't worry. I just wanted to ask if you'd come to Dad's grave with me sometime?'

There were a few seconds of silence. 'I didn't think you liked to go down there, Lucy.'

'No, I know. But I want to go now. Will you come with me, Mum?' she asked, blinking as more tears came.

'Course I will. Any time you want. You know that.'

'Thanks, Mum,' Lucy said, as her voice broke with emotion.

There was a knock at the door.

'Mum, I've got to go. There's somebody at the door,' Lucy said, wiping her face.

'Oh right. Boyfriend is it?'

'Yeah, something like that,' she replied with an embarrassed laugh.

'Do I get to meet this one then?'

Lucy thought for a moment. 'Yeah, I think so. Yeah. I'd like you to meet him. You'd really like him ... I'd better go, Mum. I love you, Mum.'

'Love you too, darling.'

Wiping her face again, Lucy put down the phone, got up off the sofa, and went to the door. It was Brooks.

'What do you want?' Lucy said with a smile.

Brooks looked concerned. 'You okay? Your face is all ...'

'Blotchy? Smeary?' Lucy laughed.

'Yeah, one of those.'

'You'd better come in. I need to tell you something,' Lucy said, wondering if she really had the courage to tell him about what had happened that morning.

'It's all right. I don't need to know, Luce,' he said in a way that sounded as if he knew what she was going to say.

'Know what? I haven't told you anything yet, smart arse!'

'Whatever you were doing when you were out this morning. I don't need or want to know. Okay? We move on.'

Lucy nodded – *Bloody hell. That was easy.*

'Well, are you going to stand there all day or are you coming in?'

'Thought you'd never ask.'

He smiled, moved to one side, and grabbed the suitcase that he had hidden out of sight. 'Any room at the inn?'

'No. And whatever you're selling, I'm not interested,' Lucy laughed.

RUTH SAT FORWARD ON the sofa and watched as the results of the general election came in. The BBC was predicting a Labour landslide. After the events of recent days, politics seemed strangely petty and irrelevant. People had lost their lives, and those responsible had finally been brought to justice. The fact that Michael Portillo, a rather disingenuous Conservative MP, had lost his Enfield South seat against all odds was mildly interesting.

Shiori stood at the doors to the patio, smoking and drinking wine. They had been chatting and drinking all night. Ruth hadn't relayed the events of the previous morning at Brookwood Cemetery. That was between her and Lucy, and no one else. Ruth and Shiori had avoided the subject of their kiss. Both of them were pretending that it had never happened. Ruth wasn't sure if Shiori was embarrassed, or whether she actually did have feelings for Ruth but was too afraid to make them known. It might have been 1997, but attitudes towards being gay were still fairly archaic in many social circles. It was something that Ruth played out in her mind when she questioned her sexuality. If she came out as being gay, what would others think? What would her mum or sister say? Her work colleagues made enough lesbian jokes as it was, even though they knew she and Lucy were seemingly 'straight'. Coming out as gay would open a new world of sniggers and judgement.

Shiori turned and headed back to the sofa. 'How are we doing?'

By 'we', Ruth knew that she meant the Labour Party.

Ruth gestured to the television which was now showing a map of the UK covered in red where the Labour Party had won seats.

'I think they've done it. We've done it,' Ruth said with a smile.

A BBC journalist stood near a man pointing to various parts of a UK map. *'Labour now has its best results since the 1930s, with record-breaking success all across here. In the Home Counties, in the South, in Surrey, and the South Coast. Up here, the Midlands and the North are almost entirely red. And, of course, in Scotland, all Labour except for the Liberal Democrats, with the Tory Party now having no seats in the whole of Scotland.'*

Shiori jumped on the sofa with an excited squeal. 'My God. It really is a landslide? Champagne?'

'Why not?' Ruth said. The bottle of wine they had shared had relaxed her, and Shiori's exuberance was beginning to rub off on her.

A moment later, Shiori returned from the fridge and popped the cork before she had even sat down. 'Here we go!'

Ruth drained the remains of her wine, put the empty glass on the table in front of her, and slid it over to Shiori to be re-filled. She needed to put the events of the last few days to one side and embrace the joy of the evening.

'Bottoms up, as I think you say,' Shiori said, clinking her glass.

Ruth laughed. 'That's only in bad American films.'

They looked at each other for a moment.

Shiori frowned and pointed at Ruth's face. 'Honey, you've got some mascara or something on your eye.'

Ruth touched her eye. 'Have I?'

'Here ... close your eyes for a second,' Shiori said, moving closer.

Ruth closed her eyes.

Then she felt the warmth of Shiori's lips against hers.

Oh my God! She just kissed me!

Ruth responded, as Shiori ran her hands through Ruth's hair.

They stopped for a moment.

'You tricked me!' Ruth said with a grin and mock indignation.

'In my defence I was just checking if kissing you was as good as I remember.'

'Well, what's the verdict?'

'It's better.'

They moved together and began kissing passionately.

Ruth pulled away and smiled. 'So ... are we going to bed?'

Shiori raised an eyebrow. 'I don't know. Are we?'

AMAZON REVIEW

If you enjoyed this book, *please* leave me
a short review on Amazon. I really
does make all the difference.
Many thanks.

Enjoy this book?
Get the first book in the
DI Ruth Hunter Snowdonia series
https://www.amazon.co.uk/dp/B08268L6L8
https://www.amazon.com/dp/B08268L6L8

AUTHOR'S NOTE

Although this book is very much a work of fiction, it is located in Snowdonia, a spectacular area of North Wales. It is steeped in history and folklore that spans over two thousand years. It is worth mentioning that Llancastell is a fictional town on the eastern edges of Snowdonia. I have made liberal use of artistic licence, names and places have been changed to enhance the pace and substance of the story.

Acknowledgements

I will always be indebted to the people who have made this
novel possible.

M y mum, Pam, and my stronger half, Nicola, whose initial reaction, ideas and notes on my work I trust implic-
itly. And Dad, for his overwhelming enthusiasm.

Thanks also go to my incredible Advanced Reading Team.
Various officers in the North Wales Police Force for checking
my work and explaining the complicated world of police pro-
cedure and investigation. My incredibly talented editor Rebec-
ca Millar who has held my hand through the rewriting and
editing process and is a joy to work with. Carole Kendal for her
copy editing and meticulous proofreading. My designer Stuart
Bache for the incredible cover design.

Your FREE book is waiting for you now

Get your FREE copy of the prequel to
the DI Ruth Hunter Series NOW
at www.simonmccleave.com[1]
and join my VIP Email Club

Printed in Great Britain
by Amazon